SHIELD OF DUTY

A FROST SISTERS MYSTERY

SHIELD OF DUTY

SCARLETT DEAN

FIVE STAR
A part of Gale, Cengage Learning

GALE
CENGAGE Learning·

Detroit • New York • San Francisco • New Haven, Conn • Waterville, Maine • London

GALE
CENGAGE Learning·

Set in 11 pt. Plantin.
Printed on permanent paper.

LIBRARY OF CONGRESS CATALOGING-IN-PUBLICATION DATA

Dean, Scarlett.
    Shield of duty : a Frost sisters mystery / Scarlett Dean. — 1st ed.
      p. cm.
    ISBN-13: 978-1-59414-855-2 (alk. paper)
    ISBN-10: 1-59414-855-4 (alk. paper)
    1. Policewomen—Fiction. 2. Supernatural—Fiction. 3. Future
life—Fiction. 4. Homicide investigation—Fiction. I. Title.
PS3604.E1538S55 2010
813'.6—dc22   2009042222

First Edition. First Printing: February 2010.
Published in 2010 in conjunction with Tekno Books and Ed Gorman.

Printed in the United States of America
1 2 3 4 5 6 7 14 13 12 11 10

For those who serve.

ACKNOWLEDGMENTS

Thanks to Thomas J. Keevers for sharing knowledge and insights on homicide investigations.

Once again, my thanks to Beth Anderson for being my reader and mentor!

CHAPTER ONE

Squad lights strobed the Southfield Heights Police Department lot as I reached the Crown Vic. As a homicide detective, I'm not used to riding in the backseat, especially when the driver is my ex-partner, Gerard Alvarez.

I admit to jealousy pangs upon seeing my sister, Kate, ride shotgun as we raced to execute a warrant. But she'd earned that spot after putting in her time as a beat cop and eventually working her way into homicide. Her success had come with a great price on my part, but I'm proud as hell of her.

Alvarez led the way with Kate monitoring the radio. She'd done well in the short time she'd been a homicide detective, and had a great partner and mentor in Gerard. The fact they were romantically involved was secondary.

Alvarez wore the stern expression I'd seen so many times when we'd worked together. Electric tension hung sharp enough to ignite plastic explosives. He sped up.

Kate adjusted her Kevlar bulletproof vest. Her expression had grown as tense as Alvarez's. The usual chatter was absent between them, and I knew they were playing out possible scenarios as they neared their destination.

I'd gotten to the station shortly before they'd taken off to serve the warrant, and the details were sketchy. From what I could tell, we were on the way to arrest a murder suspect who'd evaded the authorities for weeks. An anonymous tip had come in on his whereabouts, sparking a mad rush.

So far the case against the guy was solid, with reliable witnesses and no known alibi. I hadn't seen the original crime scene, but had heard that one seasoned detective had tossed his dinner in the bushes. Even with my four years in homicide, it never gets any easier to view a mutilated child.

An open-and-shut case, except once the suspect figured out they were on to him, he'd bolted underground for a few weeks, only to resurface just miles from the station. Now he had most of the department on their way to arrest him. He had no idea what he was in for with the crime-scene photos permanently etched into every officer's mind. Adrenaline and fiery determination pumped through their veins. The guy might be praying for the wrath of God instead of the Southfield Heights police before this night ended.

Kate broke the silence as we approached the neighborhood.

"I can't wait to get this guy."

"You're in good company," said Alvarez.

"Think he'll go down easy?"

"He's already killed once. Ready?"

"A long time ago."

He pulled the car curbside in front of the other squads. Within seconds the property swarmed with law enforcement as we rushed the small brick bungalow.

Kate and Alvarez stood beside the front door, weapons drawn. Officers took positions surrounding the home and Alvarez pounded a greeting.

"Southfield Police! Open up."

They didn't wait for an invitation, and Alvarez kicked through the flimsy door. Kate positioned herself low going in. It had been the same routine when I partnered with Alvarez; I always went in low and he took the high road. You never know what's waiting for you on the other side of a door.

Once inside, we moved cautiously through the small house.

I motioned to Kate that I was headed downstairs.

The basement door stood slightly open and I moved silently down the steps.

A shuffling sound drifted from a darkened corner where I saw an unusually tall silhouette. He was waiting on us.

Gray light spilled into the room from a window well, and I saw he stood tall for a reason. He was perched on a step stool; a thick rope pinching the skin around his neck with the tail tied around a ceiling pipe.

When Kate started after me she caught my look.

"He's got a rope around his neck," I told her.

"That's too good for him." Kate motioned to Alvarez that she was going in.

"Jason Weaver? I'm Detective Kate Frost with the Southfield Heights police. I'd like to speak with you."

"I'll jump." He edged closer to the stool's edge.

"Jason, there's no need for that. We can work this out."

"Stay where you are!"

"All right. I can talk from here."

"I don't want to talk. It's time to end this."

"If you undo the rope we can help you." Kate inched closer.

"No one can help me now."

His knees bent.

Kate lunged, grabbing his legs and holding him up long enough for an officer to undo the rope around his neck.

As Kate let go, Jason dropped to the floor but wasn't giving up so easily. He reached inside his boot and brought out a small pistol.

When his gun went off the bullet passed through my chest and out, hitting the cement wall behind me. The ricochet, luckily, hit neither Kate nor Alvarez.

Kate fired her weapon, hitting him in the arm, causing him to drop his gun.

He rolled back and forth on the floor, clutching his arm.

"Why didn't you just let me die?"

"I'm not feeling generous today." Kate dropped to cuff him.

I breathed a sigh of relief knowing the whole thing was over, and no one had been hurt, convinced once more that being dead has its perks.

When I died last year my life had been a shambles, although at the time I didn't know it. I'd started my fifth year at the South-field Heights PD in homicide, partnering with Detective Gerard Alvarez. Together we'd solved a high percentage of our assigned cases thanks to our great rapport, timing and the fact that he could intimidate Satan and I could outrun most criminals.

Socially I prefer the company of a beer and a ham sandwich, but had decided to make it official with my fiancé George Anderson. I should have married the sandwich. At age twenty-eight I felt I had put in enough workout time in the gym to prolong a sagging rump and fight the dreaded arm wattles. Life was good until I was murdered.

My peaches-and-cream complexion morphed rapidly into a blue hue only the Cookie Monster would envy and I watched in horror as my family dealt with the pain and grief of my death. Amidst the torture of standing by helplessly while life went on without me, I realized early on that my sister, Kate, then a patrol officer at Southfield, could—amazingly—see and hear me. So far she's the only one. I believe it stems from Kate's belief in all things paranormal. She's open to it and therefore can see and hear not only me, but also the spirit acquaintances I've befriended on the other side. Since my death she's taken my place as both the only female homicide dick on the force, and Alvarez's new partner.

Kate and I work homicide together, putting aside our competitive natures long enough to do some serious damage to those responsible. If anyone were to ask I'd say do not try this at home. It's not the kind of gig I would have volunteered for, but, all things considered, it's worked to our advantage. Kate is my physical link to the real world, and I can go places she can't.

I should be resting in peace but something tells me I'm in it for the long haul. My detective badge still hangs on its lanyard around my neck and I wear it proudly. No one has told me it's time to take it off. It's what referred to as a death tag, and I'm told every spirit has one. It's the item that signifies the one unresolved issue that keeps the spirit from going on to the next level. Once the issue is resolved, the spirit moves on. I haven't seen any indication that I'm ready to give up my badge yet. If and when the time is right, I'll go quietly. But, for now, I'm still on duty.

CHAPTER TWO

"You don't need a dog. You work too many hours." I checked Kate's expression. Determined frown, focused gaze, and lack of a quick comeback, told me she was considering my take on the situation.

"Stop being so negative, Linz. I've already paid the deposit and when I get back from White Crest, he should be weaned. Done deal."

Then she brightened. "It's karma, sort of. What I didn't tell you is that this woman who bred him is somebody I . . . well, it's a long story." And the brightness dimmed as quickly as it had come up.

"It's going to be a long drive," I said, hoping to encourage more detail. And I got it!

"Oh, all right. This poor woman—her name is Betty Carter—is the sister of a guy who died in custody a few years ago. An innocent guy—he got caught up in a sting operation and ended up hanging himself in the cellblock. And I'm the one who arrested him. It was awful, Lindsay . . . truly awful. I felt terrible about it at the time and I still do, although of course it wasn't really my fault. It was just one of those situations where somebody's in the wrong place at the wrong time and . . . well, you know how it can happen.

"By the time the mistake was figured out it was too late and he was dead. It just . . . happened, is all. Personally I half expected his poor sister to go buy a shotgun and come back guns-a-blazin'. She threatened to kill us all and I guess the only reason she didn't make good is because if anything happened, she'd be the top suspect. Still it gave us pause, as she seemed a bit off to start with and I'm not sure the brother was . . . all there either. I know their mother's a bit . . . weird. And worse, now, I expect. She took it pretty hard there at the time, and I can't imagine her feeling any better over time."

"Well if there's karma involved, it doesn't sound like good karma to me." Which it didn't, but then karma is a relative term when you're dead. "What—you expect the guy's sister to be happy about selling you a puppy? I'd worry it might have rabies or something."

"Oh, don't be negative. Besides, I'd be truly astonished if she even knew who I was. There was no indication of it when Jakes and I went to look at the pups. The night her brother died, there were numerous officers involved and major chaos. I doubt she even knew who originally arrested him. And of course, I was in street clothes when I went to pick out the dog. Okay, maybe karma isn't the word. Maybe the one I want is co-incidence."

I let the subject drop, hoping to move on to something that had nagged me the last few days.

Every January, Kate and her college buds take a ski trip to White Crest Mountain in Wisconsin. Every year she tries to get me to tag along, and every year I have to come up with a more creative excuse than the year before. This year, she didn't ask, so no excuses were required. I was dead. You can't get more creative than that, plus it wasn't a lie.

You'd think with a name like Lindsay Frost, I'd be a real snow bunny. The truth is, I hate cold and snow or anything that doesn't have anything to do with a bronze waiter in a Speedo offering me an umbrella drink. I tried to forget she'd neglected to ask me this year, but it kept surfacing in my mind. Unfortunately, Kate had latched onto her latest obsession like a pit bull.

"You should see him, Linz. The pup is all fur and blue eyes. He's the most handsome of all his siblings. I can't wait to bring him home. Jakes went with me to pick him out, like I said, and she absolutely fell in love with him."

Evelyn Jakes was a mutual childhood friend. She was Kate's age but we'd all grown up together in Southfield Heights. Evelyn was no sissy-girl, and preferred her last name to her first. She'd always just been Jakes to us.

Jakes ran her own catering business in a nearby town, not leaving much time for get-togethers with old friends. This year Kate had invited her to go to White Crest for a little R&R and to catch up on old times.

"You'll be sorry," I said. "You'll be chasing him all the time. Huskies are runners."

"Exactly. Can you imagine how much fun it will be to go skiing with the dog pulling me? I saw a special about it on cable. It's the latest thing. Why are you so against this?"

Before I could figure that out she glanced in the rearview mirror. "Speaking of dogs, it looks like we've grown a tail."

I caught a glance of the car in my side mirror. The older model Buick Riviera was not the best car to follow someone in. Although its engine is powerful enough to keep up, the car is too conspicuous in size and glamour. Besides, this one had been painted a ninety-nine-dollar shade of green. I couldn't see the driver clearly, though it appeared to be a male.

"Try braking a little to see if he's just a tailgater," I suggested.

"He's been on us for at least five miles. In this traffic you'd think he would have turned off by now."

Southfield Heights takes up little space on the northwest-Indiana map, with its farmland and small-town atmosphere. It reminds me of a grown-up Mayberry. The stretch of road we were on is known as Main Street, taking us through downtown Southfield where fast-food restaurants and mom-and-pop shops are prevalent.

"I can't get a good look at him. He's definitely male, blond, wearing sunglasses and a really bad mullet."

"Ever seen a good one?"

Kate squinted. "Maybe it's a hat."

A squeal of tires behind us told me he'd seen Kate looking. The Buick turned off at the light and headed west.

"Weird. Maybe you should follow him." I craned to get a plate number.

Kate continued north for several more blocks, then made her way toward the station.

"Forget him. With that haircut he's probably in search of the eighties." She nodded to herself. "I know what your problem is, Linz. You're afraid the dog will ruin the house."

My house, or at least it used to be until I'd been murdered last year, no longer belonged to me. It had done my heart good to see Kate move in, saving me the trouble of having to haunt it. I could spend as much time there as I wanted and I did. Haunting was impossible with Kate. She could see me. It had taken her a little time to get used to the idea that she could see her sister's ghost, but she'd always been a believer in all things paranormal and it came as no surprise that she quickly embraced the idea. It also came as no surprise to me that she is able to see other spirits who occasionally tag along when I visit Kate. So far, she's been the only living being who has spotted my paranormal friends and me, a fact that seems completely normal to her.

Still waiting for my answer, she waved a hand in front of my face.

"Your carpet is Scotchgarded, right?"

The fact that Kate wanted a dog had little to do with my

fears of chewed trim or urine-stained couches. Material possessions held little appeal to me now that I'd crossed over.

"That has nothing to do with it."

"What then?" She adjusted her designer blazer.

Then it hit me. Kate had moved on. Last year we had partnered up to solve my murder. We'd spent hours working together and were able to put our sibling competitiveness aside to get the job done. During my time in homicide I knew I'd pissed off a lot of people, so when my killer turned out to be a psycho with a vendetta, it held no surprise. What did shock me was finding my corpse with slit wrists in my own bathtub. Knowing I'd never off myself had spurred both Kate and me on to find the killer. Kate nearly lost her own life in the battle but got the bad guy in the end. It had been a major coup in fulfilling her dream of moving up in the department and had landed her a detective spot on the force. I couldn't have handpicked a better replacement for my vacant position. With the case solved, those days were over and I felt a little left out. Now I had to deal with being dead. It raised the question of what to do with myself.

Since then, I've tagged along on a few cases, but I want my old life back, or at least my career. Without that, I have nothing to exist for. My life had been snuffed too soon, and although most women wouldn't mind staying thirty-two forever, it had come with a price.

Throughout my ordeal, Kate had kept me sane. She'd been my anchor in a tumultuous sea of uncertainty, but, lately, she'd seemed distant and distracted, and I tried to tell myself it was simply the new job and the stresses that go with it. I feared a dog would be another distraction in her life, a life that doesn't include me like it used to.

I saw her impatient expression and forced a grin. "Okay, I'm jealous."

"Of what?"

"I'll have to give up riding shotgun. There won't be room for both of us in the front."

Kate shook her head. "You're so full of it."

"So why an Alpha male?" I tried to sound more positive.

"Stud service."

"You have a boyfriend."

"Ah, but this male has papers. I'll be able to make a buck on stud service once he's old enough."

"All men should come with papers."

My relationship track record proved it. At least papers, or the lack of, would have sent a warning and saved me a lot of grief.

She pulled the SUV into her assigned space in the Southfield Heights Police Department lot. She'd been a homicide detective for less than a year and already had her own space. It had taken me much longer.

She cut the engine.

"Some men don't need them." Kate watched as Alvarez headed inside the building.

"Don't do that to me, you know I'm physically unable to puke."

Kate and Gerard were the only two people I knew who could work comfortably as partners both on and off the job. So far they'd made it work with their sense of duty to the job, knowing how to keep it professional when needed. On the job they were both tough as leather, and at times they butted heads. Still, they were good for each other. I could rest in peace, knowing they would be all right.

If there were a couple's glam magazine they'd be on it. They complemented each other in looks with Kate's blonde tresses and blue eyes against his bronze skin and dark, piercing expression. As nauseating as it was, the truth stood that they were the perfect couple.

Kate checked her watch. "Just a few more hours to go. By this time tomorrow I'll be shooshing down the mountain. Can't wait to feel that powder against my cheeks."

"Which ones?" That was exactly why I never wanted to go skiing. I'm athletically challenged.

"I'm a good skier. Never had a bad fall," she countered.

"Who's going this year?" I hinted.

"The regulars. Carmen, Teresa, Nicki, and Pam. Oh, and Jakes."

The invitation didn't come. Maybe I'd said no once too often.

Kate grabbed her purse. "Gotta go. You coming?" She said to me as an afterthought.

"I might tag along. . . ."

The driver's door shut and I watched her hurry to catch up to Gerard.

Before I could make my ethereal exit, I noticed that green Buick Riviera turning into a lot space. It seemed Mullet Man had business at the station. I watched the guy saunter toward the building. A thirty-five-millimeter camera hung from his neck on a thick strap. I figured the guy must be a photographer, which meant something was going on at the station. I hurried to catch up with Kate.

I found her inside Chief Grady O'Connor's office, pacing before his desk.

"You can't be serious. Does Alvarez know about this?"

" 'Fraid so." His blue eyes sparkled.

"That explains his hasty exit into the men's room. Chief, please don't make me do this."

"What's the big deal? It's good publicity for the department," O'Connor said.

"But it's not good for me. Besides, I'm going on vacation in a few hours. Why not assign him to someone else?"

"He said his newspaper specifically asked him to do a special on female detectives and right now you're the only one I have. Look, Kate, it's only for a few days. He'll do ride-alongs and hang around the station. That's it. All you have to do is be nice. Answer a few questions, explain simple procedures, and let him get a good idea what it's like to be a female homicide detective."

"Why can't he just interview me and be gone?"

"I guess his newspaper is jumping on the reality thing. They want to show your life on the job."

"Two days. That's all I'll give him. And if he so much as farts, he's gone."

"You can tell him yourself. He's due in at any moment."

"Terrific. What's his name?"

"Ed Nog."

"Egg Nog?"

"No. Edward Nog. He's a photojournalist at *The Crier*. And Kate? Let's not give him anything to cry about."

I followed Kate out of the chief's office, grinning like a Cheshire cat. When we reached her office, she closed the door and turned.

"What is he thinking?"

"Who?"

"O'Connor." Kate glanced at her cabin reservation and tossed it aside.

"You're just upset because he has fuller hair than you."

"What are you talking about?"

"I think I've seen your date."

"Where?"

"You know the guy who was tailing us in the Buick?"

"Don't say it."

"Yup. The one and only Mullet Man."

There was a knock on Kate's door and Nancy Peterson from reception poked her head inside.

"Sorry to intrude. There's a Mr. Nog here to see you. He says you're expecting him."

"Yes. And I'm expecting him to stay right where he is until I'm ready for him. I'll go up front in a few minutes, Nancy. Thanks."

Kate opened a file folder and began making notes.

"What are you doing?" I asked.

"I'm trying to finish up my paperwork so I can go on vacation."

"Aren't you going to see about Mr. Nog?"

"In a while. Let him wait. After all, he wants to know what it's like to be a detective. Now he'll have an idea. We wait for leads. We wait for witnesses to come forward. We wait for autopsy reports."

"I know. I used to do your job, remember? Look, the sooner you get this over with, the sooner you'll get to your shooshing."

Reluctantly, Kate put down her pen and followed me down the corridor to the front.

She peeked through the small square of glass in the door.

"Was the guy you saw wearing cowboy boots?" she asked.

"Dog-shit brown."

"Too tight jeans?"

"He'll never father children. Which is probably a blessing."

I came up beside her and looked through the window.

Edward Nog had stretched out on the wooden bench of the SHPD waiting room. His faded boots were propped on one armrest, his head on the other. The room was little more than a wide hallway with limited seating space. On one wall, a sliding glass partition kept the public a safe distance from the receptionist; a rack of outdated magazines lined the other wall. Nog had the whole place to himself.

"Well, go on," I urged. "Fame awaits you."

CHAPTER THREE

Kate pulled open the door and forced a smile.

"Mr. Nog?" She tried not to stare at his hair.

One eyelid popped open as if that were all the energy he could offer at this point. Seeing Kate, he nodded and sat up, stretching.

"I'm sorry, I must have dozed off."

"I'm Detective Kate Frost. I understand you want to interview me?"

"Yes, ma'am. I do." He shook her hand.

His Southern accent reminded her of her uncle Jake from Tennessee.

"Actually, it's more of a reality story. Only I'll be documenting with my camera instead of a video."

"Of course. May I ask whose idea this was?" Kate asked.

"All mine. When I heard about the death of your sister and how you took her place, I thought it sounded like a good story. It kind of tugs at the heartstrings. And then my editor suggested we take it a step further and highlight the life and times of a female detective."

"I'll be sure to send her a thank-you note." Kate nodded for the receptionist to buzz them through the door. "Follow me."

Back in her office, Kate waited for Nog to enter. She stuck her head around the corner to see where he'd gone. He was taking his time, looking around, and making notes in a small notepad. Eventually, he sauntered in.

"Nice place here. Wish I had an office at *The Crier.*"

"Have a seat, Mr. Nog." Kate offered, taking her place behind her desk. "Let me call my partner in so I can introduce you. I'm sure he's anxious to meet you."

She dialed Alvarez's number and frowned when it rang endlessly. "He seems to be out at the moment. So tell me, how long have you worked at *The Crier*?"

"Been there about three years."

"I see. When would you like to start your research?"

"You just say the word. I'm here for you."

"Right. Well, unfortunately I'm going out of town for a few days. We won't be able to start until next week. Does that sound fair?"

"Completely. Are you going on vacation?"

"Yes. If you check back early next week, I'm sure we'll be able to set something up."

Kate stood to dismiss him, but he remained seated.

"I think that's great. A little sand and surf. Everyone deserves a break now and then."

"You should know up front, I won't be taking you anywhere that could endanger your hair—health."

"I appreciate that, but you don't have to change your routine because of me. That's part of my job. If I have to risk life and limb, then so be it."

"I see. Well, perhaps we can discuss the ground rules next week. Meantime, I have to cut our visit short."

"Right. Vacation. Can I ask where you're headed?"

"Well, Mr. Nog, I really don't see. . . ." She spied Alvarez heading past her office. "Gerard? May I see you a moment?"

He turned wearing a pained expression. His mouth formed a silent *"no"* behind Nog's back, but she would have none of it. Partners are partners, and if she had to suffer, then so did he.

"Please come in. There's someone I'd like you to meet."

Alvarez shook hands with Nog as Kate introduced the two men.

"And Mr. Nog will be joining us next week to get a feel for how detectives work."

"That's female detectives. This story is focused on your role as a female homicide investigator," Nog said.

"See, Kate? You don't really need me." Alvarez nearly backed into Nancy as she entered the office carrying a small package.

"This came for you a while ago, Detective. Not sure who left it, but it has your name on it."

"Pretty paper. It looks like a box of chocolates." Kate shot Alvarez a questioning glance.

He stood palms up. "Don't look at me."

"Can I get a shot of this, Detective?" Nog readied his camera.

"No. I'm not even sure I should open it."

"Is it ticking?" Alvarez teased.

"Stop it." Kate placed it on her desk. "It's cold."

"See? It probably is chocolates. Hurry up and open it, I'm starving," Alvarez said.

Kate tore at the paper until she saw the box inside. "Who would send me this?"

"One of your adoring fans?" Alvarez came up beside her.

"Back off. This is my candy." Kate lifted the lid.

A bright flash briefly blinded her.

She heard a hearty "Hot damn!" from Nog as Alvarez pulled her away from the desk.

Another series of camera flashes went off.

"Stop that!" Kate commanded Nog.

Kate leaned closer to see the bloodied appendage surrounded by dry ice. It was a woman's finger.

"Geez. You must have really pissed someone off for them to give you the finger like that." Nog stared at the box. "Are you sure it's real?"

Alvarez was on the phone to the crime lab even as Kate ushered Nog from the office.

"I'm sorry, but you'll have to leave now."

"But this is the kind of thing I need to document. This is perfect."

"Not now."

"I can see you're upset. I would be too if some goof had just made a mess of my desk. I'll be in contact with you real soon."

"I look forward to it." Like a root canal.

Kate slid her cabin reservations from under the box, careful not to touch it. She tossed them into the waste can figuring her vacation had just been cancelled.

CHAPTER FOUR

I rode along with Kate back to my old house. She had packing to do.

It had taken a lot of fast-talking from Chief O'Connor and Alvarez to convince Kate not to cancel her trip. Kate can be stubborn and I can only imagine what they had to promise her. From what she said, they'd both been right. There wasn't a whole lot she could do even if she did stay. The crime lab would analyze the evidence to determine whose finger it was. If the print wasn't in the system, we didn't stand much of a chance of finding its owner unless she showed up at our lost and found. Even then, I doubt it would do her much good. I hadn't seen it up close, but from what Kate told me, the finger had been frozen in dry ice, and still looked pretty fresh.

Kate barely spoke as she headed for home.

I tried to break the tension.

"You know the fact that the finger was sent directly to you could mean a lot of things, depending on the condition of the rest of the body. A severed finger doesn't necessarily point to murder."

She failed to see the humor.

"It could just be a matter of someone with a grudge who has access to detached limbs. I'm sure Alvarez will check hospitals and morgues for missing parts and places that sell dry ice. For now, there's nothing for you to do but go to White Crest and let the department handle it. Monday will be here soon enough."

Although I still had yet to receive my invitation to White Crest, the more I thought about it, I realized Kate's trip would provide me with a good opportunity to investigate my new world. I'd spent the first part of my spirit life solving my own murder. Since then, I'd made it a point to work with Kate as a kind of invisible shield while she got her bearings in homicide. Truth is, she didn't need much help.

With her gone for a few days, I could concentrate on learning all I could about my new existence. The break might be good for both of us. Maybe she'd be her old self when she returned.

We arrived at the house and I watched Kate kick through the snow on the walkway. It seemed like ages since I could do that, so I tried just for fun. My foot plowed through it without a mark. No snow angels for me. I still have a hard time accepting I can move things in the paranormal world, but not in the physical world. In the spirit realm we can only move paranormal things like our death tags. My theory is that our tags are the replicas of the physical world we bring with us and we're able to hold on to them because they're paranormal in nature. Apples to apples.

During my quest to solve my murder, I'd had to duke it out with a criminal I'd killed during a standoff before my death. Tanner Jean Hoyt was a military wannabe with a strange sense of justice. When she attacked me shortly after my death, her blows landed hard enough to send me flying, prompting my friend, Mike, to teach me paranormal counter moves. It was all based on concentration and focus. That explains why there's no actual contact when we attempt to shake hands or hug other spirits. We're not actively concentrating on the action.

When we move to the physical world, however, we lose the ability to move items with physical properties. Knowing this, I still forget at times and attempt to touch or grab things. Frustrating.

"You know I won't be able to think of anything else all weekend but that stupid finger," Kate said.

"Let go of it," I told her.

"What kind of message does it send?" Kate unlocked the front door.

"Well, there's the obvious. But that really depends on who it was previously attached to."

"You should have seen it, Linz. God, who would do that? And then there's that idiot, Nog, snapping pictures of it. I can't believe I have to spend time with that man."

Kate has the annoying habit of latching onto a topic. If I didn't ease her off, Mullet Man would end up with bite marks. "It will give Alvarez a little competition," I joked.

"Don't start. It was a conspiracy. Alvarez could have warned me. I could have called in sick today. But that's beside the point. How am I going to get out of this?" Kate started emptying the perishables out of her refrigerator.

"You're not. So try and focus on cold, white, fluffy stuff."

I watched Kate pour expired milk down the sink.

"Right. Did you see the way Nog stared at me? It gave me the creeps. How can I maintain a professional image with him following me everywhere? He's like a hemorrhoid."

A package of green bologna went into the trash.

"Forget about it. You're officially on vacation and your biggest concern right now should be which bottle of wine to bring."

Kate headed for the bedroom and pulled down a suitcase from the top shelf. I paced before her dresser as she folded and packed her weekend getaway gear.

I was still holding out for the invitation to join her.

"So, what's on the agenda for the gang?" I fished.

"The usual. Skiing. Drinking. Gossip. Skiing. And more drinking. I'm afraid it won't be that interesting."

Kate shoved a few condom packets in the suitcase's side pouch.

"You're worried things won't be interesting?" I grinned.

Her cheeks colored. "You never know who'll show up."

"I thought this was no men allowed."

"Normally it is."

"You invited Alvarez?"

"No. But. . . ."

"But he knows where the cabin is just in case," I teased.

She picked up the condoms again.

"I was kidding. Put those back."

"On second thought, it's probably a waste of time."

"Why?"

"Cynthia's been acting up again and I just can't see Gerard leaving the boys for a couple of days."

I knew Cynthia from my partnering days with Alvarez. Her alcohol abuse had torn them apart, and, after a bitter divorce last year, he'd gained custody of their boys, Paul and John. Since then he'd been a single man working a more-than-full-time job and had done well. Although divorced, he still had to deal with her binges while trying to salvage what relationship the boys had left with her. That hadn't always gone so well.

"What happened?" I asked.

"She was supposed to take the boys over the weekend, and Paul called around eleven the first night to tell Gerard she was passed out on the couch. He won't let her see the boys until she gets back to AA. She told him to go to hell."

"He married her," I said. As far as I was concerned he'd done his time.

"Since then he's been distracted. Can't say I blame him."

"Well, he could leave the boys with his mom," I suggested.

Kate grinned and tossed the rubbers back into her suitcase. "You're right."

"What? You don't see enough of him on the job?" I love to watch her squirm.

"Yes. No. Stop the interrogation. I haven't done anything wrong." She tossed in a sexy negligee.

"That's it. I'm steppin' out for a beer. I can't stand to watch you like this."

"What's that, happy?"

"Horny. You're my little sister and he's my ex-partner. Too many details spoil the plot." I winked and let myself fade. What an exit. My navigational skills were improving daily.

I left Kate to her packing, intent on checking in with a group of friends I hadn't touched base with for some time. When I'd worked on my own homicide last year, I met several spirits on the other side, one of whom turned into a potential paranormal guide. She was the get-answer guru when it came to learning how to function in the afterlife.

Sally O'Shannon had died tragically in a fire intentionally set by an overzealous human-rights group intent on taking down a sperm bank. Poor Sally had gone in on her day off to do some filing and ended up a human torch. I admit her cynical perspective can be annoying at times, but she was the first person I met here and she is truly someone I can count on.

I found Sally at her usual spot in the parking lot where she'd died. According to my research, it's common practice for a ghost to be drawn to his or her place of death. I'm sure there's some Freudian reason for it, but no one here seems too worried about it.

Had I known that, I would have opted to die in a Jamaican Villa surrounded by gorgeous, scantily clad men. As it turned out, I would forever be drawn to the claw-footed bathtub in my old bathroom.

Sally waved me over to where she sat on the curb, holding

her death tag, a bedraggled teddy bear. "How is it you always look perky and ready for adventure?" Her dark unibrow shelved across the melted skin of her forehead betraying one of the telltale signs of her fiery death. I thanked God for small favors glancing at my scarred wrists, compliments of my murderer. It's a sad fact we spend eternity looking like our corpse when we die, scars included. No trade-ins for a perfect body minus cellulite and arm wattles.

"Diet and exercise," I joked.

"Eternal rest, remember?"

"We both know that's not true." I tugged at the bear. "We all have our issues, right?"

I fingered the detective badge hanging from its cord around my neck. All those years spent thinking death meant permanent R&R had been wrong. Death is only a stopping place along the way to eternity where we get a chance to work out a major issue. Once that's accomplished, we give up our tag and move on to the next level.

"One day you'll figure it out." Sally smiled.

"I hope not. I have no plans to give up my shield. It's what I do, who I am."

"It might be good that you feel that way because earlier someone was looking for you."

My spine tingled. . . . Well, not literally, but the last time someone in the spirit world had been looking for me they turned out to be a stalker. It had nearly cost me my death tag and my family's safety.

I tried for casual. "Oh? Who?"

"He didn't leave his name."

"And this has something to do with my badge?"

"I'm not sure. But he asked for Detective Frost. So I'm guessing it's a professional concern. He was no newbie. Knew exactly who he was looking for and that I was a friend of yours. Said he needed to speak with you."

"About what?"

"Wouldn't say. Guess it's a private matter." She looked hurt.

I tried to think of who it might be. My contacts on this side were minimal. If I'd pissed anyone off or owed them money they were most likely still among the living. My curiosity piqued.

"Did he say where I can find him?"

"He said he'd be back."

Great. Now all I had to do was wait. With eternity on my side, I guessed I probably wouldn't break a sweat, even if I could.

CHAPTER FIVE

Since Kate's invitation to join her at White Crest hadn't come, I decided maybe it was time for me to take a little trip of my own. I opted for Daytona Beach where I could enjoy the scenery, namely bronze men in Speedos. It would be a break from the Indiana winter skies, which tended to turn the color of rancid mashed potatoes in December and stay that way through May. Even though I wouldn't be able to feel the sun's warmth, my spirit would appreciate the blue skies and sandy beaches.

It's nice not to have to rely on airlines for distance traveling, and I used my navigational skills as I concentrated on my destination. No lines, no traffic, and I didn't miss the onboard movie.

Upon my arrival, I found I was over-dressed in the blouse and pants I'd been wearing at my demise. As a kid I used to scoff at my mother's prompting to always wear clean underwear in case I was in an accident. What she didn't know was that it goes a lot further than that. You wear what you die in, so always dress in the thing you'll be comfortable in for eternity.

I took a spot amidst the crowds parked on blankets and towels on the beachfront. No need for sunscreen or sunglasses as I perused the ample display of men playing Frisbee and strutting their manliness to and from the water. Sailboats trimmed the horizon as I closed my eyes and let the crashing waves soothe my restless spirit. After a little while I walked along the beach, letting the waves almost wash over my shoes. My transparent form allowed me to see the foam rush up on the shore beneath my feet. Not as satisfying as it used to be but this wasn't about reliving familiarities, it was about creating new experiences.

I walked out into the ocean, noticing the absence of the water pressure surrounding my body and the lack of sea smell. A large wave neared the shore, and I saw excited body surfers gathering to wait to catch a ride in. I wished I could join them in feeling the rush of adrenaline it brought while speeding over the water like a sailboat. Turning into the wind, my blonde tresses stayed neatly on my shoulders instead of blowing gracefully outward. No cover-girl shot today. Still, it was just what I needed to feel human again.

Suddenly the thought of spending the weekend on a snowy mountain with dangling icicles and more muck-colored skies lost what little appeal it had had in the first place. Kate could have it. This might just become my new place to hang out. It was paradise . . . at least by comparison.

Then all hell broke loose.

At first I paid no attention to the swimmers' squeals as they played and splashed nearby. But one high-pitched scream in particular gained my attention, and it wasn't long before I realized it was a panicked cry for help.

Standing, I scanned the water for someone in distress but didn't see anyone. The pleading cries continued to find me as I hurried along the beach. I wondered what I would do when I located the person, having no physical form to pull them from the water or administer CPR with. I raced on anyway. It occurred to me that the problem might be on the beach itself rather than the water, and I turned my attention to the hundreds of sunbathers. The crowded beach left little room to survey individuals, and I scanned for any unusual movements like running or someone being attacked. Still nothing.

By now the cries had stopped and I made my way back. I

caught sight of a Caucasian child of about eight, wearing a pink bathing suit, clutching swim goggles. She stumbled out of the water, tears streaming down her face. Her high-pitched cry had been the one I'd heard earlier and I hurried to her aid. When I reached her, I bent down and realized she was a ghost.

"What is it?" I asked. "What's wrong?"

She clutched her goggles close as if I would take them from her and sniffed. "I'm lost. Can you help me?"

"Who are you looking for?"

"My parents. A big wave knocked over our sailboat."

I knew then that she'd drowned.

"C'mon, we'll try and find them."

We made our way to the concession stand where patio tables and umbrellas provided a shady place to enjoy everything from hot dogs to ice cream. As we passed a newspaper box, I saw the headline and the matching photo.

LOCAL FAMILY LOST IN SAILING ACCIDENT

The family portrait showed the same little girl with her parents, smiling for the camera during happier times. Skimming the article, I learned the whole family had drowned when their sailboat had capsized the day before.

I led the child back to the waterfront and waited. If I'd lost track of my child, I'd keep visiting the place where I'd seen her last. Suddenly the little girl squealed, this time in delight.

"There's my mom!" She pointed to a woman wearing a black one-piece bathing suit.

A look of relief washed over the woman's face as she ran to her daughter.

"April, are you all right?" she asked.

"This nice lady helped me find you."

A tall man in swim trunks and tennis shoes came up beside them.

"Thank you so much for finding our little girl. We've looked everywhere and thought we'd lost her." He extended his hand and I made the pretense of shaking. He didn't seem to notice and I wondered if he knew he was dead.

"We'd better get back to the dock," he told his wife.

They thanked me once again and April waved good-bye. I wasn't sure if they truly knew the score, but I sure wasn't about to ruin their day. If that's the way they chose to deal with their situation, it was fine by me. There are worse ways to spend eternity.

Little did I know that this little episode was just the beginning of a new way for me to spend mine.

CHAPTER SIX

Kate Frost made the final turn down the long forest road leading to the A-frame house. Its outdoor, railed second-floor
balcony ran the length of the home. She saw no trace of life
through the tall windows, but she knew in a short while the
cathedral ceiling lights and blazing fireplace would emanate an
enticing golden glow. The frosted air of vacancy would soon be
replaced with the hot gossip and wild laughter of five college
buddies on their yearly ski trip. It had surprised her when Jakes
had decided to take her up on the ski trip offer. Jakes was a
workaholic whose idea of relaxing was going over the next
month's business schedule.

Lately, she'd noticed a change in her friend, not necessarily
for the better. Although Jakes had been more open to last-
minute lunches in town, it had seemed to Kate their get-
togethers were a much-needed outlet. They'd shared long
discussions over lattes about Jakes' live-in boyfriend. Her friend
showed all the telltale signs of someone about to flush a relationship that had been circling the drain for months. Kate knew this
trip away was just what Jakes needed to pull herself together. It
would be a chance to leave behind the daily concerns and let
them go for a few days.

The word rustic never came to mind when describing her
Wisconsin weekend getaway, although the term "roughing it"
did. Anytime she had to apply manual labor to secure creature
comforts like heat and cooked food, it was rough. There were

no fast-food joints, pampering spas or gourmet coffee shops. It was just woman and the elements—and, of course, an ample supply of wine.

When she stopped at a convenience store for last-minute items like milk and butter, the woman behind the counter gave a knowing nod.

"Stocking up before the big one, huh?" The woman rang up the items.

"The big what?" Kate asked.

"Snowstorm, honey. Haven't you heard?"

"I'm used to snow. After all that's what I'm here for."

"Well I hope you're wearin' your long johns because it could bury us all."

"Thanks for the warning."

The skies had been clear and blue as she drove and Kate wondered if the woman had been having fun at her expense. A little scare-the-tourist humor. She shrugged and decided she was up for a weekend of roughing it after receiving a finger in the mail.

Chopping wood and long underwear aside, she loved going to White Crest Mountain. It brought out the nature lover and risk taker in her, as well as gave her the opportunity to catch up with her best friends from college. This year she'd be going as Detective Kate Frost, a dream come true for her. She glanced at the passenger seat at the large champagne bottle she'd brought for a toast. Tonight would be a special night.

Guilt pangs gripped her at the thought of once again leaving Lindsay behind. It's not like she hadn't invited her. Hadn't she? She couldn't recall her sister's response and wondered if she'd neglected to ask. But what was the point? Lindsay had declined her invitation every year, offering one lame excuse after another.

After losing her sister last year, she'd thought her life would take a steady downhill slide into an abyss of darkness. It almost had. Then Lindsay had returned, granted, not in original form, but she was back in Kate's life. Now that things had become almost normal again between them, she figured her sister hadn't changed her philosophy on frozen nose hairs and snow-soaked socks.

She parked the SUV near the steps and noted she was the first to arrive. No signs of Jakes yet, but she had a knack for being late. She'd spoken to her yesterday to give her final directions to the cabin. The only thing going on with her friend had been her boyfriend complaining about the trip. "He'll get over it," was all she'd said.

Checking her watch she saw she'd made better time than she'd anticipated. Kate grinned knowing that she'd get first choice of available bedrooms and she already knew which one it would be. The smallest bedroom on the west side of the home had the best view of the lake and the main road. The barren trees allowed a perfect view of approaching cars. Just in case they'd have a visitor.

It took less than fifteen minutes to settle in and realize she was freezing. Pleasantly surprised to find an ample supply of cut wood ready and waiting, she started a fire. Out of necessity, she'd learned the art of building a roaring fire, and, before long, she stood warming her fingers before the open flames. As her limbs thawed, she cuddled inside a couch comforter and let her mind wander over the hills and valleys of lust. She longed to have Gerard beside her now with a glass of wine and soft music playing. She made herself stop, realizing it would make for a miserable weekend if she did nothing but fantasize about Gerard.

Her surprise gift came to mind instead and Kate tried to push aside the image of the finger, and concentrate on more pleasant thoughts. She jumped when the front door banged open.

"Hey! Let's get this girl-fest started! Anyone home?"

Kate bounded from the couch to greet the second of the weekend warriors, Teresa Nielson, a family-practice lawyer from California.

She hugged Teresa feeling the old familiar warmth and camaraderie of her college days return. "Good to see you. How was your flight?"

Teresa's chestnut hair bobbed behind her in a ponytail as she lugged her skis across the room. "What's that joke about tired arms?"

Kate peeked out the window and gave a low whistle. "Driving a shiny convertible must be murder on your arms."

"It's the only rental car I could find." Teresa grinned.

Kate groaned when she picked up Teresa's suitcase. "What have you got in here, a body?"

"That's right. It's a test, Detective. Congratulations, Kate. I always knew you'd do it."

"Looks like you get second dibs on the rooms. Where do you want this?" Kate hauled her luggage toward the bedrooms.

"I like that little room in the back."

"Taken. You know the rules. First come, first choice."

"Shit. That has the nicest view of the lake."

"Why not take the middle room? It has the sleigh bed and the most closet space."

"Why would I need that?" Teresa grinned carting two more suitcases down the hall.

Kate sat on the king-size bed, watching her friend unpack. "So how's it going?"

"You mean since the divorce?" Teresa gave a thoughtful smile. "I used to collect figurines; now I collect men. But I find men far more interesting." She hung up another pair of jeans. "So how about you? Anyone special?"

"Well, I think I e-mailed you about Gerard."

"Right. He's your partner both on the streets and in the sheets."

"Something like that. He was Lindsay's partner before. . . ."

"Oh, honey. I'm so sorry I didn't make it to the funeral. I didn't know her very well, but I loved her because she was your sister. How are you holding up?"

Kate felt guilty. She no longer considered her sister dead. They saw each other every day and it seemed little had really changed between them except her sister's physical properties. No one could see or hear her except Kate. She realized that before the weekend was over she would most likely have more heartfelt condolences to contend with. Of the five women in the weekend group, only Nicki Jordan, Pam Mallard, and Jakes had made it to the funeral.

A rush of activity sounded in the other room, and Kate knew the weekend had begun.

She and Teresa greeted the rest of the gang with plenty of hugs and kisses and enough laughter to rattle the eaves. Nicki Jordan led the pack with Pam Mallard and Carmen French following.

Kate was thrilled to see Nicki's Golden Retriever, Beaver, bounding through the door offering a friendly bark and chin kisses for everyone.

After they'd settled in, the group sat before the fireplace toasting Kate's success and then raised a glass to Lindsay's memory.

"Thanks everyone." Kate looked around at her friends wishing Lindsay hadn't missed it, and wondering what had happened to Jakes. She had tried her cell phone several times with no answer.

Nicki Jordan sat with her back against the couch finishing the last of the frozen pizza with Beaver nuzzled beside her. Nicki's waif-thin figure gave no indication of her ravenous appetite.

Kate supposed she burned a lot of calories as a high-school gym teacher and girls'-basketball coach. A love for sports and her high energy made Nicki the perfect fit for the high school set. Her blonde spiked hair and piercing green eyes gave her a younger look for her twenty-eight years.

The love of her life was her dog, and she rarely went anywhere without him. She gave him the last morsel from her plate and lifted her glass once more.

"To great friends and even greater shooshing!"

"Hear, hear!" A round of voices went up.

"I can't wait to get out there tomorrow morning. Anyone sleeping late gets a wedgie."

"You and what army, Nicki?" Teresa wanted to know.

"I'm an army of one."

"That's battery, you know."

"That's not your thing. Stick to what you know." Nicki grinned.

"That's a laugh. How's it look for a family-practice lawyer to get divorced? Apparently I didn't practice enough."

Pam Mallard refilled everyone's glasses. "You look healthier for it."

Teresa raised her glass. "I'll take that as a compliment. Besides, you know all about health. By the way, do you have any new tales of the crypt to share?"

Pam had become the group's resident storyteller. As a surgical nurse at a Chicago hospital she never seemed to run out of anecdotes and stories both funny and frightening.

"I might have a few tucked away for a late-night campfire."

"Count me out unless you want a bed partner. I can't sleep after hearing those stories." Carmen French shook her head, causing her large hoop earrings to dangle. The Jada Pinkett look-alike held up a manicured hand. "The scariest thing I can handle is the news that home-mortgage rates are skyrocketing.

But as for all that cut-it-up sew-it-up stuff? Uh-uh."

Kate laughed knowing the real Carmen was a lot tougher than she let on. Raised on inner-city streets, she'd probably witnessed more horror and tragedy than Pam could come up with. She'd fought to avoid the gangs and trouble so prevalent near her home, intent on making a future and a fortune. And she had. After college, she'd moved to Florida where she used her real-estate broker's license and business degree to corner the market on oceanfront properties.

After two more bottles of wine and a generous portion of gossip, Kate realized the sun would be making its appearance in only a few short hours, and Nicki wasn't kidding when she threatened wedgies to anyone sleeping in. With that in mind she called it a night.

Early the next morning, Kate decided they didn't make room-darkening shades dark enough to suit her. The nightstand alarm clock glowed a neon eight A.M., but she detected no signs of life from the other room and tugged the pillow over her head for more sleep. Wedgie be damned. Besides, she'd made sure her firearm was in plain view on the nightstand to deter any would-be wedgieists.

A harsh knock sounded from the front door, and she listened carefully a moment hoping it was just the wind. Another series of hard pounds sounded loud enough to get her out of bed barefoot and sleep-logged. She wrapped the bed comforter around her and headed to the living room.

"Okay. Stop with the banging." She checked out the window to see a man wearing a hooded ski parka, faded blue jeans and black work boots. His gloved hand rose once more to knock.

Kate hurried to open the door and let the early bird have it when she was taken off guard by his alarming bearded smile.

"Good morning. I'm Ted Burke, caretaker." He held out a

box of donuts.

Kate tucked a strand of blonde hair behind her ear and stepped aside to allow him in. He stamped the snow from his boots on the mat and proceeded to the kitchen.

"Quite a party, huh?" He nodded to the glasses and empty wine bottles on the coffee table as he went.

As long as she'd been renting the cottage on White Crest, she'd never recalled seeing or meeting the caretaker. Was this some new service compliments of the A-frame's owner? Her sleep-deprived brain finally caught up with the situation, and she followed the man into the kitchen.

"You can just set them on the table." She straightened to her full five-foot-eight height and went into detective mode. "Is there something I can do for you, Mr. Burke?"

"No. I just wanted to make an appearance and let you know I'm around if you ladies need anything. Quite a few cars out there. Are you expecting anyone else?" His line of vision moved toward the back bedroom.

"There's plenty of room if we get more company, Mr. Burke." Kate tried to steer him toward the door.

"Well, then. I'll leave ya my cell phone number." He tore a sheet of paper from a notepad on the rolltop desk and scribbled his information. "That ought to do it." He handed it to Kate.

She barely glanced at it, feeling her annoyance at the early intrusion and his lack of manners. He did bring donuts, she chided herself.

"What's going on?" Teresa trudged into the living room in her satin robe and matching pink scuffs. "Oh. We have company."

"This is our caretaker, Mr. Burke," Kate said.

Teresa closed the distance between them, her hand extended. "Nice to meet you. I knew it was too good to be true that my friend here had actually chopped wood for a fire yesterday. That had to be your handiwork."

Kate appreciated Teresa's ability to adapt to any situation. She guessed years spent smoothing the ruffled feathers of her clients under some very delicate negotiations had trained her to deal with almost anything.

"Thanks for the compliment." Kate frowned.

"Yes, ma'am. That was me," Burke said. "I took the liberty of getting the place ready so you could dive right in and have fun." He glanced once more at the coffee table.

"Yes, well, that was very thoughtful of you," Kate started for the door hoping he'd pick up the cue.

A warning beep from a laptop on the rolltop alerted Teresa she had a message. "Excuse me," she said as she sat at the desk. After pressing a few keys, Teresa frowned. "Damn thing is locked up."

Before Kate could open the front door, she saw Burke lean over Teresa's shoulder to study the computer screen. "These things do that. Here, try this." He tapped a couple of keys and waited less than a second. "There. You're back in business."

"That's amazing. I never have any luck with it when it locks up. I simply shut down, curse and try again. Thank you, Mr. Burke."

"No problem." He made his way to the door then, stopping beside Kate to say, "Like I said, call me if you need anything."

CHAPTER SEVEN

My attempt at a mini-vacation had backfired. Although I felt a sense of satisfaction in helping April and her family, it kind of ruined my getaway. No longer in the mood for tanned skin and sandy crevices, I thought about the mysterious man who'd visited Sally in search of me. I hate surprises, unless it involves money or sex, and in my current condition neither one would do me much good. Still I had little choice except to wait and see if he came back around. I'm not a patient person so waiting for some dead guy to show up looking for me lasted about ten minutes. I think. No real way of telling time here. I guess eternity is all you need to know.

I decided to look up another friend of mine, Mike Blake, a cop killed in the line of duty about a year before I came on the scene. He'd helped me out on my case last year by showing me some paranormal self-defense moves. His physique and green eyes had given me pause when I realized sexual attraction doesn't end at death. Unfortunately, my relationship track record and the fact that I didn't know the first thing about pursuing an affair on this side gave me enough reason to reconsider.

Mike admitted he still had feelings for his wife although there wasn't a chance that he could ever act on them. I didn't take it personal and figured some things just need to run their course. We decided to remain good friends as a safety net for both of us.

My father always called me obstinate, and I suppose he was right. It seems I always take the less-used door to arrive at my destinations. It isn't in me to do anything like everyone else. I prefer to say I walk my own path.

So far all of the spirits I've met revisit their place of death occasionally, making it easy to find a person when you want them. Personally, a bathroom can be a necessary place to visit, but I wouldn't want to live there, so I invented my own special place. Growing up, my parents liked to take me and my sister Kate to a wooded picnic ground where we could spread a blanket under mature trees and eat our lunch. Maybe that's a little *Leave It to Beaver,* but that's the place I thought of when I decided to create my home away from home. Since the spot is paranormal in nature, I found it easy to create, meaning I didn't have to actually plant trees or get permission from the park district to stake my claim. I simply imagined it and started hanging out there. My paranormal crime team consisting of Sally, Mike Blake and an acquaintance of Mike's, coroner Dr. Warren Saint, all like it so much that they visit my spot more often than I do. Frankly, I'm flattered. Guess that makes me the Michelangelo of the spirit world.

And that's where I found Mike Blake sitting under a tall oak, picking at a piece of tall grass growing wild in the shade. Yes, I even put in a few weeds to give a more authentic look.

He grinned and started to get up.

"Sit," I told him. "You look far too comfortable to move." I plopped down beside him.

The set of his narrow jaw told me he'd been in deep thought about something so I tried to sit quiet and wait for him to say something. I'd learned the technique from my ex-partner, Gerard Alvarez, in interviewing difficult suspects. He was the god of patience and could sit in silence longer than any marble statue. Most criminals found it nerve-racking, and they usually started talking within minutes. It had worked for me on occasion, but only if the suspect had a dire need to use the washroom. I didn't have Gerard's knack.

I was relieved to see Mike toss aside the weed and turn my way. Not one to mince words, he said, "Kathy is getting married."

Ouch. Kathy was his widow and although her obligations to Mike had been officially severed when death did them part, I knew it hurt him.

"I'm sorry, Mike. Do you know the guy?"

"Yeah. He's a cop. Can you believe that? Our marital problems stemmed from my career. Too many hours and stress. That's all she ever complained about. And, to top it off, he's from my department."

I sat in silence unsure what to say. My own relationship history was riddled with unfairness and screwups, but never anything as painful as this.

"And I worry about the effect of this on Michelle. She's only eight and she's already lost one father figure in her life in the line of duty. What happens to her if this guy gets hurt or killed too?"

I averted my eyes from the gunshot hole in the chest of his police uniform. I knew the chances of that happening were slim. Small-town police forces lose few cops in the line of duty, but it had happened to Mike so I kept my stats to myself. Right now Mike needed to vent.

"Can I help?" I asked, unsure of how lame it sounded.

His green eyes held my gaze and he moved closer. For a moment I thought he was going to try and kiss me, and I wondered if it was even possible in spirit form. But then he gripped my chin even though I didn't actually feel it, and said, "You've already done it. I know how hard it is for you to let someone have the floor. Thanks for letting me blow off some steam."

"I'm not sure that was a compliment, but I'll let it slide because one, you're under duress, and two, you're right."

We both tensed, when a section of tall grass behind us rustled and bent forward.

"Who's there?" I called.

Mike took the lead, stepping in front of me; a move I'm not used to as a seasoned officer. I let it go, knowing it was his chivalrous nature more than a male ego thing and stepped to his side.

"I said who's there?" My gaze scanned the row of bushes.

Mike signaled for me to take one side of the brush while he moved to the other. Before we went too far, a tall wiry white male stepped through looking somewhat lost. His dark eyes pinned me with an even darker stare.

"You Detective Lindsay Frost?"

"Who wants to know?" I didn't like this guy.

His caterpillar eyebrows eased into two lines again and I saw his jaw muscles relax. He took a slow drag from his cigarette.

Mike stood beside me, arms crossed over his broad chest, as if waiting for the guy to say or do the wrong thing. My hero.

The man finally extended a hand my way as he moved past Mike. "Easy there, big fellah. Even in spirit form you outweigh me by at least fifty pounds. I'm not here to start trouble."

"Why didn't you answer me when I asked who you were?" I made the pretense of shaking his hand, much like Muffy sharing an air kiss at the yacht club.

"I wasn't sure who you were. I never expected to show up in a forest looking for you. You have to be careful where you navigate; the natives aren't always friendly. Besides, what were you going to do, shoot me?"

"Point taken," I eased up. "I'm Detective Frost. What can I do for you?"

His tan business suit reeked of lawyer or perhaps accountant, and I briefly wondered if there was some sort of death tax I'd neglected to pay. I could see the telltale signs of his death from the gaping exit wound in his forehead with evidence of bone fragments and mushy gray matter. His forehead had taken on a misshapen, lopsided look. I've witnessed my share of autopsies and from the looks of the hole it was apparent he'd been shot from behind. His death was most likely a professional hit. Then everything fell into place when he told me his name.

"I'm Rico DiCianni. Perhaps you've heard of me?"

Who hadn't? He was a well-known mobster with Chicago ties. He'd originally set up shop in northwest Indiana as a used-furniture dealer, dealing in more than dusty couches and beaded lampshades. In the end he'd been found stuffed into one of his own dressers, each drawer housing a different body part. It's a good thing he'd died of the gunshot wound or he'd literally be in pieces right now. A reminder that the way a person looks when they die is how they spend eternity. That little fact had helped me solve my own murder.

Mike stood silently by, never taking his eyes from the man. I knew he didn't trust him. But I'd grown curious, wondering what a guy like this wanted with me.

"Yes, I'm familiar with your history. What can I do for you?"

"I want you to find out who murdered me." Although he'd been puffing on the cigarette throughout our conversation, it never got any smaller. I figured it must be his death tag.

"You realize I'm dead, right? I don't work homicide anymore."

I could see this was a man who hadn't heard the word "no" more than once or twice in his life.

"There's no need to try and kill me with that look, Mr. DiCianni. It won't do you any good."

He looked away, nodding. "Okay. I guess things don't change much after death. What's your price?"

"I don't have one."

"Everyone has one."

Mike stepped in front of him. "She told you she doesn't. Your visit here is over."

"I don't think so." He blew smoke in Mike's direction.

I intervened before Mike took him out—again.

"Listen, Mr. DiCianni, I'm really not interested in working homicides any longer." Something caught in my subconscious, and I mulled my last statement over while he took another drag.

"That's not what I heard. You solved your own murder not long ago."

"That was different. I had little choice if I wanted closure for my family and myself."

"Isn't it your sworn duty or something? Serve and protect and all that?"

"Well, yes. . . ."

"Then that shouldn't change just because you're dead. If you solved your own murder why not mine?"

He had a point. I recalled my mini-vacation and April's family. It seemed I was still in the serving capacity, dead or not.

When I'd held my badge for the first time, it felt solid. It felt right. When I left the earth, I'd taken it as my death tag. What was it I'd told Kate? "It's who I am. It's what I do." Ol' Rico was right. It was my duty until I give up my tag.

"All right, Mr. DiCianni. . . ."

"Please, call me Rico."

"Rico. I'll hear you out and if I think I can help you, I will. But I'm warning you I can be brutally honest. If at any time I don't think you're on the level with me, I'll shitcan your request into eternity. We clear?"

I saw Mike take a seat on a downed tree log, shaking his head. Since it probably wasn't a headache, I figured he'd given up on me. His expression said he was only sticking around because he wanted to see how deep I could dig myself.

So be it.

When I learned the details surrounding Rico's death, I figured I could help. He had a long list of possible suspects and knew the actual name of the hit man. What he wanted to know was who ordered the hit.

"Aren't you the least bit angry with the guy who pulled the trigger?" I asked.

"Nah. He was just following orders. Doin' his job."

"Interesting." I knew the world of organized crime took a different view on many things, but that surprised me. "So tell me, Rico. If I find out who ordered the hit, what will you do with the information. It's not like you can enact revenge."

"Like you said it's a matter of closure. I can wait. He's got to die sooner or later."

"Ah, so your motive is payback. What are you planning to do?"

"Can't tell ya that."

"Why not?"

"Because then I'd have to kill you."

When I didn't laugh, he shrugged. "Just a little mob humor."

"Very little." I paced the thick grass before him, thinking hard.

Was this something I should get involved with? Probably not. Could I be taking on more than I could handle? Considering I had no job, no love life—make that no life at all really—I supposed not.

Would this come back to bite me in my ethereal ass? Most likely.

But right now I needed a diversion. And Rico's words kept repeating like a bad song in my head. *Isn't it your sworn duty?*

I turned in time to get a face full of smoke from Rico's cigarette. At least secondhand smoke was no longer a health concern.

"All right Mr.—"

He raised a stump of an index finger to correct me. Somewhere along the line he'd given a pound of flesh or at least a quarter.

"Rico," I amended. "I'll look into it. Where can I find you if I need you?"

"Forget about it. I'll find you." With that he disappeared into the tall grass, a trail of smoke lingering behind.

CHAPTER EIGHT

After Rico left, I waited to see what Mike would have to say. He remained seated on the downed tree log, a smirk twisting his full lips.

"What?" I asked sitting beside the log in the grass.

"Thank you."

"For what?"

"For making me forget my own troubles for a while. Nice to know I'm not alone."

"Misery loves company. But I'm not really miserable. This is really a good opportunity for me."

"To do what?"

"Since solving my own murder, I've been kind of, you know, in limbo . . . wait, poor choice of words. I've been wondering what I should do next. I suppose you could say my main issue has been taken care of. We found my killer."

"I'm listening."

"Well doesn't it strike you as a little odd that my death tag didn't disappear after I resolved the issue of my death? I mean technically, I should be at the next level right now. Whatever that is."

I'd seen firsthand what happens to spirits who settle their issue. It's actually quite beautiful. First their death tag disappears and then the person's image fades gently away. The man I saw move on had the most wonderful smile on his face as he went.

Mike's frown told me I was onto something.

"That means my murder isn't all there is, to whatever death issue I'm supposed to work out. I hate to admit it, but Rico is right. I have a sworn duty to serve and protect, and that's what I'm going to keep doing."

"Explain how you plan to work homicide."

"I'm going to hang out a shingle. One-Eight-Hundred-Who-Dunnit. Free Frisbee to the first fifty customers."

"Very funny. But you still haven't told me how you're going to do it."

"I did it before. With Kate's help."

"Kate has a job. I understand why she worked with you the first time, but now you're talking about a permanent thing. You better think it through."

"You're right." After a beat I said, "Okay. Done."

"I can see you're in one of your moods."

"I don't have moods. I'm a professional."

"That's right, Lindsay. You are. And a pro always has a plan. What's yours?"

He had me there. If Kate opted out, I had no contact person in the department. Since no one could see or hear me it would be impossible to ask questions and gain file access. I felt my ego deflate as I paced the green grass before me, asking myself how I could save face. I'd broken one of my own hard-and-fast rules; never jump in. It had saved my ass countless times on the job.

As I paced back I nearly ran into Mike's broad chest.

"Oh, you're still here." I turned the other way.

"I'm not going anywhere. You need me." He grinned.

"As well as me." A voice sounded from behind.

I turned to find my coroner buddy, Dr. Warren Saint, making his way toward us. His full head of snow-white hair gleamed against his crystal blue eyes. He still wore the lab coat he'd had on at his death at the morgue, where he'd dropped dead of a massive coronary. As corpses go, he'd gotten off lucky with no outward signs of his death.

"Doc. It's great to see you." We made the pretense of hugging. "So what brings you to my special place?"

His fuzzy brows furrowed. "I seem to have heard some discussion about you going into business. Not that I was eavesdropping you understand, I was simply on my way to visit here when I overheard the two of you."

"So you already know my dilemma."

"Yes, I do. But it doesn't seem as grim as you might think."

"Really?" I shot a glance at Mike. "What's your take?"

"Trust your instincts. First you need to ask Kate. She might be more willing than you think. Why not give her the opportunity to answer for herself?"

"I plan to. But Dr. Saint, Mike is right. She already has a job, and it's a job that calls for quite a bit of OT and mental energy. If she can't or won't do it, I'll completely understand, but that will leave me in a bind."

"It's a challenge, I agree, but not impossible." He continued as he polished his death tag scalpel with his sleeve. "I suggest you talk with Sally. Perhaps there is a way to gain access to the physical world in a limited way, short of possessing someone's body."

That idea definitely didn't appeal to me. I'd seen the damage it could do.

"Good idea. You're a saint." I hugged him again.

"I've heard that." He chuckled.

"What are you going to do about Rico?" Mike asked.

I explained Rico's request to Dr. Saint.

His mustache twitched in concern. "Be careful with that one."

"I'm dead. What can he do, fit me with a pair of cement shoes?"

"He's been dead a long time. I'm sure he has a trick or two up his proverbial sleeve."

"It shouldn't be too hard. All I have to do is find out who put a hit on him."

"I'd still watch it. As a detective you should know you can't trust a criminal under any circumstances."

Dr. Saint was right. In life I never would have made a deal with a guy like Rico DiCianni. I'd been off the job too long and had gone soft.

Mike must have caught on to my thought train, offering me a subtle nod.

"He's got ulterior motives." I could feel my creative juices flow. "I can't see a guy like that owning an ounce of patience. He's not going to want to wait till the guy dies. If Rico has a way to enact revenge, then I want to know what it is. Chances are, he's found a way to manipulate in the physical world. Looks like I need to pay Rico a little visit."

"What are you going to tell him?" Mike wanted to know.

"We have to negotiate the terms of our agreement. If he wants me to find his killer, then I want to know his little secret."

"Wouldn't it be wiser to contact Sally? She's more likely to give you an honest answer if she knows it." Dr. Saint's worried expression reminded me of my father the day I told him I wanted to join the police department. So I told Dr. Saint the same thing I told my father.

"This is something I have to do on my own."

"What if he doesn't cooperate?" the doctor asked.

"Then I'll make him an offer he can't refuse."

I don't know a detective who hasn't utilized the services of a snitch. I knew several, but had only met one so far on this side. That surprised me. A snitch's life is a crapshoot, but no one grows up *wanting* to be a snitch. Usually, a set of circumstances forces someone to choose it. Most often it's a matter of supporting a habit or supplying basic food and shelter. Either way, once you're pegged an informant it sticks.

If I'd met one on this side, there had to be more. I made my way to the edge of town known to be frequented by prostitutes. Yes, even in the quiet town of Southfield Heights, there are those unpleasant elements that the town folk would rather not think about. It was law enforcement's job to see that they didn't have to. In the process, cops knew where to look.

My destination gave new meaning to the term seedy little bar. The black windows peeked out onto Beacon Street from faded gray wood siding that looked too rotted to hold them. This section of town known as the Beacon district from the street corner where the bar stood was notorious for prostitutes. I figured if I hung out here long enough I'd meet someone who might know a little history on Rico.

My instincts were right and I soon spotted a tall blonde almost wearing a red halter and skimpy shorts. Her long legs and stiletto heels gave her a giraffe look as she paraded her sashaying hips down the walk. I waited patiently at the corner, knowing what was coming.

Her lit cigarette landed at my feet. "You don't belong here, bitch."

She wore the telltale signs of her death like a permanent necklace. Eyes saturated with tiny red dots told me the rest. Strangulation.

"Oops. Did I take your corner? I'm new here." I stepped aside and let her take my place near the light pole.

She ignored me, looking down the street as if waiting for someone.

"You come here often?" I asked.

She turned as if surprised I was still there. "It's my turf. Get lost before I tear your hair out."

I lifted my badge so she could fully see it. "You might want to rethink that."

She sniffed. "Think that scares me? What are you going to do, arrest me?"

Okay, she had me there.

"I'm looking for information."

"And I should care because?"

"Look, uh. . . ."

"No names. You know that. You want information, it's gonna cost you."

I made the pretense of checking my pockets. "I'm all out of cash. You take credit cards?"

"Look, smart ass. Just get on with it so I can get back to work. Not all of us have the convenience of a clock to punch."

"Ever hear of Rico DiCianni?"

I caught a slight widening of her eyes that she hid behind a fake cough. She was no Academy Award winner.

"Hasn't everyone?" She recovered.

"What do you know about him?"

"He was murdered. No great loss as far as I'm concerned."

"Did you know him personally?"

"I never get personally involved with my clients."

"Who killed him?"

"Never heard. It was a hit."

"Who ordered it?"

"Don't know. Look, are we through here?"

She pulled out a pocket mirror and checked her lipstick when a potential patron strolled in our direction.

"What can you tell me about his murder?"

"It's a family affair and you should stay the hell out of it."

With that, she turned her back on me to personally greet her gentleman caller.

CHAPTER NINE

Rico's Used Furniture had been out of business for several years. The building stood along Route 41, backing up to farmland with a view of more farm fields across the highway to the west. The only other business stood about a mile down the road. I'd never understood how businesses stationed so far off the beaten path stayed open, but, in Rico's case, the store had served as a convenient front for his other activities.

With its owner long gone, the building had fallen vacant until a couple of doctors had opened a practice here, breathing new life into a place of the dead.

I'd hoped not only to survey the original crime scene, but also perhaps meet up with my new client to discuss our agreement. Mike tagged along as officers do on many searches. It gave the whole situation a professional feel and I slipped easily back into my detective mode.

With no signs of Rico, I started the process of investigating the crime scene, which by now had been greatly compromised. The parking lot had been repaved, the building repainted, a new sign hung, and, of course, any evidence of Rico's demise was long gone. I had nothing to work with.

"I'd like to say I've seen worse, but it would be a lie. There's nothing here." I walked around the building to see where the Dumpsters were kept. According to Rico, that's where it had happened. Mike followed.

"All I have to go on are Rico's details, and, given the fact that he was the victim, it isn't much."

Mike never said, "I told you so." For that, I was grateful. Instead he started nosing around the back door for clues. "So what did he tell you?"

"He'd been working late at the store doing paperwork and cleaning up. When he'd taken the garbage out back, a guy came up behind him and he knew what was coming. It was too dark to see who it was, but he recognized the voice as a guy by the name of Jimmy Bones. Rico said the guy told him to kneel down, and, before he had a chance to say a Hail Mary, he saw bright light explode behind his eyes and everything went black. Like I said, not much to go on."

"What do you know about Jimmy Bones?" Mike asked.

"Small-time hood who apparently graduated to murder. Last I heard he was in pretty tight with the Santini family. But they're mostly into the casinos. I can't say what the connection is to DiCianni."

"That's another question for your client."

"It's getting to be quite a list. But meantime, I'm going to run this like I would a normal homicide. I usually don't have access to the vic's point of view, so why should this be any different? I want to get a feel for his last couple of days. He's already told me his side, but I need to get a fresh view."

"So what's next?"

"Find Jimmy Bones. It's not often I already know the killer when I start a case. If that turns into a dead end, I'll need to interview his family, namely his wife."

"That I have to see." Mike crossed his arms over his chest.

"Don't be so negative. One time I interviewed a comatose patient."

"And how did that go for you?"

"A little slow at first, but I'd dated enough to get through it. Actually, the man could communicate if I asked yes or no questions. He flinched his eyelids once for yes and twice for no."

"But he could hear you. DiCianni's wife can't."

"Sometimes the best information isn't spoken. I can tell if a person is lying just by the way he moves his eyes. Besides, people tend to fabricate or invent information to please interviewers. I can visit his wife without her knowing, and look for clues or behaviors that might be important."

"In other words, you're going to spy."

"Right."

"But it's been several years since the man's death. By now I'm sure the topic of his death doesn't come up very often. And any evidence that might be lying around is probably gone."

"It's still worth a shot."

"All right. So where do we find Jimmy Bones?"

That was a good question. Normally, I would search the computer for his address or to see if he'd been incarcerated. With Kate off risking frostbite, my options were limited. But I knew one person who might be able to help.

"C'mon. Let's find Sally."

When I couldn't locate Sally at her usual spot, I felt the old job frustrations bubbling up. I was feeling more like my old self. This kind of stuff came with the job.

I sat on the curb in front of Tri-City Labs, and patted a spot beside me for Mike.

"Sit. It might be a while." I fidgeted. "You'd think with all the geek geniuses that have passed away, they would have come up with some sort of paging system here."

"We're supposed to leave all those things behind. Although I met a guy who had a cell phone for a death tag," Mike said.

"Really. Did he get any calls?"

"Nah. The line was dead too."

"It's probably for the best. Could you imagine the roaming charges?"

"You two ought to do stand-up."

I grinned at the sound of Sally's voice coming from behind us.

"We were turned down for *Saturday Night Live*." I scooted over to make room for her on the curb.

"Uh oh. You've got that look in your eyes. What did I do now?" she wanted to know.

"We need your help."

"I think I can pencil you in."

"Sally, I need to find a man by the name of Jimmy Bones."

"Living or spirit?"

"Living. I have no idea where he hangs out or lives."

"This wouldn't have anything to do with that guy with the crater in his head would it?"

"Yes. Can you help us?"

"That's a tough one. It usually takes some sort of image of the person or knowing where they are to navigate to them."

"Is it even possible to manipulate the physical world?"

"Not that I know of."

Mike looked my way. "Plan B?"

"Not yet. There has to be a way to get to Jimmy Bones."

"I really hate to do this, but it looks like I need to contact Kate."

"What can she do from Wisconsin?" Mike asked.

"More than I can do from eternity."

CHAPTER TEN

I know I'd vowed not to bother Kate on her vacation. But this was an emergency. It took little time to find my sister shooshing down a high slope with snow spraying into the wind and a look of exhilaration on her face. Her rosy cheeks came compliments of Mother Nature although I felt no sense of cold. The sunlit sky and absence of freezing temperatures made me rethink the whole ski-trip idea. There'd be no risking life and limb on the bunny hill, and, even if I fell, no one would see me. Just call me peekaboo. Perhaps I would tag along next year if invited.

The tricky part was trying to figure out how to get Kate's attention without her ending up in a tree. My past attempts to warn her of my arrival had been lame at best. I decided to wait at the bottom of the slope in hopes she'd see me on the way down.

I watched her coming faster and smoother than anyone else. Her friends followed behind, most of them laughing and falling mid-slope. A blonde with short spiked hair in an ice-blue snowsuit zipped past Kate nearly cutting her off.

"Take that, Frost!" She laughed.

The unexpected move didn't rattle Kate and she crouched to speed up.

As they neared the bottom, I waved and caught the hesitation on Kate's face. She shooshed her way to a row of trees and waited for me.

"Nice moves, Sis," I said.

She removed her goggles and rubbed her eyes. "I can't believe what I'm seeing. You finally decided to join us?"

I shrugged. "No skis. But you all look like you're having fun."

"Yeah. We are." I saw her glance toward the main road.

"Any visitors?"

"Not Gerard, if that's what you're thinking. But Jakes never showed up. I've tried to call her but keep getting her voice mail."

"Maybe she changed her mind."

"She would have called."

"Listen, I won't keep you. But I need a favor."

"What's up?"

"I need to use the department computer to look up a hit man. His name is Jimmy Bones. Ever heard of him?"

"Sounds familiar. Why do you need to find him?"

"One of his vics came to me for help. He wants me to find out who ordered the hit."

Her chapped lips formed a low whistle. "You sure know how to pick 'em."

"He picked me. Remember the DiCianni hit a few years ago?"

"That was a bit close to home. I was working when the call came in. Not a pretty sight."

"Well, he wants to know who's responsible."

"And you agreed?"

"Why not? It's my duty."

"I think you're off the hook, Linz. You don't have to do this anymore. Tell him to go to hell."

"In a way he's already there. All the guy wants is closure. It's the same thing I wanted."

Kate nodded. "What do you want me to do?"

"Can you call John Turner at the station and have him look up the information on Bones? Tell him to print it out and lay it on your desk. Then I can take a look myself. That's it."

"John is a fellow officer—not my personal secretary. I'm sure he has enough to do running the K-9 unit."

"Are you kidding? He's got a crush on you."

She formed a cheesy grin. "He does, doesn't he?"

"Kate—"

"All right. I'll call him when I get back to the house. He's working evenings this week."

"Thanks. I owe you."

"Yes, you do, and don't think I'm not keeping score."

With that, she slid her goggles back into place and took off toward the house.

I love it when a plan comes together. Unfortunately, this one didn't. When I arrived at the Southfield Heights police station, I found the papers that John had printed for Kate—face down.

In a futile attempt to save my pride, I tried blowing them off the desk, then shoving them, but to no avail. I have nothing solid to work with. Finally I plopped my rear on top of them and rested my chin in my hand. Shit.

"Sulking doesn't become you, Detective Frost."

I jumped at the voice.

Rico leaned in the doorway smoking his cigarette looking like a young Dean Martin, except for the head wound.

"Where the hell have you been?"

"Close. You're good, Detective."

I took a seat behind Kate's desk, or at least levitated there enough to look like it. "We need to talk."

"I'm listening." He blew out a stream of smoke.

"I want to know the real reason you're so interested in finding who ordered the hit."

"Peace of mind."

"I think you're lying, and I think you've found a way to manipulate in the physical world. You're planning revenge."

His dark eyes pinned me. "I would like nothing more. Unfortunately, that's not the case."

I wasn't sure I believed him, but he'd taken his stand and I knew that wouldn't change. If he'd found a way, he sure wasn't going to share it with me. I couldn't back down now and risk looking weak so I played my bluff.

"Here's the deal, Rico. If I find out you're lying, we're through. I won't work your case and any information I have stays with me. Got it?"

"You leave me little choice. But, as I've said, I don't possess those skills."

"I'm looking for Jimmy Bones. Any idea where I might find him?"

"Sure. I can take you to him." He turned to leave.

"Where are we going?"

"To see Santini."

We passed through a Spanish-style structure into a marble-tiled foyer, greeted by the tinkling sound of fountain water where an eight-foot cherub bathed inside a clamshell. Piped-in music hovered overhead—Vivaldi, I think—as we made our way past a winding staircase down a wide hall.

The sound of pots clanking told me we'd found the kitchen, and, even though spirits don't have a sense of smell, I knew the bubbling sauce on the stove would be to die for.

A woman no taller than five feet high stood behind the stove, tasting the steaming contents of a ladle. What she lacked in stature, she made up for in looks. Blonde—number twelve, sparkling blue eyes compliments of Bausch & Lomb, and an ample bust courtesy double implants. All woman and then some.

A shorter woman with salt-and-pepper hair and an olive complexion stood with her back to us at the sink. Her wide girth revealed hours taste testing the finest cuisine. She rattled off something in Italian, and the blonde at the stove answered in a not-so-authentic accent.

Rico nodded toward the blonde. "That's Santini's wife, Eliza."

"Who's the cook?" I wished I could smell the food.

"Santini's mother. Doesn't speak a word of English. And she can't stand Eliza."

"I bet that makes for fun at the dinner table."

Rico grinned. "Poor Eliza thinks 'putana' means 'my pet.' "

"Sorry. I took French in high school."

"Whore."

"Excuse me?"

"That's what it means."

"I'll make a note of that. So where do we find Jimmy?"

"Follow me."

The elaborate dining room held a table long enough to seat twelve. Pearl-white candles glowed from the candelabra standing in the center, surrounded by white china place settings and utensils of gold. Baskets of fresh bread, probably homemade, olive-oil flasks, and several bottles of Chianti stood randomly placed among the guests. I watched as platters of gnocchi, swimming in red sauce, and large bowls of insalate passed up and down the table. I knew my stomach would be growling—if I had one.

Rico nudged me from my daydream. I checked my chin for drool and drew my attention to his pointed finger. "That's Santini."

At the head of the table sat a fifty-something man who clearly loved his mama's cooking. Santini weighed no less than four hundred pounds, and I wondered how much olive oil it took to lube him into the narrow dining-room chair.

Full jowls jiggled as he spoke, all the while shoveling forkfuls of dumplings into his mouth in between gulps of wine. His eyes were onyx against an olive-colored complexion, and I had no doubt he'd taken after his mother's side in looks. Thick wavy hair lay in an ebony wave over a high forehead. His very presence said Santini was a man to be reckoned with.

The rest of his guests looked like clones in their suits, watchful eyes and attitudes. As the conversation flowed in Italian, I was lost to eavesdrop and looked to Rico to translate.

"Not much going on. It's regular business; blackmail, money laundering and gambling. That little weasel on the end is Jimmy Bones."

Bones reminded me of any one of the neighborhood snitches I'd incorporated on the job. For some reason, nutrition seems to be low on their priority lists, making them all on the skinny side with dark circles under their eyes. Jimmy's suit sagged where it should have hugged, giving him a pathetic look. I watched his eyes darting back and forth between his comrades, as if trying to catch subtle threats. I guess when you're a hit man; you have to sleep with your eyes open. Jimmy looked as though he hadn't slept in years.

"So there ya are. Go at it." Rico sauntered away.

"Hey. Don't leave me here. You have to translate."

"I can tell you they aren't saying anything about me. I'm history."

I had to get to Bones but didn't know how. So far, the only thing I'd been able to achieve in the real world was a little static on a police radio.

Then it hit me. The house music system, now playing Italian opera, worked a lot like a radio. I'm electronically challenged, but I do know where there's a radio, there's the potential for static.

I concentrated on the fat lady singing and focused on the wall speakers beside the wall switch. At first, nothing happened so I tried again. Screeching feedback split the airwaves causing the men at the table to clutch their ears.

Santini jumped up from his chair, nearly taking it with him as he headed for the speaker. He fumbled with the knob, cursing like a sailor. I may not know Italian, but curse words are identifiable in any language.

Several men drew their weapons, or should I say pocket cannons. I saw nothing smaller than a .44 Magnum, which would have easily taken out any top-heavy opera star.

Mama Santini rushed in screaming, hands waving in the air with Eliza following behind trying to calm her down over the piercing sound.

I heard the word *putana* several times as she pushed her daughter-in-law aside on the way toward her son.

As the men raced from the room to search for the source of trouble, I saw I had Jimmy Bones all to myself.

"Jimmy," I said loudly. I heard my voice echo through the wall speaker.

He turned ready to fire. "Who's there?"

Surprised my plan worked, I had to think quickly. "You were the trigger man on the DiCianni job."

His lips tightened. This guy might be scrawny, but he wasn't easily spooked.

"Who are you?"

"Doesn't matter. Who ordered the hit?"

I saw his weapon lower. He glanced around once more to be sure he was alone.

"This some kind of joke?"

"I'm dead serious."

Rico smiled. He was thoroughly enjoying this.

"What if I don't feel like saying?"

"Radio static is just the beginning, pal. Think of all the electronics at my disposal. Ever had electrolysis by bidet? It's quite a shocking experience."

"All right. What's the big deal? DiCianni is gone. Who cares who ordered it?"

"Bzzztt."

He jumped. "Francesca DiCianni! Okay? Ya happy?"

Rico turned three shades paler than he already was. Francesca was his wife.

"Are you sure? Don't lie to me."

"I swear on my mother's life I'm not lyin'. The way I heard it, she knew he had cancer and didn't want him to suffer. So she did the only thing she could think of to ensure he went quick and painless-like."

That was good enough for me. Twisted, maybe, but it was too crazy to be a lie.

"Hey, Jimmy. Do me one more favor."

"What's that?"

"Get a better suit."

When Rico and I left, the Santini household was still in an uproar. I heard someone mention an exorcist, and saw Jimmy crossing himself. My work was done.

I hardly knew what to say to Rico. His own wife had put a hit on him. Back at my special place, he stood staring off into the sun.

When he finally spoke, his voice was surprisingly tender. "She did that for me."

I expected anger, swearing, even the use of putana, but he didn't do any of that.

Instead he said, "All those years, I cheated on her. It's part of the business. It's expected. I always provided for her and the kids, they never went without the best of everything. But I wasn't a loving husband. Throughout my lifetime I stole, lied, and murdered. So when the doctor told me I had lung cancer, I figured it was my just deserts, ya know? Figured I had it coming. But Francesca couldn't let it be. She didn't want to accept the fact I was dying. When I wouldn't go ahead with treatment, she came up with one of her own."

"It must have been hard for her, Rico. It sounds like she loved you very much."

He nodded, took one last drag from his cigarette and began to fade. "Thank you, Detective. You did your job and I appreciate it."

He was gone then, leaving me to realize that like it or not I was still on the job.

Chapter Eleven

Kate sat in her SUV in front of a small grocery store several miles from the cabin. The day's skiing had exhilarated and exhausted her. She couldn't remember laughing so hard in a long time. When they'd decided they were missing a few necessary items for their evening pajama party, like wine, munchies, and more wine, she'd volunteered to go. The time alone would give her a chance to call Gerard—away from her friends' good-natured teasing. Kate parked in the far corner of the lot, and dialed her cell phone.

Tourists, bundled in winter wear, looking uncomfortable and clumsy, lugged bags of essentials to their cars. It seemed everyone was loading up for the weekend. An earlier report on the radio confirmed the store clerk's warning of an approaching winter storm guaranteed to dump several more inches of snow. The thought of fresh powder made her anxious to hit the slopes tomorrow even if it meant another day away from Gerard.

She smiled at the sound of his voice through the cell.

"You didn't break a leg did you?"

"Thanks for the vote of confidence."

"It's just the thought of you lying helpless in bed for a few days gets me excited."

"I don't need to break a leg for that to happen. Why don't you come visit me?"

"You know I'd love to, Kate, but I have the kids this weekend. Cynthia never showed."

Kate knew Gerard's ex-wife hadn't made things easy on him since the divorce. Gerard had custody of their two teenage boys, Paul and John, and worked hard to create a happy, stable home life. It angered Kate that the woman seemed to take every opportunity to upset that life and show complete disregard for any of their feelings. She reminded herself that alcoholism is a disease and Cynthia wasn't completely to blame. Still, it's a treatable disease and she resented the woman's refusal to stick with AA.

"I'm sorry. Are the boys upset?"

"They're used to it."

"It looks like we've both been stood up. Jakes never showed, either. I'm a little concerned because she's not answering her cell or home phone. Do you think you could stop by her house and see if everything is all right?"

"No problem. I'll take a ride before I head over to Ridgeway Park. I plan on taking the boys ice skating tonight."

"Don't *you* go breaking anything."

"I promise all my parts will be in working order when you get back."

"Did you find anything out about the finger?"

"No missing body parts at local morgues and the only place that sells dry ice in the area mostly sells commercially. Occasionally they get people asking for smaller quantities for parties, but they don't keep records of those sales. They simply sell it out the back door of the warehouse."

He turned and said something to Paul, then said, "The natives are restless. Can I call you later? By the way, how are things going?"

Kate barely heard his question when she saw Ted Burke get out of an old gray truck and cross the small lot toward the store.

"Kate? You there?" Gerard asked.

"Yes. Sorry."

"Everything all right?"

"Fine. I just saw someone . . . it's nothing."

"Listen, I have to let you go."

"Go ahead. Call me later." She disconnected and slouched down as Burke passed the front of her vehicle.

She decided to wait until he finished his shopping and left. The guy gave her the creeps and she wanted to avoid another encounter.

The skies overhead grew darker as time went on and she checked her watch. How many groceries could one man need?

As the first snowflakes fell, she knew she shouldn't wait any longer. She headed inside the store, hoping to dodge him.

"Kate!" Burke waved on his way over from the deli.

She began filling her cart as he caught up.

"What a coincidence. Everything all right at the house?"

"Yes, thanks. We're all set." She tossed in a bottle of headache reliever.

"Well, like I said, call if you need me." He headed for the checkout counter.

On the way back to the cabin, Kate fought her inner demons to figure out why Ted Burke bothered her so. He'd been thoughtful, except for the early-morning wake-up call, polite, and had even fixed Teresa's laptop.

She slammed on the brakes, skidding a short way on a patch of ice. Her mind replayed her recent encounter with him, catching on something he'd said. He'd called her Kate, but she'd never told him her first name.

On her way back to the cabin, Kate decided to keep her encounter with the strange caretaker to herself. She didn't want to alarm her friends and ruin what was left of their trip. Besides it could stand to reason that the A-frame owner had mentioned her by name since she'd made the reservations.

As she drove, she realized that their three-day getaway went by faster every year. Perhaps they should think about extending their yearly jaunt to four days. Except that would force her to be away from Gerard an additional day. Perhaps they needed an addendum to their "no men allowed" rule.

A short time later, with the groceries put away and the fireplace roaring with yellow warmth, Kate gathered with her friends for a pajama party, sipping their drinks.

"Who would have thought we'd still be having pajama parties at our age?" Teresa drained her glass and disappeared down the hall.

"Here's to terminal teen-hood!" Nicki laughed.

Kate raised the suggestion about extending their trip by another day and was surprised at the positive response.

"Hank will probably go live with his mother. I swear the man can't function without a woman in the house. Last year he was waiting on the front porch when I returned. When I asked him why, he said he was hungry."

Teresa nodded. "I think it's a wonderful idea. It seems our weekend time feels shorter every year."

"You seriously want to trade the beautiful California weather for snow?"

"I can have sand and surf anytime. This trip is important for me. I haven't touched my laptop since this morning and probably won't have time for the rest of the weekend. This is my escape from the daily grind. I'm sure we all need that."

"Except Kate, now that she has a boyfriend," Nicki teased. "Or are you already in need of a little time out?"

Kate waved her suggestion away.

"I can't imagine working with my boyfriend. It's enough we've lived together for the past three years," Carmen said.

"C'mon guys. It's no big deal. Gerard and I keep a professional relationship on the job. And off the job, we make sure we don't mix business with pleasure."

Kate caught site of a shadow in the nearby window. No one seemed to notice but her and she let the others take over the conversation. She tried to analyze what she'd seen, but it had been nothing more than a moving shadow. A wisp of blowing snow? Tree branches bending in the wind?

Kate moved to the door and double-checked the deadbolt. She wished she could grab her weapon, but it would be a little hard to conceal in flannel jammies. Not wanting to raise an alarm, she decided to wait and see.

"Well, ladies," Pam stretched. "I think I'm done here."

"Me too. I want to catch some of that fresh powder tomorrow morning before we have to start packing it up." Kate used the opportunity to check out the window. "It's coming down pretty good."

"Kate's right. I'm going to bed. See you all in the morning." Nicki headed down the hall with Beaver bounding after her.

After everyone else had gone to bed, Kate crept back into the now-darkened living room. Her eyes scanned the yard's perimeter as she checked each window. She saw nothing but white moonlight and thick forest.

A sudden glint of silver bounced against the darkness at the far end of the property. Trees lined the area and Kate knew from there the property sloped down a steep ridge. If you didn't know where you were going it would be easy to fall over it. Her eyes scanned her friends' cars parked in front and down the sloped drive as far as she could follow it. Nothing.

She braved the elements and opened the front door to stand on the wooden porch. The only sound was the eerie wind slicing through the barren trees. Her gaze caught a rabbit's trail across the wide yard in the moonlight. But rabbits don't glint in the night. Whatever it was it had been something shiny like metal.

Rubbing her hands together, she decided to go inside. After bolting the door behind her, she stood before the glowing fireplace embers and replayed what she'd seen. It remained a mystery. The wine and the hour were wearing her down, but a sense of foreboding filled her.

A quick stop in the kitchen provided a cup of instant coffee to keep her alert. Tonight would not be a night for sleep. She covered up on the couch with the thick comforter from her bed and watched the last of the dying fireplace embers go dark. Her hand rested against the cool steel of her weapon as she waited.

CHAPTER TWELVE

Kate saw the slight rise of the ground too late to swerve. For the few seconds she was airborne, her stomach dropped like she was riding a roller coaster. As Kate tumbled downhill, her skis flew off, she lost her poles somewhere along the way and she found herself counting each agonizing bump. The whole stunt probably took less than thirty seconds, but felt much longer.

She didn't bother to move when she stopped. If she waited long enough she'd either die of exposure or embarrassment. Heavy snowflakes pelted her face and she realized conditions were fast becoming blizzard-like. She heard her friends calling as they headed her way.

"I'll take humiliation for two hundred, Alex." Kate moaned and tried to get up.

"Wait! Don't move." Pam leaned over for a closer look.

Kate ignored her. "Relax. The only thing wounded is my pride."

The rest of the gang gathered around, concern etched on their faces, until Pam lost her footing and fell.

"Hold on there, girlfriend." Carmen reached out to help her up and let out a yelp when her skis slid out from beneath her. She landed hard on her bottom, sending up a snow cloud. "Damn, that hurt."

Teresa unlatched her skis and sat. "I'm not taking any chances."

"Last one standing! I'm queen of the hill!" Nicki raised her poles in glory.

Kate saw her chance and shoved Nicki's right ski causing her to topple over face first.

A snowball fight ensued amid the heavy snowfall, and Kate relished her last few moments on the hill with her friends. In a few hours she would be on the road toward home and Gerard. Suddenly her spirits rose. She hadn't realized how much she'd missed him.

He'd called late last night to tell her that he'd gone by Jakes' house: no one had been home.

"That's not like her. Something's wrong," she'd told him.

"Maybe she changed her mind," Gerard said.

"I don't like this. Are you sure they were gone?"

"No one answered the door and the place was dark. Eight in the evening is kind of early for bed."

"Someone should have answered. She has a live-in boyfriend."

"Well, while the cat's away. . . ."

She'd heard the smile in his voice.

"I see. Is that how it is?"

"Not me, cariña. I'm behaving and waiting for you."

She'd just adjusted herself on the not-so-comfy couch when Gerard asked, "Is everything all right, there?"

She'd decided not to mention the strange things she'd seen, or thought she'd seen outside the cabin. There hadn't been much to tell and it would have caused him to worry.

"Fine. The only thing missing is you."

After they'd hung up, she'd gotten up and looked outside the window once more.

The front yard glittered with snow diamonds against the bright moonlight. As beautiful as it looked, she'd wished for the morning sun to bring an end to the uncertainty of the night.

Back at the cabin, Kate inspected the damage of her fall and saw the telltale signs of bruising. She turned before the full-length mirror and slipped her underwear down a few inches to catch a glimpse of her purple rump.

"That's a beaut." Nicki leaned in the doorway grinning.

"I like to take souvenirs home with me. By the way, where's Pam?"

"Cleaning the snow off the cars. It must be eight inches thick! I thought we were done with the snowstorm, but it's really starting to snow hard again. We need to get out of here before we're snowed in. Why don't you let me put your suitcase in your SUV for you while you finish up here?"

"Thanks. Here you go." Kate tossed her the keys.

Kate turned the other way. Most of the bruising was on her right. "Well, there goes my centerfold shoot."

A few minutes later, Nicki returned.

"What's up?" Kate asked.

"Bad news. I've been listening to the radio and they've just reported road closures in our area. It looks like we aren't going anywhere for a while."

Kate grinned. "And that's a bad thing?"

"It is when I have to be back at work on Monday. I'd better go tell the others they can wait with the packing."

Kate eyed her cell phone on the bed and thought about calling Gerard to tell him the news. Although she couldn't wait to get home, the trip was always a great stress-buster that left her ready to get back to work. She decided it wouldn't be such a tragedy if they were stuck here one more day. This year the getaway had also provided a distraction to get her mind off another pending issue, one that could change her life forever. Her thoughts were interrupted by screams.

"Will you guys grow up?" Kate grinned.

Footsteps pounded down the hallway toward her room. The screams had become panicked cries.

"Kate! Come quick!"

Teresa grabbed her arm, dragging her toward the front door. "You aren't going to believe this."

Kate winced at the pain but allowed it. Something was very wrong. When they reached the front porch, she saw Nicki and Pam had gathered behind her SUV staring into the back. Carmen bent over and retched into the bushes.

"Guys. This isn't funny." Kate watched them back away as she stepped closer.

When she glanced inside her vehicle, she felt her own stomach lurch. She'd seen her share of corpses on the job as a beat cop and more recently working homicide. It took a lot to make her flinch. This was different.

The scene was surreal. It took her a moment to realize what she was looking at was human.

"Tell me this is some sick joke. It's not real, is it?" Teresa asked.

Kate studied what resembled life-size doll parts that had been stuffed into the back. The severed limbs lay stacked on top of the torso. She leaned in closer to inspect the body. Her nose told her that it was human, and she realized that the parts, including the torso, had been cast in some sort of plaster. There was a noticeable lack of blood; just the ragged edges of muscle and tendon left at the edges of each piece. Cable had been cast into the body parts at strategic areas of the shoulders and hands like a marionette.

Her stomach knotted when she realized what was missing. The severed finger had only been the beginning. She carefully moved to the front of the vehicle, seeing nothing but clean snow with no visible prints. The murderer had gone in through the back to place the body. By now her friends' heavy boots would have destroyed any footprints when they started to load the vehicle.

As she inched closer to the front, her heart raced. Something odd lay in the front seat. Her breath caught at the site of thick auburn hair. It partially covered a severed head cast in the same material as the body. A pair of green eyes stared back at her through the pasty white covering. Kate closed her eyes when she recognized the face. It was Jakes.

"Who is it?" Pam's voice quivered.

She fought back tears, trying to maintain a clear head and professionalism in front of her friends.

Teresa leaned over her shoulder. "Good God. What a mess."

"Stop. Don't anyone move." Kate reached into her jacket pocket and brought out her digital camera. "I'd hoped to get a picture of everyone before we left, but didn't think it would be quite like this."

"Kate. I need to move." Pam looked like she might bolt any second.

"Pam, listen to me. This is a crime scene. Don't do anything until I get some pictures. Then I'll tell you how to step away."

When she finished she explained to Pam, Nicki and Teresa how to avoid disturbing important evidence. The fresh snow had provided her with shots of footprints further back from the car, although they could belong to any of them. She discovered what seemed to be snowmobile tracks leading up the drive, but they offered little in the way of evidence. Unfortunately, the prints and track marks would most likely be lost as evidence when the snow melted. She had no way to preserve them but with her camera. Looking around she knew the crime scene had already been compromised with everyone traipsing back and forth with their luggage. When it was over, she knew there wouldn't be much to work with, and she wondered if that had been intentional on the part of the killer.

Carmen leaned beside a tall pine beside the SUV, rubbing her face with snow. "I'm not moving from here till that body is gone. Have you called the police?"

"She is the police," Nicki reminded her.

"Well, somebody has to come and take that car away or my ass will be frostbitten by tonight. I'm stayin' right here."

Teresa sat on the A-frame's front step trying her cell phone. "Damn. I swear I'm a jinx when it comes to all things electronic."

"What's wrong?" Nicki asked.

"No signal." Teresa tossed her the phone.

"She's right, Kate. Try yours."

Kate saw her phone too had no signal. "No good. Must be the weather. I'll use the landline. Let's go inside for now and warm up."

"What about the body?" Nicki pointed to the car.

"The roads are closed for now; we have no choice but to leave it." Kate turned away.

Inside, the group sat silent, as fresh snow blanketed the crime scene. Kate frowned at her dead cell phone wondering what the hell she should do next. The cabin's landline was out of service as well, leaving them with no contact with the outside world. She had no way to get in touch with the authorities, and, according to the radio, the main roads had been closed indefinitely. It looked like her wish had come true and they'd be spending another night on White Crest Mountain.

Pam and Nicki had busied themselves in the kitchen cooking, although no one seemed to be hungry. Carmen had retired to her bedroom complaining of a headache, and Teresa sat in silence on the couch nursing a martini. Kate took a seat beside her.

"Hey. You all right?"

"As all right as can be expected." She turned to face Kate. "I'm so sorry about Jakes. I know you grew up together. Any idea who might have done this?"

"Nothing solid. We won't be able to process the scene until tomorrow and by then much of the evidence will be snow covered. By the way, I think you'll be losing your laptop temporarily. Until we prove otherwise, that creepy caretaker is a person of interest, and his prints are on the keyboard."

"Are we prepared if anything else happens?"

"I have my gun, if that's what you're asking."

"Good. I figured you did." She got up holding her empty glass. "I need a refill. Can I get you anything?"

"I'm fine for now. Thanks."

Kate wished she could afford the luxury of a drink, but someone had to stay alert. It looked like she was back on duty.

CHAPTER THIRTEEN

Kate tugged the comforter up to her chin and watched her breath wisp into the frigid living-room air. Bright sunlight poured through the windows but did nothing to warm her. With the wall clock's hands sitting stubbornly at five after three, she knew the power had gone out. Her wristwatch confirmed they'd gone five hours without heat and she started a fire in the fireplace.

Wrapped in a comforter, she peered into the front yard itching to get out to the crime scene. Several inches of fresh snow dampened her hopes and she regretted she hadn't tried to find more evidence last evening. With the sun setting fast, and everyone so upset, she'd just wanted to get them inside away from the gruesome sight. Now all evidence was buried.

"Damn."

"I'll second that." Teresa stood behind her wearing layers of clothing. "Power's out, huh?"

"Yes. Since about three."

Teresa glanced outside toward Kate's vehicle.

"I can't get that image out of my mind. Does it ever go away?" she asked Kate.

"Yeah. When it's replaced by a new one."

"Glad I don't work homicide."

"I need to get out there and work the scene, but the snow coverage has compromised it."

Teresa held her gaze. "You all right?"

"What do you mean?"

"Your friend has been murdered and you're strictly business. It's okay to cry, you know?"

Kate took a deep breath. She fought the familiar sting in her eyes.

"Not now. Jakes needs more from me than tears. I'm not so hardened that I don't feel the pain, but I can't let it get in the way. I can't help but feel that I'm partly responsible for her death."

"How can you say that?"

"This murder is personal. Now it's up to me to get this guy before he strikes again, if that's his plan. I can't afford to let emotions cloud my judgment. Does that make sense?"

"A lot more than you think. I'm really proud of you, Kate. Now tell me what can I do to help?"

"Nothing. Even I'm at a disadvantage with the snow coverage."

"You took pictures yesterday. Can you bring them up on your digital camera?"

"If the battery isn't dead."

Kate sat on the couch reviewing the crime-scene pics. The first showed a clear shot of Carmen puking in the background. Lovely.

She scanned through the shots, stopping to study one in detail. She'd captured a clear shot of the snowmobile tracks or whatever they were, and something else. She squinted to see a black object poking up through the snow several feet from the tracks, but couldn't make it out. Whatever it was, it still had to be there buried under the new snow.

She shut off the camera and headed to her bedroom.

"Where're you going?" Teresa rubbed her hands before the fireplace.

"Outside where it's a little warmer."

In the front yard, the camera's battery light flashed, signaling an imminent loss of power. Kate hurried to snap several more shots of the yard and then she carefully dug around the area where she'd spotted the black object in the photo. Her gloved hand grabbed a cylindrical object and she dusted the snow off to see it was an empty film container. No one in the cabin had brought a thirty-five-millimeter camera. So, who had discarded this film container here? she wondered.

Tossing it into a Ziploc baggie, she continued her search for clues. Gently sweeping the freshest-looking snow away from the older packed snow underneath, she saw a set of footprints. Her digital camera gave her two more shots and died.

It was hard to be sure, but the footprints looked different than the sets closer to the car. These weren't snow boots, and had a pointed toe and had left no tread mark. They looked like cowboy boots.

After twenty minutes of searching for clues, her fingertips were numb and her teeth chattered. She went inside and huddled before the fire, thinking hard about her find.

"You say there're two killers?" Teresa sat on the couch.

"No. I said there are two distinct sets of footprints."

"Same thing. Where else could the second set have come from? None of us traipsed that far toward the edge of the property."

"I'm trying to keep you out of this," Kate warned.

"As a friend or a detective?"

"Both. You may be called as a witness."

"Of course I will. I'm the lawyer, remember? That doesn't bother me a bit."

"I hope the rest of the gang feels the same way."

"I'm not so sure about Carmen. They better hand her a barf bag if they intend to show her crime-scene photos."

"I heard that!" Carmen came into the living room.

"Well, it's true." Teresa moved over for her to sit.

"Just because I tossed my grits, doesn't mean I can't handle myself in court. Besides, I don't need to review the photos. That image is permanently burned into my brain."

"We have to catch the guy before you can testify," Kate reminded them.

"What *we?*" Carmen said. "You're the detective. I'm not going anywhere near that car. You figure it out."

"I will. As soon as I can get in touch with the authorities and get a real investigation going."

Pam screamed from the back room, and Kate grabbed her gun from the coffee table. Footsteps pounded the hallway as Nicki followed close behind.

"What happened?" Kate met them halfway.

"There's someone outside!" Pam pointed to the back room.

"Everyone stay here. Make sure the front door is locked." Kate headed toward the bedrooms.

She checked each window and saw nothing but snow-covered trees and a lone squirrel. Beneath Pam's window she saw the same boot print she'd seen near the film container.

Back in the living room, everyone sat huddled before the fireplace.

"There's a set of footprints outside your window, Pam. What did you see?" Kate asked, grabbing her coat.

Pam's eyes were wide. Her gaze shot from Kate to the gun and back. "I was making the bed when I felt someone watching me. When I looked up, I saw a man staring through the window. He had his hands cupped around his face to see in and I didn't stick around to get a good look."

"Lock the door behind me," Kate ordered.

"Wait a minute, girlfriend. Is that a smart thing to do with Jack the Ripper running around out there? You shouldn't go out there alone," Carmen said.

Kate disengaged her revolver's safety. "I'm not alone."

Outside, the sun burned away the last of the early-morning haze, and Kate could feel the temperature rising. At least her fingers were no longer numb and she held her weapon ready as she inched her way around the wide house.

When she reached Pam's window, she clearly saw the boot prints and searched the area for other clues. She followed tracks around to the back, where they went off into the woods. To follow without backup or a radio would be stupid. Where was Lindsay when she needed her?

She concentrated hard, hoping her message would get through, and called to her sister, feeling a little foolish, and hoping the girls wouldn't hear her.

"Lindsay, where are you? I need you."

She waited, hearing only the rustling of another squirrel in a nearby tree.

Kate waited a few more seconds and tried again, this time trying to visualize her. She'd known Lindsay to be summoned only one other time, but that was by a known psychic. Although Kate believed in psychic abilities, it didn't make her Jeane Dixon.

Turning, she gasped. Lindsay stood behind her, grinning.

"Don't do that!"

"What?" Her older sister laughed.

"Sneak up on me. You need to warn me when you arrive."

"Sorry. I don't have a cowbell handy. What's up? I thought you were leaving today."

"Can't go."

"Car trouble?"

"You might say that."

"I'm no mechanic."

"Right now I need you to help find a Peeping Tom slash murder suspect."

"Who died?"

"It's Jakes."

"Evelyn? My God, what happened?"

"I can't explain now. I need to find this guy before he gets too deep into the woods."

"I'll go ahead of you. Have you called anyone?"

"Phones and power are out. It's just you and me for now."

"Then I'd say this guy is in real trouble."

CHAPTER FOURTEEN

I hadn't bothered to ask Kate for a description. After all, how many suspected murderers could be lurking in the woods? The trail seemed endless and I wondered how fast a person would be able to walk in the snow without snow boots. Whatever the guy had on his feet they had to be soaked and difficult to walk in by now.

I couldn't digest the news about Jakes. It seemed impossible that our vivacious, fun-loving friend had been murdered. But then, so had I.

Turning back a moment, I motioned to Kate.

"Nothing yet. Want to keep going?"

"We're almost to the main road."

I followed the footprints with Kate several yards behind.

It felt good to be back on the trail of a suspect, a real living being. The last time I'd stalked an offender, she'd been a spirit and it hadn't seemed real. The idea that Kate had summoned me to help gave me hope that we could work together on a regular basis. There was one thing that bothered me as I approached the main road and waited for her to catch up.

"How did you know how to call me?"

"I read it on FindAnyone.com." Kate picked up her pace.

"You seem to be catching on to this life-after-death thing a lot faster than I am. What did you do?"

"Same thing you do when you want to find me. Concentrate and focus. It worked. And I'm glad too, because I hear there's no text messaging on your side."

We stood at the top of the hill where the main highway cut a path through the forest. A ribbon of wet blacktop in front of us revealed a recent plowing and, of course, no sign of our Peeping Tom.

"Look"—Kate pointed west—"here comes a snowplow."

She crossed the pavement, flagging her bright-orange ski hat high above her head.

I checked the road for oncoming traffic. "What are you doing?"

"Tempting fate." She continued down the middle of the plowed road, flagging the plow.

I try not to be negative, but I'm dead and that makes me the ultimate poster child for the It-Can-Happen-To-You campaign. Knowing my sister's stubborn nature, I knew better than to bark orders, so I tried a different approach.

"Did you keep my Road Kill Cookbook by any chance?"

That got me a frown and a raised brow, but not the result I'd wanted.

To my amazement, the mammoth plow came to a graceful stop, and Kate ran up to the driver's side, looking smaller and more vulnerable than ever.

"Hey there!" She called up to the man poking his head out of the window. "I'm Detective Kate Frost with Southfield Heights homicide."

"You're what?" The man's stubble told me he was working on some serious overtime.

"I'm a police detective and I need to ask you a few questions." Kate climbed onto the step below the door.

"Kind of a strange place to do an interview, wouldn't you say?" I saw the man's bloodshot eyes scan the road.

"Yes, sir. . . ."

"Call me, Pat. Sir is my father's title." He grinned.

"Okay, Pat. This is important. Have you seen any westbound traffic within the last ten minutes?"

He winced as if in pain, rubbed an arthritic-looking hand under his chin and nodded. "Yeah. I sure did. An older-model car passed me about five minutes ago."

"Did you see the driver?"

"Not really. See, Bertha here"—he patted the steering wheel—"won't let my eye wander on a day like today."

"Do you recall anything as far as description?"

"He seemed to be goin' a little fast for the conditions."

"How do you know it was a he?"

"No woman would drive a car that ugly."

"You didn't happen to catch a plate number by any chance?"

"Like I said, I try to keep my mind on my work. One thing I can tell you is that it's the only car I've seen all day."

"Can you radio something into your dispatcher for me?"

"Sure."

Kate gave him the information to pass on to dispatch about getting in touch with local authorities for White Crest, and to Alvarez back home.

"How are the local roads looking?" Kate asked.

"Fair. I'd say they'll be safe by late evening."

"Evening? I can't wait that long."

Pat eyed her carefully. "Patience is a virtue—"

"That I don't have. But what I do have is a melting crime scene and a thawing corpse."

"You sure have your share of problems. I'll tell ya what. I'll radio a good buddy of mine and see if I can't get him to get to your area right away. It's the best I can do."

"Thanks, Pat. If you're ever in Southfield, I owe you a beer."

"I'll hold you to it."

We headed back down the hill to await the cavalry.

95

★ ★ ★ ★ ★

Our wait wasn't long. Police cruisers with lights and sirens blazing broke the snowy calm surrounding the A-frame home. Kate's friends peered intently out the wide windows watching the parade of police and forensic personnel working the crime scene. I took in all the action, making mental notes, trying to keep all of the new names and faces in order. A man in a black trench coat caught my eye with a look that said *GQ* had really missed a good thing, as the man was definitely magazine cover material. I'm a sucker for great eyes, and his laser greens bordered on hypnotic. I was grateful he couldn't see me with my tongue hanging out. Kate, however, had to stifle a grin at my reaction when he came over to introduce himself.

"Detective Frost, is it?" He extended his leather-gloved hand.

"Yes. Please call me Kate. And you are?"

"Detective Pete Milner, homicide. I'm sorry your vacation ended on such a sour note. We're really quite peaceful up here on White Crest. Can you walk me through your initial findings?"

As Kate took him through the evidence, I wandered over to the SUV housing the victim.

A sixty-something woman, in a jumpsuit and down jacket hovered over the torso. Her ID badge told me she was Thelma Phillips, Coroner.

"Dr. Phillips? Are you ready to load the wagon?" a man in a green parka asked.

"I don't think we'll need it, Jeremy. Looks like we're taking in the whole car as evidence."

She took her time documenting the vehicle's contents, which had been carefully placed inside. I couldn't help thinking that although the corpse had been brutally presented, the casting and placing of each body part seemed like a woman's touch.

The usual who, what, where questions were running through

my mind. One: who wanted poor Jakes dead in such a gruesome way? Chances are there was some sort of message in the way she was killed and positioned that might point to an answer and possibly a solid lead. I saw Jakes' open eyes staring my way through the plaster and wondered what she'd seen last.

Kate came up beside me with Detective Milner. She handed him the photo stick from her digital camera. "Sorry I can't show you my shots. The battery died, and we've been without power since three this morning."

"No problem. I appreciate your work. But I have to ask, doesn't it seem a bit coincidental that the body was placed in *your* car?"

"I'd been warned before this, but didn't have any idea what might be coming. I received a severed finger in a package in my office the other day. Somehow, this is personal."

A uniformed officer interrupted, saying, "Detective Frost? Looks like the phone lines are back up. You have a call inside the house."

"Thank you. Excuse me, Pete. I have to take this call."

I watched the uniforms cordoning off the already-secluded area. It was a place that saw little foot traffic, except for squirrels and Peeping Toms.

CHAPTER FIFTEEN

Kate felt a wash of relief at the sound of Gerard's voice. She relayed the recent events, wishing he were standing beside her.

"Are you all right, cariña?"

"Yes. Wish you were here."

"I'm on my way."

"Don't. There's been a snowstorm and the roads are barely passable. I'm hoping to be able to leave by late this afternoon with Pam. There's not much more for me to do."

"Kate, I'm really sorry. I hate feeling helpless with you so far away."

"I'll be fine. It looks like a good crew working the scene."

"Who's the primary detective?"

"Pete Milner. Do you know him?"

"No. Does everything look in order?"

"If you mean, does he play by the book, I'd say very much so. He's professional. I turned over my photos and took him through my findings. It's out of my hands now."

"You and your friends will be called as witnesses."

"I've already told them."

"How are they holding up?"

"Fine after a few martinis. Since Teresa and I are the only ones who saw the caretaker, we'll be spending our afternoon with a sketch artist. Detective Milner spoke with the landlord. Turns out he never hired a caretaker, so this guy Burke is definitely a person of interest. And how are you getting along without me?"

"I'm not. Hurry home."

"That's nice to hear."

"That I'm miserable without you?"

"Yes."

"Glad I could tickle your fancy. Speaking of which, will I see you tonight?"

Kate felt her cheeks warm. "This isn't a secure line, Detective. Are you sure you want to go there?"

"There are many places I want to go. But we'll talk about that later."

"It'll be late by the time we finish here. I'll call you when I get in."

"I'll be up."

"I love it when you talk dirty."

"Just come by."

"I'm riding with Pam so I'll see if she'll drop me off."

"Hurry home."

"No, that's not it. The chin was narrower," Kate told the sketch artist as she sat in the cabin's living room. She fought the urge to pace. "I feel incredibly stupid. I'm trained to focus on details, and I can't even picture the guy clearly enough to get his chin right."

Detective Milner smiled. "This time you're the witness, not the cop. It makes a world of difference."

"How did Teresa do?"

"Actually she did pretty well. We'll compare the two sketches and see what comes up. Relax, you're doing fine. Why don't you go get a cup of coffee and take a short break?"

"Sounds good." Kate went into the kitchen.

Lindsay nodded toward Milner as he stepped outside and headed toward the crime scene. She pretended to wipe her chin. "Too bad I'm dead."

"He's married," Kate mumbled.

"How do you know?"

"Wedding ring. Subtle cologne. Slight paunch."

"That still doesn't make him married."

"He told me his wife's name."

"Oh. Well, in that case, I'm taking off. I want to get back to reality."

"Checking up on Mike?"

"Something like that."

Kate watched her fade then headed to the bedroom to collect her belongings. She had the feeling this would probably be her last trip to White Crest. It angered her to know the person who'd done this had not only taken away her childhood friend, but also the cherished place to gather with her friends.

After finishing up with the sketch artist, Detective Milner told all of them they were free to leave. A short time later, Kate hugged each one of her friends good-bye in the driveway.

"Hey, same time next year? I'll bring the barf bag." Nicki yelled to Carmen as she got into her rental car.

"You're hysterical. I hope you get fleas in your gym shorts." Carmen waved with a smile and backed down the long drive.

"And what about next year, guys?" Nicki turned to the other three. "We can't let this guy win. We should do it to honor Jakes' memory."

Kate appreciated the gesture, and it showed that her friends weren't as traumatized as she'd feared. Her mind wandered over the evidence and what message the murderer was trying to send her. She hoped there wasn't more to the whole picture that might put them all in danger at some point.

"Hey, Kate. Would you mind driving? I'm still pretty shaken up about everything. I just can't focus," Pam said.

Kate got in and started the engine. "We'll have a great time. I have to warn you though, I sing a pretty raunchy version of a hundred bottles of beer."

Pam moaned at that, and Kate felt some of her tensions ease. For the next four hours she kept her mind on the road while Pam snored mercilessly in the passenger seat.

The drive gave Kate plenty of time to consider the case, but, by the time she reached Southfield Heights, she still hadn't come up with anything solid. Slowing up in front of Gerard's house, she found the idea of leaving the details up to the White Crest authorities quite appealing. Right now she had her own issues to resolve, like making up for lost time with her partner. Besides, he might be able to help her come up with the connection between herself and the murderer.

She almost second-guessed her idea of a late-night visit when she recalled that the boys were home. Still, he'd told her to come by. Pam offered to take her equipment home and let Kate pick it up another time. Kate waved good-bye from Gerard's front porch.

A living-room light told her Gerard was still up, probably watching television, and she knocked at the front door instead of ringing the bell.

When he opened the door, his smile eased away any second thoughts and he pulled her close inside the doorway.

"I missed you." His lips grazed her ear.

"Me too. Right now, can't even think of the reason I went."

He pulled back a moment. "Are you sure you're all right? No one followed you or anything strange?"

"I'm fine. Now."

"Can I get you something?"

"Only you."

On the couch, Kate allowed the chaos of the past twenty-four hours to settle as she laid her head against Gerard's chest. As

101

the quiet filled her, she felt herself growing drowsy and shook herself awake.

"I better get going before I fall asleep. Any idea how I'll get home?"

Gerard held on to her hand as she stood. "What's the hurry?"

"If I don't go now, your boys will find me on the couch in the morning with wrinkled clothes and sleep drool on my cheek. I'm sure that's a visual they don't need."

"The boys are gone."

"Cynthia?"

"No. A sleepover at their friends."

Suddenly Kate felt wide-awake.

"Really?" She eased back onto the couch.

"And I don't think the couch is very comfortable. Trust me, I know. Personally, I'd suggest the bed."

Before she could answer, he kissed her deeply, extinguishing all reservations and igniting the fire within. She sucked in a breath when his hands touched her where she desired most and realized that after all of the times they'd shared his bed, she'd never felt the need to be with him so urgently before. She moaned as his lips trailed her neck and down past her bare shoulders. Her hands greedily sought to touch him and she helped unbutton his jeans, before discarding the rest of her clothing.

She closed her eyes and realized how much she'd missed his bronze skin so hot against her own. Her tongue savored his taste as she caressed his broad shoulders and they moved together in the night. Her last thought before drifting off to sleep was if absence makes the heart grow fonder, three days at White Crest could be potentially volatile. She promised not to let that much time go by again.

The next morning at the department's gym, Kate performed a

series of stretches before starting her workout. The building stood next to the station, and it housed a weight room and sparring ring and had enough room left over for public self-defense classes. Officer Jake Tucker taught them weekly on Saturday evenings. Kate teased him that the only reason he'd volunteered was because the class consisted mostly of women. He'd countered that he was the best guy for the job because he felt an obligation to the community, beside the fact that he was a third-degree black belt. Although true, Kate knew he was also a hopeless flirt.

Gerard had gone to pick up the boys after dropping her off, intent on meeting back at the gym for a sparring session.

"You mean another one," he'd grinned over breakfast.

She smiled now at the thought of their night together, when the weekend's horror had briefly faded. Pulling her hair into a ponytail, she realized today would be back to reality and that meant dealing with Jakes' death.

Her body needed a workout to loosen up the stiff muscles from her fall, and her mind needed the diversion. As she finished her last set of stretches, she decided to start with the speed bag. Each hit released a small amount of tension, and, as her pace grew faster, so did her accuracy. Her mind reviewed the weekend events, causing her to relive the frustrations of helplessness and the loss of a close friend. After a while the drone of fist hitting bag became a white noise that allowed all of her concerns to surface.

Her mother stood a firm believer that trials make a person stronger. If that were true, Kate figured she should be as sturdy as the Rock of Gibraltar. Her mother had set the example by surviving her oldest daughter's death with grace and composure and had seemed to grow stronger for it. Kate hoped she could match her mother's resilience. Recent and upcoming events were slowly taking their toll and she hated herself for allowing it.

"Get off the pity pot, Frost." She hit the bag harder.

Her concentration broke when a figure came up beside her.

"Let me know if the bag talks back." Officer Jake Tucker said with a grin.

Kate remained focused on the bag.

"You pummel that thing any harder and it'll end up in the weight room," Tucker said.

Kate stopped, feeling invigorated. "Really? Last time it ended up at the station on O'Connor's desk." She offered a grin and arm-swiped her sweaty forehead. "It's all yours. I'm headed for the heavy bag."

Even after the stretches she'd done, it took her a few minutes to work through the pain in her legs. She served up a series of kicks that sent the bag swaying. Jakes' green eyes flashed in her mind.

Bam! Thrust kick.

She recalled the petrified looks on her friends' faces at the scene.

Another thrust.

A faceless silhouette formed in her mind as she tried to picture the animal that'd done it.

Several punches and a roundhouse sent the bag swinging. She stopped briefly to catch her breath. Tears stung her eyes. She refused to cry here. God, not here.

The bag took more of her wrath as she forced herself to think of something else. But it wasn't a pleasant memory or happy future event that came to mind, and a claustrophobic fear consumed her. Suddenly she felt the urge to run instead of fight. As she replayed the words that had changed her life forever, it became more difficult to maintain self-control.

Her hands throbbed from the punches she'd inflicted and she

realized she'd taken her workout too far. Thankfully, Gerard entered the gym and headed her way.

"Looks like you've already had your sparring session." He eyed her carefully.

Grabbing a towel from her workout bag, she dried her face and neck.

"Naw. I'm just getting started."

"Uh-huh. Want to tell me what's wrong?"

She stopped suddenly, feeling physically exhausted and emotionally drained. Her throat tightened as she fought the fatigue and her emotions.

"I let the weekend get to me. Coming here was probably a mistake. Instead of releasing tension, it only made things worse."

"You need a vacation from your vacation. Maybe a nice lunch at your favorite place after this?"

"I really should get back to the office."

"They're not expecting you back until tomorrow. Why not take advantage?"

Kate closed her eyes as he brushed a lock of hair from her face. "You're not in this alone," he said softly. "We'll get through both of these challenges together."

She wished it were true. But no matter how much Gerard wanted to be there for her, she knew there was one challenge she'd have to face alone. Before she could answer, his cell phone rang.

His expression turned dark and he turned away to finish the conversation. She heard him break into Spanish, recognizing a few choice words she'd learned on the job as his partner. Her suspicions told her it had to be Cynthia.

Kate decided to give him some space and got on a stationary bike. This was something she could do with little effort and pain while allowing her body to wind down. She missed the summer weather where she could take her ten-speed along the trails behind the courthouse and burn a few calories while getting some fresh air. She closed her eyes and visualized the mature trees and fresh air, reminding her it wouldn't be long until spring.

When she opened her eyes, Gerard had vanished. Another officer had taken over the speed bag, and no one else remained except Jake Turner.

He caught her puzzled expression and came over.

"You lookin' for Alvarez?"

"Where did he go?"

"He took off muttering something in Spanish. I didn't bother to ask."

Her lunch plans left open for the moment, she decided to go into the office after all, where her date with a sack lunch wouldn't be cancelled.

Chapter Sixteen

Kate waved good-bye to Pam as I paced in her living room. It had taken both of them to haul the ski equipment and her suitcase into the house and then I had to wait for gossip and hugs before Pam left. Patience is not one of my virtues, especially when I have something on my mind. I was glad to see Kate back home, anxious to find out any details she'd learned about the murder, and to hit her with my brainstorm. This case provided the perfect excuse to bring up the topic. So why did I feel apprehensive?

Kate hummed while she sorted through her suitcase.

"You're in a good mood. All things considered, the weekend to White Crest must have done you some good."

"It wasn't the weekend away as much as the homecoming." She winked.

"Why don't we talk about something less nauseating. When are they doing the autopsy?"

"I don't know. Gerard is going to call today."

"Back to him, are we?"

"I'm stalling. I'm not due back on duty for another twenty-four hours, yet I know I'll be there today. Every minute I let by is time for the bastard who killed Jakes to get away."

"Speaking of work—"

"I'm trying not to." She tossed her ski goggles onto the closet shelf.

"Okay. I'll try you again tomorrow."

107

"Try me again for what?"

"Nothing. I better get going. The paranormal softball league is meeting—"

"No . . . wait. Tell me."

I knew it would work. Kate can't stand suspense or secrets or any form of waiting. Now I had her.

"I have an idea."

"Oh no, Lindsay. Not again."

"Just listen."

I told her about my recent case involving Rico and how it had sparked an idea.

"There are probably a lot of people on the other side who need my services to find closure. Since I still have my death tag, I suppose it means it's not time for me to move on yet. Kate, what if this is what I'm suppose to be doing?"

Her silence told me she was mulling it over.

"All I'll need is your help once in a while for the physical details I can't get to. We'll be like Simon and Simon."

"Who?"

"Remember that show about the two brother detectives?"

"No."

"Forget it."

"I already did."

"We know we make a good team. Why not give it a try and see what happens?"

She shut the empty suitcase and lugged it to the closet. Her silence had become nerve-racking. Perhaps I was on the wrong track with this. When we were kids, I could usually talk her into anything. I had the upper hand as the big sister, but now I was the dead sister, the one who shouldn't even be here. Had I become so insecure that I was willing to grab the first idea that came along and run with it? Why couldn't I just go to my eternal rest like everyone else?

I was so involved with my internal monologue that I almost missed what she said.

"Almost like solving cold cases."

"What? Oh right. Except we have the advantage of being able to get vital information from the victim."

"That might just work, Linz. I don't know how much time I'll be able to spare, but it's worth a shot. We could help a lot of people. I know I'll need you to help me with Jakes."

"Wow. That was easy."

"What do you mean?"

"I didn't know if you'd go for it."

"Just trying to help you."

That hurt. I never thought of myself as needy. I'm too independent and bullheaded for that. The tables had turned and Kate was the strong one now, making me feel dependent on her. It was a role I'd never had to play before.

I'd tripped over my pride before and saw the potential for it to happen again. Like it or not, I needed Kate and if I wanted to pursue my new goal I needed to get down to work.

"Great." I tried to sound enthusiastic.

Kate's cell phone interrupted me and I listened to her take the call.

"Kate Frost. Right. I see. I'll be there."

She disconnected saying, "Sorry, Linz. Looks like I have to go in today. You were saying?"

"Great."

A squad had dropped Kate off at the rent-a-car in town, and, soon after, we were on our way to the station. She filled me in on the details as she drove.

"Any new clues?" I asked.

"Detective Milner isn't saying too much, but Gerard did manage to find out the autopsy is scheduled for today."

"It could be Milner is holding out because he knows you'll be called as a witness. I could eavesdrop on the autopsy if you'd like."

"That's cheating. How soon can you leave?"

I left Kate in search of Dr. Warren Saint in his morgue and found him observing an autopsy being done by someone else. He was not happy!

"No, no. That's not the proper technique." He shook his head at the new coroner.

The man continued the procedure oblivious to the dead doctor's concerns.

"Dr. Saint?" I approached.

"What's that? Oh. Detective Frost. Not expecting anyone to address me here. Gave me a fright."

"Sorry." I glanced toward the table. "Anything interesting?"

"Run-of-the-mill heart attack. But this joker is turning it into a Wes Craven production. Completely unnecessary."

"Dr. Saint, I need your help."

"Wonderful. Let's get out of here before I puke."

"You have a weak stomach?"

"For unprofessional work, yes."

We decided to meet at my special place in the woods.

"Now what can I do for you, Detective Frost?" the doctor asked, settling himself on a nearby tree stump.

"Please call me Lindsay. I need to view an autopsy today and wondered if you could lend a professional opinion. I've observed them before, but I'd like a second pair of eyes to make sure nothing is missed."

"Be glad to. I only hope the coroner does a better cutting job than my replacement."

"I don't think that's going to be a problem."

Dr. Saint stared at the cast body parts on the morgue table. "I see what you mean."

Dr. Thelma Phillips and her assistant peeled off the white material covering each of the limbs and stood back a moment to observe.

"We'll need individual weights and measurements," Phillips said.

"And a definite ID," Dr. Saint added as if he could be heard.

I nodded. Although the victim was most likely Jakes, they had yet to remove the casting material from the head.

"This woman was found stuffed into Kate's car?" Dr. Saint asked.

"Right. It's actually a childhood friend of ours. Somewhere in all this it's meant to be personal for Kate."

The coroner's assistant snapped a series of photos, then leaned in close to the severed end of an arm. "Looks like hacksaw marks."

I hoped Jakes had been dead before the mutilation occurred. Not only for mercy: if she died after the mutilation, her spirit would spend eternity in pieces.

"I count nine phalanges," the assistant said. "Looks like a middle finger is missing."

"That's our girl," I said.

I watched the coroner carefully cut and peel the covering from the face. Jakes' green eyes remained fixed on something above as the doctor tugged away the last of her tomb. The one thing I recall vividly about Jakes was her near-perfect complexion. She'd been told countless times that she should consider modeling. But Jakes had had her own rules, her own style, and prancing down a catwalk in a skimpy dress did not appeal to her. That's one of the reasons she and I had gotten along so well. We'd both been tomboys. Kate had always shown a more prissy side, with her designer this and that, and the fact that she wore makeup before any other girl in school. But she and Jakes had hit if off and become close friends.

Dr. Phillips cleaned Jakes' face and stood back. "What a lovely woman. A goddamn shame, I tell you."

I agreed with her there. Any murder is a shame, but this one was close to home.

I thanked Dr. Saint for his time and left him back at his morgue, where another autopsy had started. The good doctor hurried over to supervise, shaking his head when the attendant dropped the pruning sheers into the chest cavity.

CHAPTER SEVENTEEN

Kate found Alvarez in his office. His dark brow furrowed enough to let her know he wasn't happy.

"What's up?" She hoped it wasn't more Cynthia drama.

His expression softened. "Hey, sorry about this morning. I owe you a lunch."

"Forget it. I had to get back to my mountain of paperwork before my desk collapsed. Any news?"

"I just got off the phone with Detective Milner. He doesn't know much more than we do."

"Did Milner check out the caretaker?"

"Dead end. The name Ted Burke didn't turn up anything promising and the A-frame owner stands by his story that he never hired a caretaker. The cell phone number Burke gave you doesn't exist. Looks like your bearded buddy was up to no good."

"That's a lead."

"How do you figure?"

"Find the caretaker. Find the killer. It's too coincidental that the two aren't connected."

"You're probably right, but there's no trace of him. He's long gone."

"Maybe not. If this whole thing is directed at me, then he knew I would be at White Crest. That tells me he's local to this area."

"Who knew you'd be going?"

"You, my parents, and several people here."

"Who did you get to bring in your mail?"

"My eighty-year-old neighbor. I seriously doubt that she did this crime."

"What do you recall about the caretaker?"

"Well, we can assume he lied about his name. However, I asked John to run the name Ted Burke through the computer for me. You never know what it will turn up."

"What else?"

"Not much. He seemed to have computer skills, because he did some impressive troubleshooting on Teresa's laptop. I thought that a bit odd for a guy who supposedly spends his time raking leaves and fixing leaky pipes."

"What about age, height and build?"

"I'd say about thirty. He stood approximately five-nine and seemed large boned, but he was wearing a parka so it's hard to be sure. He had sandy-brown hair and a scruffy beard. Green eyes. Nothing that really stands out."

"What did he drive?"

"A rustic gray Chevy pickup."

"You're a detective. You should be able to come up with more than that." Alvarez grinned.

"I was half asleep. Besides, he distracted me with donuts."

"Ah, the old donut distraction ploy. Works like a charm on cops."

Officer John Turner stuck his head inside the office and held up some paperwork. "Detective Frost?"

Kate smiled at his formality. He wouldn't call her Kate in front of Alvarez.

"What do you have for me, John?"

"I received the employee list from Miss Jakes' secretary." He handed her the information. "It's all there."

"I owe you, John."

Alvarez stared at her after John left.

"You realize he has a major crush on you, right?"

"Who?"

"Officer Turner."

"Oh. I hadn't noticed," Kate lied.

She scanned the list with her partner looking over her shoulder. "Here. This guy, Percy Smith."

"Why does he stand out?"

"He worked for Jakes, apparently. And he's an ice sculptor."

"So?"

"He has the right tools."

"Anyone can buy a hacksaw."

"Yes, but see this notation next to his name? He's recently been canned."

"I'd say we need to take a little trip to see the ice man."

Alvarez pulled the car curbside in front of the house and cut the engine. "Looks a little bedraggled."

Kate snorted. "I've seen sharper looking port-a-potties."

"You ready?"

"I'll call Hazmat."

The walk hadn't been shoveled in a while, and the snow reached just above Kate's kneecaps, creeping inside her boots. She trudged her way toward the living-room windows and noticed tan curtains resembling onionskin, hanging limp in the windows.

She cringed at the grimy glass and came away with soot-covered hands when she cupped them to look inside.

"I bet he's at Home Depot buying glass cleaner."

"And a doorbell." Alvarez pounded on the front door.

"I saw a family of rats heading toward the next house with their luggage."

Alvarez pounded again.

"Hold on." Kate headed across the yard to a neighbor's house. "Excuse me," she called to a woman in a faded winter coat retrieving the newspaper. "I'm Detective Kate Frost with SHPD." She flashed her badge. "May I speak with you a moment?"

The woman raised an eyebrow. "Detective, huh? What'd he do?"

"Is that the home of Percy Smith?"

"You oughta know. You're the cop."

"I'm sorry, I didn't get your name."

"I didn't give it to you."

Kate spotted a rusted old Chevy parked on the street in front of the woman's house. "Is that your car?"

The woman shot a glance at the vehicle then back to Kate. "It's my son's."

Kate slowly reached into her pocket for a pen.

"Wait," the woman said. "He's out of work right now and can't afford plates."

Kate eyed her carefully.

The woman nodded toward Percy's home. "Smith's a pretty good neighbor, mostly. He's kind of let the place go. Come to think of it, I haven't seen him for a couple of days. He's not in trouble, is he?"

"Does he work?"

"Yeah. He's some sort of artist. Does ice for parties."

"What time does he generally return home?"

"He doesn't seem to have a regular schedule. Comes and goes at all hours. I couldn't say. He lives a different sort of life."

"Define different."

"Well, he's into all that sun-worship stuff. Spends a lot of time at the nudist colony in Berkfield."

Kate handed the woman her business card. "I'd like to speak with him. Can you see that he gets this for me?"

"Sure." The woman glanced at her son's car again.

"Your son might want to keep the car in the drive until he gets plates."

"Oh. Right. Good idea. Thanks." The woman hurried toward her house.

Alvarez came up beside her. "You find out anything?"

"He prefers to go sans pantaloon."

"What?"

"Au natural. Turns out Percy is an ice sculptor who regularly visits the Sun City nudist colony."

"Maybe we should go check it out."

"The nudist colony?"

"Why not? We might get a clearer picture of this guy."

"That's what I'm afraid of."

In the car, Alvarez's cell phone rang. Kate tried to tune out the conversation with his ex-wife. Sitting beside him, she realized it was impossible.

His jaw muscle tensed as he spoke.

"No, Cynthia. I told you I can't make it. You'll have to pick the kids up."

Kate hummed softly to herself and looked out the passenger window.

"I'm not keeping the boys from you. They're looking forward to going."

Blessedly her own cell phone rang as he broke into Spanish.

"Frost here."

She smiled at the officer's familiar voice.

"Hey, Kate. It's John Turner."

"What can I do for you, John?"

"There's a photographer here to see you. His name is Ed Nog."

"Shit."

"You got that right. He says he can't leave till he talks to you."

"Can't or won't?"

"Can't. Says he has some photos you'll want to see. But you're the only one he'll show them to."

"Tell him to wait. I'll be there shortly."

Alvarez disconnected his call and sped up. "Change of plans. I have to take care of some personal business. Can I drop you off at the station?"

Kate swallowed the slight. She knew his problems with Cynthia were just that—*his* problems. But she felt left out when he didn't confide in her and wondered if he'd ever let down his guard.

She reminded herself he was used to doing everything on his own. Cynthia's drinking had forced him to become the breadwinner, mom, dad and babysitter. It would take a while for him to learn to trust someone and she knew patience was the answer. Still, it rankled when he referred to the situation as "personal business," as if she were a stranger. Cynthia's behavior had become intrusive in their relationship, and had crossed from his personal business into her business.

She bit her tongue once again knowing he didn't need the added stress of a high-maintenance girlfriend. Let it go, she told herself. And she did, with the promise to take it up when everything calmed down.

"Sure. It looks like I have some business of my own to attend to."

CHAPTER EIGHTEEN

I located Kate in her office interviewing Mullet Man. She barely gave me a nod when I appeared in the corner. My news about the autopsy would have to wait. Her situation looked far more interesting so I listened in.

"How did you know about White Crest Mountain?" Kate downed two aspirin without water.

"I don't want to say too much now and get into trouble."

"You're already in trouble, Mr. Nog."

Yeah. Look at that "do."

I sauntered around to her side and reviewed the notes she'd made.

Name: Edward Allen Nog. Was at White Crest Mountain the day of the murder.

"Wow," I said out loud.

Kate ignored me, and focused on her next question.

"If you've been withholding information about an ongoing murder investigation, you could be in a lot of trouble. On the other hand, I'm listening." She pinned him with a heated stare.

I taught her that one. It worked too, because suddenly he sat up stick straight, which made his mullet taller. He looked like a rooster about to crow.

"See I know we weren't supposed to start our shooting till this week. But when I saw that finger I knew it had to be a worthwhile case. I had to follow up."

"That's not following up—that's stalking. I could have you

arrested for that. Better yet, I think I'll call your editor. . . ."

He blanched. Not a pretty sight.

"Wait! Don't do that. I'll get fired."

Kate put down the receiver.

"Okay, let me just say that—do I need a lawyer?"

"If you don't finish, you'll need a doctor."

"Gotcha. Like I told you, I followed you to White Crest."

"How did you know I would be there?"

"I saw the reservations on your desk. You know you really should be more careful."

"What did you say *The Crier*'s number is?"

"Okay. Okay. When I got there, I saw where you were staying and I went and rented a room in town. By that time it was too late to do anything so I crashed at the hotel."

"Go ahead."

"The next morning, Saturday, I got up early and saw that creepy fellah in the beat-up truck at your door. But, since you let him in, I figured he was okay. Then, later, he followed you to that little store and I thought that was kind of weird."

"The fact that you were following me, as well, never seemed strange to you?"

"No, ma'am. I was working."

"I see. Then what happened?"

"Well, the next day you took a nasty tumble on the hill. . . ."

"You got pictures of that?"

"Yeah."

"Continue."

"Here's where it gets interesting." When he smiled, his crooked front teeth pointed at her. "I found a place down the road. It's nothing more than a log cabin. I figured that's where the caretaker might be staying, and, since his truck was nowhere to be found, I had a look around. I peeked in the windows and about tossed my cookies. The place was a wreck, with overturned chairs, and what looked like blood all over the floor."

Kate glanced my way and I knew we must be onto something. She picked up her phone and asked the receptionist to get her Detective Milner.

"Please, continue, Mr. Nog. What did you do next?" she asked him.

He ran both hands through his hair, making it stick out in two points. Apparently he used enough product to keep the look alive, only now he looked like he had horns.

Kate coughed to conceal a laugh and regained her composure nicely.

"Well, ma'am, I kind of jiggled the doorknob till it gave."

"You entered a crime scene?"

"No. Not technically. I stood in the doorway and snapped a few shots."

"Why on earth would you do that?"

"Well, with you being a cop and all, I figured you might appreciate the help. You know, crime-scene photos taken by a professional? That's when I hightailed it over to the A-frame to find you, but when I got there, I saw everyone gathered around the back of your SUV and I knew you ladies had problems of your own. I guess you know the rest."

"Did you reload your camera at the A-frame?"

"Yeah. Why?"

"Because I found an empty film canister. And I'm assuming that was you playing peekaboo in our cabin window?"

"You saw that?"

"I think the hair gave you away."

"You like that, huh?" he winked.

"Well, Mr. Nog, that's quite a tale. At this point I'm not even going to press charges for stalking, trespassing on private property, disturbing a crime scene, and withholding evidence— especially the withholding evidence. And do you know why?"

"No, ma'am."

I grinned at Kate. "Because that last part is a lie. It's not illegal to withhold evidence."

She ignored me.

"Because you're going to turn over those pictures. Am I right?"

"Now just hold on there, I can sell those for a pretty high price. I was just being honest with you so you could solve the case. You can have the photos, but I want to retain the rights."

I saw Kate bite back her first response. Now that, I didn't teach her. I would have been all over the guy, and not in the way he would have wanted.

"Look, Mr. Nog. I can and will take those photos, but I would prefer to do it the nice way. The nice way being that you hand them over to me with or without a smile, I really don't care. The not-so-nice way is where I arrest you for all of the above and I get to smile."

"Arrest me for what?"

"We'll think of something." She raised a brow.

"I see your point. When would you like them?"

"Now."

"I'll need to run home and get them."

"I'll go one better than that and have an officer escort you there and back. Sound good?"

"I, uh. . . ."

"Oh, and don't forget the one of me on the hill." She picked up her phone and dialed for an officer.

After Nog left with his six-foot, muscular date, I watched Kate pinch the bridge of her nose.

"You feeling all right?"

"Headache's almost gone. But I thought I might rupture myself trying not to laugh."

"You handled it like a pro."

"I can't believe he followed me there. And even though he was at the crime scene, I don't even consider him a person of interest. He's too dumb."

"I don't know. Kind of convenient how he showed up for the finger photo as well as the murder. You might want to rethink that theory."

"I'm going to check him out with *The Crier*. Other than that, we have only one other lead."

She filled me in on her suspicions about the nudist, Percy Smith. Before I could tell her I thought it sounded like another dead end, her phone rang.

"Yes. That's correct, Detective Milner. I'm waiting on the cabin photos now. I'll send you copies as soon as I get them." She hung up and nodded at me.

"They've already found the cabin. A real mess, but not the original crime scene. Not enough blood."

"Maybe we'll get lucky and the guy made a mistake."

"I hope so. By the way, how did the autopsy go?" Kate asked.

"No doubt it's Jakes. And it looks like the murderer used a hacksaw to slice and dice. No other evidence like prints or fibers. Unless we can trace the hacksaw, we have nothing to go on."

"He's one sick pup."

"And he's made sure to keep you involved. We need to find this guy before he tries something else. Meantime, maybe I can contact newbies on the other side to see if I can find Jakes. Not sure where the new-recruits terminal is, but I'll work on it. Hey, maybe we should take a run over to—"

Just then, Alvarez stuck his head inside her office.

"Care to grab a bite to eat?"

"Sure. It will give me chance to update you on the case. Let me finish up here and I'll catch up with you."

Once he was gone, Kate shrugged at me. "Gotta go."

I hid my disappointment. "Me too. I'm meeting Mike for dinner at Chez Dead."

"Have fun. I'll catch you later."

"I'll probably order the finger sandwiches!" I called after her, but she apparently didn't hear me.

I wandered about her office, the same four walls that used to be my office space. Times had changed. Our lives had changed. Gone were my awards and certificates, my photos, and of course my police teddy bear from Build-A-Bear. That one had been a gift from Richard Kelter, one of my kids at the Special Olympics. I'd helped out for years with the softball event, and still attended in spirit.

I'd had some pretty good times in this office, some pretty bad ones too. I shook my melancholy mood and scanned Kate's desk, noting it was just as cluttered as I used to keep it. Percy Smith's address was scribbled on a notepad and I thought about checking it out to see if the mysterious Mr. Smith might show up.

Then I saw something that scared me more than all the criminals and crime scenes I'd encountered. Kate's desk calendar revealed an appointment tomorrow for an ultrasound at Dr. Karr's office. As sisters we shared many things, one of them being the same gynecologist. I briefly considered pregnancy, but knew Kate too well. If she suspected she was pregnant, I would be the first to know. It frightened me to think Dr. Karr had found something serious enough to warrant an ultrasound, and it worried me even more that Kate hadn't confided in me.

CHAPTER NINETEEN

Kate sat behind her desk, viewing Edward Nog's photos, passing each of them to Alvarez. There were forty in all, but only thirty-nine on her desk after her shoving the one of her fall from grace into her top drawer. The rest showed a time line of events from Kate's arrival at White Crest to the discovery of the body in the trunk. As annoying as the photographer was, there stood a chance he might have captured crucial evidence.

"Maybe the department should consider assigning photographers to all of its detectives." Alvarez examined the crime-scene photos.

"I hate to admit it, but he knows how to capture a shot. Hopefully it will lead us somewhere."

"By the way, when I spoke to Detective Milner, he said the cabin is quite secluded and looks like it's been abandoned for years, until recently. He also said there wasn't enough blood to be the primary crime scene. It looks like Jakes was killed elsewhere. Looking at these photos I can see why this was the perfect place to hide. Look at this."

Kate saw the wide shot of the forest surrounding the cabin. She'd missed the dilapidated structure on her ski runs because it stood so far off the beaten path. No one would see it unless they were looking for it. And that told her the murderer knew what he was looking for when he got there.

"Perhaps he's a White Crest local. Anyone who could make their way in and out of that area with a body has to be familiar with the land. Trust me, I found out firsthand about unseen bumps in the road."

"I'm sure Milner is already on it," Alvarez said.

Kate pored over a photo of the inside of the cabin. A kitchen chair had been turned over on its side. Bits of plaster were visible on the kitchen table and floor.

"Milner has to find something in all this mess. Somewhere in here, the murderer made a costly mistake." Kate took another look at the photo.

"What kind of message is this guy sending by plastering the body, then cutting it up? And he took a big risk by going to all the trouble of putting the body into your car."

"I'm not sure I understand the significance of the plaster. It's as though he's creating the image of a doll."

"Right. Like those puppets that dance." Alvarez struggled to find the right word.

"Marionettes?"

"That's it. According to the coroner, each limb had a thin cable attached as if to control the victim's movements."

"I think you hit it. It's all about control," Kate said. "If this is a revenge killing, it might have a lot to do with the killer's feelings of lack of control, or just the opposite, and that now he is in complete control. Maybe he's telling us he holds the strings and we all better dance to his music."

"Anyone in your past play with puppets?"

She waited for the punch line, but saw he was serious. "No. Can't think of any cases that are remotely close."

Kate slid the photos aside and went through the file once more.

"What about Percy Smith? I'd like to know where he fits into this whole picture."

"Heard anything from his neighbor?"

"No. I'm not holding my breath. If he is in hiding we need to find him before he gets too deep."

"No one has seen him. Where do you want to look?"

"If he did take off, he'd need cash, and I'll bet he had some sort of severance pay or check coming from Jakes. I think it's time to talk to Jakes' receptionist."

"He's such a talented ice sculptor, but a real jerk. Jakes fired him last week," the receptionist told Kate.

Susan Scoffield wrung her hands as she spoke. Her blue eyes were rimmed in red and her rosy nose completed the set.

Kate glanced around the quaint office and noted the tasteful decor. It made the small office look much grander than it was and she recognized Jakes' eloquent touches. Framed photos lined one wall over an oak credenza. In each picture, Jakes stood beaming with several employees or a smiling bride and groom. The photos told a story line of an entrepreneur at work, building her business one customer at a time, with talent and a beautiful smile. Kate missed her friend.

Susan blew her nose. "I can't get over it. She was such a kind person. And you think Percy did it?"

"We just need to speak to him. How long did he work here?" Alvarez asked.

"Oh, about two years, I guess. He used to be quiet and polite, but, after he'd gained notoriety over his work, he started to change. That's when all the trouble started between him and Jakes. She wouldn't tolerate his tardiness and his rude attitude toward the other employees. That's all he was, just another employee, but he refused to believe it. It got so he wouldn't help with anything. All he wanted to do were his sculptures."

"When did you see him last?" Alvarez asked.

"Last Thursday when he picked up his final check. He bragged that he was into something bigger than this little catering business. You don't think he meant something like this do you?"

"That's what we're trying to find out." Kate handed Susan her card. "Will you give him this if you see him?"

"I sure will."

On their way to the car, Kate shook her head. "Wipe that grin from your face," she told Gerard.

"I don't know what you're talking about."

"You know this leaves us with the only other place Smith is known to hang out—the Sun City nudist colony."

"It's our only lead on the guy."

"I can't believe it's open year-round."

"Well, clothing is optional. I'd imagine. . . ."

"I bet you do."

Kate was relieved to see Sun City's general manager, Bob Ilkerson, fully clothed.

"Come into the back and we'll talk." He led the way into a cramped office. "Have a seat."

Kate hesitated before the leather chair, wondering how many bare bottoms had been planted there.

"We're here about one of your members. Mr. Percy Smith," Alvarez started.

"Ah, yes. Very popular guy. Is he in trouble?"

"Not really. We just need to talk to him. When did you see him last?"

"Two Saturdays ago. We had a singles dance."

"Dance?" Kate asked.

"We have them on a regular basis. Folks have to have something to do during the winter months. As you can imagine, camping is out this time of year."

"So when will he be back in?" Kate asked.

"Not sure. He talked about going out of town for a while."

"Do you know if Mr. Smith owns property in Wisconsin?" Alvarez asked.

"No. I don't believe he does. If so, he's never mentioned it."

"Do you happen to know what kind of car he drives?" Kate wanted to know.

"Older-model Dodge. Green. He's not one for pomp and circumstance. Just plain ol' Percy."

"I see. Well, thank you for your time, Mr. Ilkerson." Alvarez handed him his card. "Will you see that he gets this when you see him next?"

"Of course. Oh, and let me give you some information about our facility. I think you might enjoy it. We have our own sand dunes, swimming pool and spa, and of course a spacious clubhouse with a really hopping dance floor. It's a great place for people of all ages to make new friends and have fun. Clothing is optional, so it truly is a place for everyone."

"Everyone?"

"Well, there are those who are a bit shy, but I tell them we're all God's creatures, great and small. Nothing to be ashamed of. If you two are interested, come back and see me. I'd be happy to show you around."

They thanked him and headed back to the car.

"Another dead end," Kate mused, leafing through the pamphlets.

"Anything interesting?"

"Everything seems on the up and up. They even have a list of rules."

"Such as?"

"This one seems a bit obvious—caution when building campfires." She scanned the list. "No tree cutting, which I assume includes stray branches. Oh, and friendly pets are allowed."

"Pats?" he asked.

"Pets."

"Want to join?"

"I'm allergic to sunscreen."

"Aw, c'mon, Kate. You've never considered throwing caution to the wind and going naked?"

"Only in the shower, and I get plenty of caution-tossing on the job."

Kate stuffed the pamphlets into her purse. She'd recycle them later in the trash.

"So what do we do now?" she asked. "The mysterious Mr. Smith is nowhere to be found. The way I see it, he had motive, means, and opportunity."

"But that only makes him a person of interest. I guess we have to wait for him to show himself."

"That shouldn't be a problem. He seems to get a lot of practice."

The hot shower spray felt good on Kate's aching muscles. Her bruise had turned a lovely shade of green but still felt sore to the touch. Gerard had dropped her off, after she declined his offer to scrub her back. She didn't quite understand her own reasons for turning down the chance to spend time with him, but he didn't press for an explanation. Perhaps working and playing together had become too much and it was time for some space.

She took advantage of the time alone, to let recent events sink in—especially their progress, or lack thereof, on the investigation. This case held more emotional power than any other, except for Lindsay's. With no time demands upon her, she gave herself the full spa treatment with a hot oil hair treatment, manicure and pedicure. The only thing missing was one of Gerard's wonderful massages, which would have been welcome on her aching muscles. She reminded herself that absence makes the heart grow fonder, or at least less guarded. By the time she got out she realized it had been well over an hour. An hour well spent, she decided, and dropped her towel.

When she reached for her nightgown, her hand hovered over the open drawer, frozen. Her head cocked slightly trying to make out the sound she'd heard coming from her living room. A low sound of music seemed to be coming from the stereo. She didn't recall turning it on before she went into the shower.

She silently cursed herself for leaving her weapon on the kitchen counter. The same place Lindsay had left her weapon the night she'd been murdered. Throwing on a pair of workout pants and a shirt, she padded barefoot down the hall, staying close to the wall. The music grew more distinct as she drew closer to the living room and she recognized it as some sort of Broadway show tune she should probably know the name of.

Crouching low to peer around the corner, she saw the room remained empty of intruders. A quick check of the kitchen showed no signs of intrusion, and, from there, she proceeded to secure the entire house. After confirming she was truly alone, she fished a pair of rubber gloves from her jacket pocket and pushed the button on the CD player. The machine opened to show a best-loved-show-tunes CD that she didn't own. Holding it up, she saw a juicy fingerprint waiting to be matched. Earlier, she'd looked forward to showering and getting to bed, but that had changed. Fueled by excitement at the new lead, she dressed quickly, pocketed the CD and drove straight to the station. With any luck, Gerard would still be up and able to meet her there.

CHAPTER TWENTY

"What do you mean it's Jakes' fingerprint? She hated show tunes!" Kate spilled coffee down the front of her workout shirt.

Alvarez handed her a roll of paper towels. "It is what it is. Someone is screwing with you. They printed the CD for future use. Now they're playing a psychological game with you, and, if you don't settle down, they're going to win."

"All right. You're right." Kate paced before his desk. "And there were no other prints on it?"

"None. This guy isn't stupid. But somewhere along the way I'm sure he's made a mistake. They all do. We just haven't found it yet." He worked a bright-blue ball in his left hand.

"What is that thing?"

"It's for working out the tension and stress of everyday life." He tossed it to her.

She gave it a few squeezes. "Soft and squishy doesn't do it for me. I need to pummel the crap out of something." She pitched it back to him, nearly knocking over his coffee.

"Hey, don't look at me when you say that." He offered a rare smile.

She stopped herself from saying something flirtatious, recalling her notion of too much time together.

"Are you feeling unusually stressed?" Kate asked instead.

"Yes. Thanks to your recent house guest."

"So what do you suggest?"

"We find out how he got into your house without leaving a

trace. What is he—a ghost?"

"You never know."

"What?"

"Nothing. It's just so incredibly frustrating."

"It's also incredibly dangerous that you have so little protection. I hate to bring it up, but Lindsay refused to put in an alarm system. I hope you'll at least consider it." The stress ball disappeared in his hand, compressed into ballooned bulges between his fingers.

"I'm a cop," she reminded him.

"Exactly. A lot of people have grudges against cops. Lindsay's death proves it. Don't be foolish, you're not superwoman."

Kate bit her lip. She hated to admit defeat, but he was right. If something happened to her, it would devastate her parents to lose another child. Besides, if something happened to her, Lindsay would kill her.

"All right. I'll see about it."

"Don't see about it. Do it." Gerard's eyes pinned her.

"All right! But that still leaves us with this." She held up the CD. "It's a clue. As sick and twisted as it might be, the CD is a clue. What significance do Broadway show tunes have in all this? I'm a rock 'n' roll girl myself."

"It might not be about your taste, or lack of. I'm partial to Latina."

"I never would have guessed." Kate smiled.

"Do you recall which song was playing when you first heard it?"

"I'm not up on my Broadway musicals. Besides, it's just the standard compilation CD, with a wide variety of songs. No theme."

"I think you should let the crime team have a look at your house in case something else was left behind."

"They won't find anything. I've already gone through it. It's easier for me to spot something out of place because it's my turf."

"So how did he get in?"

"I'm guessing the window well in the basement. It never did lock properly. It was still cracked open a bit when I checked, and, unless there was an awfully big wind, it would have stayed closed."

"I'll send someone over to print it in the morning."

"Thanks, but I really doubt he slipped up there. I saw no footprints outside or in. It's not likely he was careless enough to use his bare hands."

He checked his watch. "Why don't you go home and get some rest, then take the day off tomorrow to secure your house? Get someone out there with an alarm system and have that damn window fixed."

Kate knew he meant well, but she had a full list of things to do before her appointment with Dr. Karr.

"I'm already taking half a day tomorrow. Maybe I'll try and schedule something in the afternoon."

"Please don't let this go, Kate. It's important." His expression had softened.

She went around his desk and kissed him on the cheek.

"What was that for?" he asked.

"It was a tease. I'll catch you later."

"Where are you going?"

"To call around for prices on moat digging. Think they charge extra for the alligators?"

She felt the sting of the stress ball hit her bruised rump.

"Hey!"

Kate turned to see him wearing a satisfied grin and looking much more relaxed.

CHAPTER TWENTY-ONE

I still didn't know if I should bring up Kate's doctor appointment, so I kept it to myself. For now. Watching her pace in our living room felt like old times, and I rejected the idea that anything could be wrong with my little sister.

"So the alarm system won't be installed until next week. But at least the window is fixed," she told me.

"I should have installed an alarm years ago. Might have saved my life. But, then, if a criminal wants in bad enough, they usually find a way. That's part of the reason I never did it."

"You were too cheap." Kate laughed at me.

I think my eyes widened in shock when she showed me the estimate, but I couldn't be sure.

"I rest my case," she said. "Fingers, bodies and a CD. What kind of disjointed sicko are we dealing with? Why can't I get normal psychopaths like everyone else?"

"For now I suggest you stay alert. This guy's behavior doesn't fit any profile. What do we have right now?"

"So far all of Jakes' employees have come up clean. The only one who stands out is Percy the nudist," Kate said.

"No priors?"

"I'm a step ahead of you. I ran Percy's history and found that he'd been arrested for lewd conduct a couple of years ago when he wandered off the colony's property and onto a golf course. Not sure how that happened, considering there's barbed wire surrounding the grounds, but apparently he survived. No other

135

crimes except for being naked."

"So we're not talking about a hardened criminal here," I said.

"I suppose that depends on his mood at the time."

"I have to tell you this guy doesn't come off as a murderer," I said.

"That's what Gerard said. And so far we haven't been able to locate Percy. I'm beginning to wonder if something has happened to him."

"Anyone else of interest?"

"Jakes' live-in boyfriend, Ken Stevens. I've never met him, but, from what she'd told me, he's a real prize. She'd planned to break it off with him after White Crest and felt sure he knew something was up. Maybe this was a crime of passion."

"It seems too methodical and pre-meditated for that. And then what's the message to you?"

"I don't know. Like I said, we never met."

"We need to find him."

"Gerard is working on that. Right now I have a court appearance."

"What about later?" I hoped she'd mention her doctor appointment.

She never batted an eye. "We'll see what happens. You're coming in with me aren't you?"

"Where?" I prepared to offer my sisterly support.

"To work. I'm hoping we find Ken Stevens and I'd like you along."

"Oh. Sure. You can count on me."

After Kate left for court, I forced down my concerns for her and headed for my picnic spot. She would tell me when she was ready. I should keep my big nose out of her business. Still, I fought the feeling that she was pulling away from me, and it felt cold and lonely.

I found Sally O'Shannon at my picnic area, on her hands and knees, pulling up my imaginary weeds, with her teddy bear on the ground nearby.

"Hey! Don't do that," I called on my way over.

She yanked out a hefty, imaginary dandelion and tossed it aside. "Do you really want this in your perfect getaway?"

"Yes. I put it there when I created this place."

"You mean you *want* weeds?"

"It's more realistic; the way I recall it from my memory."

Sally got up, brushing imaginary dirt from her hands. "I was just bored and looking for something to do."

"Good. I have an assignment for you."

She beamed. "Really? What is it?"

"I need to find someone."

"Did you visit their place of death?"

"Tried that. No sign of her." I thought I had, anyway, but . . . were we sure exactly where Jakes had been killed? Not really.

"How long ago did she die?"

"Less than a week."

"Hmm. She should be there. Most newbies spend a lot longer than that at their spot."

"I didn't."

"That's because you got lost. Luckily, I found you."

Technically, I'd found her, but I knew better than to argue. Besides, what Sally said was true to a certain extent. If not for her, I would have been another lost soul in the great beyond. She'd taken me under her wing and taught me what she knew about existence on the other side. The girl could write a manual.

"So where do we look next?" I asked her.

Sally paced before me clutching her bear. The weeds she'd pulled had faded against the grass where she'd tossed them. New ones had appeared in their place.

"It's kind of soon for her to have a residual haunt."

I'd learned that a residual haunt is when a spirit has a life situation they're compelled to repeat until they correct the mistake. Unfortunately, many ghosts get caught up in them and never get out. They spend eternity repeating the same scene.

"Could she have gone on to the next level?"

"It's possible. Obviously, I'm no expert. And there's no way to question those who have done it. I've never known anyone who's gone on and then returned."

"There's no Internet search for missing persons here?"

"Not until Bill Gates joins us here and gets to work."

"So it's a dead end?"

"The deadest."

"Great. Unless I find her, my case is pretty much the same."

I tensed when the tall bushes behind me rustled. The last time that happened, it had been a mobster. This time it was Mike Blake. Although physically impossible, his green eyes showed brighter for some reason.

"You look happy. Did you win the lottery?" I asked.

"Just about." He grinned.

"Do tell." I patted a downed tree trunk for him to sit beside me.

"I think there's trouble in paradise."

I looked around.

Sally rolled her eyes. "He said 'paradise.' This isn't it."

"I think Kathy is going to call off the wedding."

"Oh, that paradise. What happened?"

"I'm not sure. All I know is they had a big blowup last night and he didn't stay there."

"That's great, I guess."

"Of course it is. She's not ready to get married. It's too soon."

Sally decided to excuse herself on the pretense of having something important to attend to. That left me free to speak my mind.

"Mike, you said yourself the two of you were nearly over when you passed. Maybe she is ready."

"Hey. Whose side are you on?"

"Even if she calls it off, what's in it for you? There's no hope of reconciliation. Don't you want her to move on and be happy?"

He shook his head and I waited for his rebuttal. Instead he said, "You're right. I know you're right. But I just can't get it out of my head."

"That's because you see her every day." I rested my spirit hand on his as best I could. "Maybe it's time for you to move on. Stop punishing yourself."

"It's easier for you. You have Kate. But I'm completely alone."

"You have me." And I meant it. I know I'd vowed to hang up the relationship gloves, but, with Mike, it didn't feel like a battle. He'd turned out to be a true friend and we had a lot in common, beside the fact we were both dead.

Face it, Frost, you're hot for him.

His look caught me off guard and I didn't know what to say next. He simply stared at me with the most tender look I've ever seen. I held his gaze, and, when he leaned in, I swear I felt heat surge between us.

When he'd taught me paranormal self-defense moves shortly after I'd met him, he'd instructed me that making contact is simply a matter of willing, or picturing it in your mind. After some practice, I'd taken him down without much effort. Apparently, it was a matter of mind strength as opposed to physical. It had proven a lifesaver—no pun intended.

We'd come this close once before and stopped, and I'd always wondered if it would be possible to have a physical relationship in spirit form. I was about to find out.

This time neither of us stopped or even hesitated. I'd never had to focus on a kiss before, but this was my first time, so to speak, and I didn't want it to be awkward.

I pictured the perfect kiss and leaned into him. At first I didn't feel anything and I peeked one eye open to make sure I hadn't missed the mark. Then my form began to tingle just like it does when the juices get flowing in physical form, and I sensed his touch. It felt as real as any sensation I'd ever had; yet no physical properties existed. It filled me with heat until I had to pull away.

"I've never felt anything like that. It was the most intimate experience I've ever had." I watched his reaction.

He made the motion of stroking my cheek. "And that was just a kiss."

I knew what he was thinking and it intrigued me to think there might be more. Much more.

CHAPTER TWENTY-TWO

I had the decency to wait in Dr. Karr's waiting room while Kate went in for her ultrasound. She didn't know I'd followed. Since she still hadn't mentioned it I decided not to. This was new territory for me. Kate had never kept a secret from me before, in part because she just couldn't do it, but also because I read her diaries. Now I felt scared that this concern was on a different level than anything she'd ever gone through before. I wondered if Alvarez knew.

The waiting room was filled, but being dead has its advantages. I didn't require a seat, and the receptionist didn't harass me for a co-pay. The mood was pleasant enough with moms and dads-to-be, paging through outdated copies of parenting magazines. Still, I was restless and paced for thirty minutes, wondering what my sister was going through and if she'd be all right. I finally settled where she wouldn't see me when she came out.

It seemed a little strange for me to be worried that she might die, having gone through it myself. In life, I'd feared death because of the unknown. Now I knew better—being dead was a little boring and I'd met some strange people. It was a lot like dating.

If Kate crossed over I'd have her with me and I'll admit that wouldn't be such a bad thing. But my fear for Kate stemmed from the fact that she might just go on to the next level without me. What would I do without her? Selfish? Yes. Human. Absolutely.

Finally, I saw Kate come through the door.

"Kate?" A very pregnant woman called out as my sister passed by.

"Ellen." Kate stopped and smiled.

"How've you been? I haven't seen you since Vonnie's birthday." Ellen started to get up.

"Stay put. I wouldn't want you to spring a leak," Kate teased, taking a seat beside her.

Ellen patted her belly. "Any day now. I'd be grateful to spring something. So what brings you here? Anything you want to tell me?"

Yeah, Kate. Anything you want to tell me?

"Just an ultrasound. I found a lump in my breast."

"Oh no. Is it serious?"

"Won't know till they get the results. I'm not too worried."

I watched the two of them chat, thinking that Kate had confided in a woman she only saw at bridal showers and Tupperware parties. *What about me?*

It took everything I had to walk, or rather, disappear, out of that room. I was pissed and wanted to confront her but realized she probably needed space right now.

Since Kate wasn't overly concerned, it seemed I was overreacting. She'd come to me when she was ready. I guess she'd learned to keep secrets somewhere along the way.

I forced myself to focus on the case—our case. I'd missed out on the nudist-colony visit, but that was my own fault. If I hadn't been lip-locked with Mike, I might have been in on the fun.

Reviewing what we had so far took all of fifteen seconds. It boiled down to a dismembered body—sent to Kate as a message, clearly—and no sound suspects. I didn't consider Percy Smith to be a solid lead. Although he had motive, means, and opportunity, he didn't strike me as the type. I figured the best way to get inside his head was to get inside his house. Fortunately, I didn't need a warrant.

I left Kate and put my nervous energy to good use. When I reached my destination, I saw that the Smith residence could have benefited from a little reconstruction in the form of demolition. Even though I'm dead, the place gave me pause as to its structural soundness. Perhaps Percy the nudist had abandoned it for good, wherever he was.

The home remained vacant throughout my search, not even a mouse. If Percy had fallen victim as well, there were no outward signs of struggle. Although sparsely decorated inside, it stood neat and fairly clean.

I literally stuck my head in the refrigerator, to check for moldy food and outdated milk, of which there were both. His pantry showed the telltale signs of a single guy living on anything nuke-able. No dishes in the sink, and the table had been wiped clean.

With no piled-up mail and newspapers, I figured one of his neighbors must have been taking them in. His bedroom closet sat filled with empty hangers and his underwear drawer had but one pair of boxers. It looked like Percy had indeed left town. The question was why.

I checked the bathroom shower and sink for signs of recent use and found no fresh spit or wet washcloths. Several half-used tubes of prescription hydrocortisone cream lay on the counter next to a box of cotton balls. Making a mental note of the doctor's name, I continued my search and saw the bathroom waste can had been emptied, yet he'd left the tubes on the counter. Since Percy seemed to be quite the neatnik, I wondered if he'd left in a hurry.

Moving on, I found his bed tightly made beside a nightstand covered with even more crumpled tubes of hydrocortisone cream. I considered bedbugs as a possible reason and moved on to safer territory.

The absence of a car in the cluttered, single-unit garage raised the question of whether Percy's absence was intentional or not. Had he fled or was he a victim of foul play?

I snooped around stacked boxes on the floor and inspected his tool bench, wishing I had solid hands to move things. I still hadn't figured out how to maneuver physical objects and wondered if it were even possible. Maybe I should contact Uri Geller.

There was nothing of particular interest among the usual guy stuff, unless you consider that there really wasn't any. No cans of motor oil, greasy tools or crumpled beer cans. Surprisingly there were no nudie chick pics either. The garage overflowed with picture frames and blank canvases of all sizes. Tubes of oil paint and numerous paintbrushes of varying thickness lay strewn on the workbench. Propped easels lined the perimeter of the garage. Not too strange if you're an artist, yet none of the canvases had been painted on.

My last stop on the house tour was a small room that served as an office with a computer seated on a small wooden desk. The walls were covered with prints of some of the great artists of our time, from Van Gogh to Rembrandt. Nothing by Percy Smith.

I was startled when Percy's phone rang, and I noted the answering machine showed twelve messages.

"Percy?" A man's voice came through the machine. "Bob here. I think I know the real reason you're staying out of sight. And I don't blame you. But you can't hide forever. We don't judge here at Sun City. By the way, the cops were here looking for you. Call me when you get this. Oh, and your tools are safe."

Bob the nudist. I shoved that visual away and decided to find Kate.

Kate had gone back to her office.

"Damn," she said, hanging up the phone.

"What's up?" My tensions rose when I considered it might be Dr. Karr's office.

"I just got word that my puppy is sick. I won't be able to pick him up till next week."

"Will he be all right?"

"The breeder said it was just a virus. He should be fine. It looks like I'm going to be buried under a pile of work for the next few days anyway."

"I don't miss that part of the job. But I have some good news for you."

I filled her in about the message from Bob.

"That's probably Bob Ilkerson, he's the general manager."

"Well, Bob knows something we don't and I think we need to pay him a visit."

"You're just dying to get in there, aren't you?"

"Why not? I can see them, but they can't see me. It should be a riot."

"I hate to disappoint you, but last time he was fully clothed. If you want to see the fun stuff, you'll have to catch one of their weekend dances."

"Puts a new twist on the Hand Jive."

"You forgot swing dancing."

"I wonder if they have bouncers?"

Kate grabbed her coat.

"Where's Alvarez?" I asked.

"Had to take his son to the orthodontist. Braces."

"Guess it's just you and me."

"How am I going to ask Bob about his message when I never

went to Percy's house?" Kate asked.

"You fudge the truth."

"You mean lie?"

"No. I said fudge. You're not going to tell him about the message. Right now we're just looking for him to tell us something warrant worthy."

"What's my reason for going back?"

"You're interested in club membership?"

On the way to Sun City, I told Kate about Percy's possible skin affliction.

"I doubt if his doctor will tell us much. Patient confidentiality and all," Kate said.

"Well, it's worth a try. So far it's all we have on him."

Kate sat in her rented car in the Sun City parking lot. "I can't believe I let you talk me into this."

"What's the big deal? You aren't actually going to join. Are you?"

"What if he's naked this time?"

"Do it for Jakes."

"She'd be rolling on the floor laughing at this."

"Oh yeah. She always loved to see you in trouble."

"All right. For Jakes."

Inside the clubhouse, I followed Kate to the general manager's office. We passed the spacious dance floor, and my imaination went into overtime, causing me to giggle.

"Bunny Hop?"

"Stop it," Kate warned.

"Detective Frost?" A man crossed the floor wearing jeans, and a plaid flannel shirt.

"Mr. Ilkerson. I was just looking for you," Kate said.

"What can I do for you?"

As a child, the one thing my sister could never get away with was a lie. Her cheeks would turn bright red and she couldn't look the person in the eye. It took years of coaching on my part to teach her how. On this day, she did me proud.

"I've been looking over those brochures you gave me and I think I might be interested in membership." Her cheeks never even tinted.

"Well, that's wonderful. C'mon back and I'll get the paperwork started."

"Mr. Ilkerson, I'm wondering if you might show me around first."

"Sure. Where would you like to start?"

"I'm specifically wondering about lockers and undressing rooms." She flashed her most flirtatious smile.

"Of course. Follow me."

Inside the coed locker room, Kate browsed for any sign of Percy's locker.

"Have you heard from Mr. Smith yet?" she asked Bob.

"No ma'am. I'm not sure when he'll be around again. But I'll give him your card."

"Well, I'm just wondering. What if he comes in while you're out? Perhaps you could stick the card in his locker?"

"See, I really couldn't do that because we aren't allowed to go into members' lockers."

"Why don't you tape it on the outside. You see, it's very important that he contact us."

"I suppose it wouldn't hurt."

"Thank you. I'll wait here while you get the tape."

She moved to view the showers, dismissing him.

He returned after a few minutes and went to a locker in the back.

"Now, he'll be sure and get it. If you'll follow me, I'll show you the handball court."

I shrugged as she followed him. Handball?

I found Percy's locker and stuck my head inside. It remained empty except for shower gel and shampoo. No tools.

When I found Kate, she was in Bob's office looking over the paperwork. I motioned to her that I hadn't found anything.

"Well, Mr. Ilkerson," she started. "I'd like to take this information home and think about it. Everything looks wonderful but I'll have to check my budget before committing."

"I understand. But I think you'll find it's well worth it. We have a lot to offer here. It's a great little community."

As I watched Kate trying to get out of the office gracefully, I nosed around. In the far corner beside a magazine rack, I saw a green canvas sack with a wooden handle sticking out. It looked like it could belong to a hacksaw.

Kate caught my find and nodded briefly. She made an excuse and left the office heading toward her car.

"I'll bet those are Percy's tools," I said.

"We still don't have enough for a warrant. If they are tools, they could belong to anyone."

"Which brings us right back to square one. Where the hell is Percy Smith?"

CHAPTER TWENTY-THREE

Kate smiled when Gerard poked his head into her office.

"We found Ken Stevens. Care to take a little ride?"

He explained in the car.

"Stevens is a computer-repair man at Super Geeks over in Chesterton."

"Jakes mentioned he had computer skills."

"How long were they together?"

"Maybe two years. They've lived together for the past year. Does he know about Jakes?"

"I don't think so. He's been off the radar for a few days. Hasn't been answering the phone and no one's at home."

They pulled into the mall parking lot near Super Geeks.

"I wonder why he hasn't reported her missing?" Kate asked.

"That's a question only Mr. Stevens can answer."

Inside the computer store, they found the manager.

"I'm George Gates," he grinned wide. "I've heard all the jokes. And, no, I'm not related to you-know-who. Now what can I do for you, detectives?"

"We're looking for one of your employees, Ken Stevens," Alvarez said.

"Ken's on a repair call right now. He should be back shortly."

"Has he been out of town recently, Mr. Gates?" Kate asked.

"He had the weekend off, but as far as going out of town, I couldn't say."

"What kind of car does he drive?"

"He has a pickup truck, but he uses the company car for calls."

"Is his truck in the lot?" Alvarez asked.

"Yes. That gray one." He pointed out the window.

"Thank you. We'll wait outside for him."

Kate recognized the truck. It looked like Ted Burke's. She peered inside the cab but saw nothing that actually confirmed the truck was one and the same. Still, in her mind, Ken Stevens was fast becoming a suspect.

A short time later, a compact car bearing the Super Geeks logo parked in the lot. Kate nudged Gerard.

"I think that's our guy."

A trim, clean-shaven man exited the vehicle and headed toward the computer store. Kate was disappointed to see he looked nothing like Ted Burke.

They caught up with him before he entered the building.

"Ken Stevens?" Alvarez held up his badge.

The man stopped, staring at Kate.

"Yes. What do you want?"

Kate recognized his voice. And, up close, his eyes.

"I'm Detective Kate Frost and this is my partner, Detective Alvarez." Kate stepped closer, showing her badge. "We need to speak with you about Evelyn Jakes."

"Have you found her?" He wouldn't look at Kate.

"Is she missing?" Kate pinned him with a stare.

"Well, I don't know about missing. She was supposed to go out of town for the weekend, but never returned. Maybe she just decided to go away for a while."

"And when was she expected back?" Alvarez closed the distance between them.

"Sunday."

"This is Wednesday. Have you contacted the authorities?"

"No. See, things were a little shaky between us lately. Do you know where she is?"

"Yes. Can you tell me when you saw her last?" Kate asked.

"Thursday afternoon. She was packing."

"Where was she going?"

"Skiing."

"Where?"

"White Crest Mountain in Wisconsin."

"Did you follow her there?"

"No."

Kate saw the telltale signs of a lie on his cheeks.

"I think you're lying. Try again."

"All right. I did, but I never saw her. Where's Evelyn? What happened?"

"She's dead, Mr. Stevens. But something tells me you already knew that. That's why you didn't bother to call the police when she didn't come home."

"I swear I didn't know. How did she die?" The color had drained from his face.

People were starting to stare on their way into the store.

Kate softened her tone. "Why don't we go straighten this out at the station? You're not under arrest, but I'm sure you don't want to have this conversation in the public eye."

"Yeah. Okay. But I need to tell my boss."

"We'll wait." Kate moved to keep an eye on him inside the doorway as he spoke to his boss. She glanced back at the truck.

"I'm almost positive that's the same truck I saw Ted Burke get out of at White Crest."

"Even if it is, we need more evidence. The fact that he followed his girlfriend isn't enough to arrest."

"How about prints? I know Ted Burke's prints are on Teresa's laptop."

"Still not enough. Let's get him to the station and see what happens."

Ken Stevens sat stiff and scared at the wooden table inside one of the station's interview rooms. He toyed with his watch as if it were the most interesting thing he'd ever seen.

Kate sat across from him, trying not to pounce. The thought of him hurting her childhood friend lessened her self-control and she worked hard to remain calm.

Alvarez entered with bottled water for everyone. He set one down before Stevens.

"Are you comfortable?" he asked as formality.

"Uh, yes, sir. What is it you need to know?" Stevens took a sip of water.

Alvarez shoved a couple of crime-scene photos of Jakes in front of him.

Stevens' eyes bulged and he cupped a hand over his mouth. It took several seconds for him to open his eyes and stop gagging.

"Take them away, please," he pleaded.

Alvarez slid them back inside the folder.

"What did you do that for? I think I'm going to be sick."

Kate pulled a waste can beside his chair. "We need answers."

Stevens nodded, taking a cleansing breath.

"I'd like you to start at the beginning." Alvarez paced before the table. "All we need to do right now is clarify a few unclear details. You said your relationship with Miss Jakes had become a little shaky?"

"Yes. We've been living together about a year and I thought things were going all right, but, lately, it seems she's been pulling away."

"How so, Mr. Stevens?" Kate asked.

"Oh, you know, like spending more time at work. She has

plenty of people to run her business, but she started working more parties than usual."

"What about White Crest Mountain?" Kate wanted to know.

"Her friends invite her every year, but she never goes. It surprised me when she said yes this time, and I thought maybe she was meeting someone."

"So you followed her there?"

"Yes," he said sheepishly.

"To do what?"

"I wanted to see for myself. If she had someone else, I figured I had the right to know."

"Go on." Kate reined in her temper.

"She never showed up. I waited and watched and drove around the town to see if I could see her car, but she wasn't anywhere to be found."

"Did you try to call her on her cell?"

"Yes, but she didn't answer."

"Wasn't that cause for concern?"

"Well, yeah. I thought she was avoiding me."

"Were you concerned for her safety?"

"No. I didn't see any reason to be. I knew she was going and she went. End of story."

"When is the last time you saw her?" Kate tried to catch him in a lie.

"I told you, I haven't seen her since Thursday night."

"What did you do when you realized she wasn't at the cabin?"

"I . . . I had to see. I had to get inside the house where her friends were staying."

"How did you do that?" Kate leaned in.

"I dressed up so she wouldn't recognize me if she was there."

"And did your plan work?"

"I'm afraid it worked too well. That's how I met you, Detective Frost."

153

"I was wondering when you'd get to that. So you are the mysterious Ted Burke?"

" 'Fraid so. I'm sorry for the charade, but I wanted to find Evelyn."

"Where have you been for the past few days?"

"I rented a room in town, not far from the house where you stayed. After realizing Evelyn had lied about going to White Crest I decided to stay a few days. It was quiet and gave me a chance to think things out. I knew when I returned home, she would probably break it off with me."

"We'll need the hotel information."

"Sure."

"Did she have any enemies?"

"Not that I know of."

"What about problems at work?"

"None. Except for the guy who did her ice sculptures. He turned out to be high maintenance and she finally decided to quit offering the service. She fired him."

"Would that be Percy Smith?"

"I think that's his name. Like I said, we'd drifted apart."

"I suggest you don't do any more drifting."

"What do you mean?"

"Right now it looks like you were the last person to see her alive."

"You seriously think I killed her? That I could do that to her?"

Kate held him with a look.

Finally he said, "Am I under arrest?"

Kate glanced at her partner. That was the magic question.

"No, Mr. Stevens. Not yet," Alvarez said.

When the interview ended, Kate watched their best lead toss his empty bottle in the waste can and walk out.

She bagged the bottle carefully.

"I don't think we're going to need that," Alvarez said from the doorway.

"You never know." She sealed the bag.

"He's not our guy."

"I guess we're back to Percy."

"The interview with Jakes' parents didn't shed any light on possible enemies or motives either," Alvarez said.

"It seems every lead takes us to another dead end. I feel like I'm letting Jakes down."

"You can't blame yourself, especially if you want to last in homicide. Unfortunately, some cases are never solved."

"Not this one. It's my duty to solve this, no matter how long it takes."

Alvarez stopped short of saying something.

"What? Tell me," Kate said.

"Nothing." He reached to take the bag. "I'll get this to the lab."

"Not so fast." She pulled the bag out of his reach. "I want to know what pearls of wisdom you're keeping from me."

He hesitated, then gave in. "You know, Kate, I think so far we've been pretty lucky working together. We have a good track record."

"Right. So what's the problem?"

"No problem. I just think you need to accept how homicide works."

"Go on." Kate had the feeling she wouldn't like what he was about to say.

"This case . . . I don't know. I think. . . ."

"You think it will go unsolved. Another cardboard box in the storage room."

"It's a very real possibility."

"I don't like those odds. You need to stay positive."

"Tell me honestly. If this case involved someone you didn't know, would you feel the same?"

"Yes, why?"

"I don't want you to be overly disappointed if it doesn't work out."

"Are you saying I'm too close?"

"Yes and no." He held up a hand to stop her rebuttal. "But I think your closeness to the victim is what will ultimately drive you to success, if this case can be solved. I just don't want you to take on too much. You have a life outside of this job, and right now you need to take care of yourself."

"You're right, Gerard. But my life and career are entwined. It's who I am. I know when to step back, and right now isn't the time. Not until the job is done."

CHAPTER TWENTY-FOUR

I stood beside Kate at Jakes' graveside, watching the mourners say their last good-byes. Alvarez had opted to let Kate go alone because she was a family friend. Although there was an ongoing murder investigation, he'd decided there was no need to overwhelm the family with too much police presence.

Jakes' parents held tight to one another as if to prop one another up. Their lost, vacant expressions reminded me of my own parents at my funeral. That had been the hardest part for me. I had hated feeling helpless to comfort them and let them know I was really okay. If not for Kate acting as their fortress, I'm not sure I would have accepted my own death as gracefully as I did, and have.

Kate glanced my way as if checking my status.

"I'm all right. If you don't mind, I think I'll work the crowd," I said.

I followed Kate's gaze to a tall man with dark hair, tears streaming down his cheeks.

"Who's that?"

"Stevens," she said under her breath.

Since Jakes' murder didn't seem to be a random act of violence, it was a safe bet the killer might show up to see the fruits of his labor. As I made my way through the crowd of about one hundred people, I saw the family members standing closest and crying the hardest. My focus was on the outer sector where distant relatives and friends stood shoulder-to-shoulder offering nothing but grim frowns. It was here, among the dry-eyed souls that I sought a potential murderer. Instead, I found Ed Nog.

I hurried back to Kate before the priest finished.

"Mullet Man is here," I said.

Her eyes widened.

"Relax. No camera."

She closed her eyes and offered an "amen" as the mourners started to break up.

"I have to find him," she murmured into a hanky.

"Be careful what you wish for." I grinned.

Ed tapped her on her shoulder. "Hey there."

"What are you doing here?" she turned to ask him.

"I'm just paying my respects."

"Did you know Evelyn?"

"Not directly. But I did the photos when you found her. I felt like I should be here."

"Is that the only reason?"

"Well, no. I was hoping to see you and find out when we could start working together again."

"We never worked together."

"Look. You still have my photos. I was real nice about that and I'm not going to press to get them back. Consider them a gift. But now I need something to give my editor, and, so, I'd like to start over. When can I finish my story?"

I thought Kate was going to slug him. Instead, she turned on him and said, "There is no story, Nog. I solve murders. If you want juicy reality journalism, go follow some local politician."

"Chief O'Connor already gave the okay for this story."

"Then eat at his dinner table tonight. Right now I have more important things to do than babysit a reporter."

She turned and headed toward Jakes' parents.

★ ★ ★ ★ ★

The funeral luncheon took place at a popular restaurant in town called Lakeside Oaks. It rested on a hill overlooking a small private lake surrounded by tall oaks, where ducks and geese glided across the water, providing guests with a show of serenity. In the summer, patrons could dine outside on the spacious patio that ran the length of the building. Today the frozen water lay covered with powdery snow, and the oaks waved barren branches in the icy wind.

A large section of the dining room had been reserved for the funeral guests and eventually everyone took their seats after murmured greetings and tender embraces. The priest from Jakes' parents' church said a brief prayer and invited everyone to recall their best memories of Evelyn as they dined in her honor.

I stood to the side watching the gathering. The group had dwindled to about fifty people, consisting only of the closest family and friends. Nog had had the good sense not to stick around for the free lunch, and I saw Kate relax a bit in his absence. As platters of food made their way down the long table, I found no good reason to stay. Food no longer held any interest for me, although I'd caught sight of the dessert table on my way in. Deceased or not, anything dripping in chocolate still held an appeal.

I decided against the frustration of trying to finger swipe the frosting off a piece of three-layer cake and instead went in search of Nog. It didn't take long to locate him in his beat-up Riviera heading down Main Street. Country music blared inside the car as his fingers tapped a beat on the steering wheel. It took all the willpower I could muster to stick out the second verse as he bellowed along off-key to the music. When he'd finished his lament about a cheatin' wife and a dead dawg, he turned down the sound and turned into an apartment-complex parking lot.

The yellow brick building held twelve units and I followed him to a third-floor apartment in the back. Inside, I was surprised to see ol' Ed had a knack for decorating and—unlike with his hair—he'd kept up with the latest styles. The traditional green shag apartment carpet was absent, replaced by a light beige weave that looked thick enough to bounce on. Touches of teal and mauve complemented the earth-toned shades of the furnishings. Not bad for a photojournalist working at a small-town newspaper.

A second bedroom sufficed as an office slash darkroom, where his film developing equipment sat along one wall opposite his computer and file cabinet. Framed photos of the Chicago skyline and some of the city's most unique buildings lined the walls. He was actually quite good.

He pulled a digital camera from his coat pocket and hooked it up to the computer, bringing up the photos on the screen. I leaned close to see a variety of shots from Jakes' funeral, including the mourners' cars and close-ups of their license plates. I cursed loud enough behind him that I thought for a moment he'd heard me when he turned to look over his shoulder.

Each shot violated the family's privacy, turning it into a potential tabloid disaster, and I wondered what the creep planned to do with them. When Kate found out, he could kiss his coif good-bye because there wouldn't be enough hair left to gel into place. I almost felt sorry for the guy. Almost.

At home, Kate stripped off her black dress and heels. She punched the start button on the coffee pot and headed toward the bedroom.

I followed.

"Can you believe that little jerk showed up at Jakes' funeral under false pretenses? He doesn't care about her, he only wanted to get back in my good graces."

160

"Maybe his pretenses aren't so false. I told you before he has a way of conveniently showing up at the right time."

"You seriously think he has brains enough to pull off a murder like this and get away with it?"

"I've seen worse. But that's not all."

Kate's eyes narrowed when I explained about the photos he'd taken at the funeral. As her sibling, I'd seen that look many times growing up. It wasn't good.

"That bastard. What's his motive for that?"

"If he has anything to do with the murder, it's so he can relive the memory. If not, he's probably going to go to the paper with them."

"Those pics are mine. I thought I was done with that little weasel, but it looks like I'll be paying him a visit today. Meantime, we need to find Percy Smith. He's the missing piece and I do mean missing. If there's foul play he might be a victim as well. At least we can connect him to Jakes and the fact he can't be found. The search of Jakes' house didn't turn up anything. Not one clue. I just haven't worked the case hard enough. Starting tomorrow, things are going to change."

"Sometimes you have to let things come to you. The hardest part of detective work is the waiting. You've followed every lead."

"It's not enough."

"It feels that way at times. Maybe you're too close."

"Jakes was my friend."

"She was mine too. But if you're too involved you might lose site of the whole picture."

"The only picture I see is the one of Jakes in the back of my car. Until I get this guy, I won't be able to put that to rest."

She cursed at a runner in her stockings and pitched them into the waste can.

"Damn!"

She seemed unusually upset. The Kate I knew didn't rant, she did a slow simmer until she boiled. This was neither. My instinct told me now was the time so I took the gamble.

"Are you scared?"

She turned my way, her blue eyes brimming with tears.

"They were only nylons, Linz." She forced a smile.

"Kate, I know about the lump."

She never batted an eye. "I figured you'd find out. Was I talking in my sleep?"

"I saw the appointment on your desk calendar. It wasn't intentional snooping."

"Dr. Karr's office called this morning. I'm scheduled for a biopsy on Monday morning."

If I'd had blood it would have run cold. Instead, I said, "Does Alvarez know?"

"Yes. He's taking me."

It hurt more than anything to know she hadn't confided in me. Once again I felt abandonment pangs making me feel left out of her life.

"I wish you would have told me."

"I know I should have, but there never seemed to be the right time. And I didn't want you hovering over me."

"There's not much I can do about that." I tried to lighten the moment.

"Linz, you've already died. One of the reasons I couldn't bring myself to tell you is that I'm not ready to deal with my own mortality."

"And seeing me makes it too real."

The hurt must have shown on my face. I'd become a painful reminder that she could die too.

"That came out all wrong. What I meant is that you're not really gone to me. I still have you. It's my own silly fears that I have to deal with."

There wasn't a whole lot I could say in rebuttal. Still, she'd given me a lot to think about. Perhaps it would have been much kinder on my part to just go on to my eternal rest and let my family, especially Kate, grieve and get on with life. As it stood, I'd prevented my sister from doing that and now she was going through pain she wouldn't have gone through if not for me.

"I'm here if you need me," I said, and faded from view.

CHAPTER TWENTY-FIVE

I usually avoided Mike's place of death, but when I didn't see him at my picnic spot, I figured that's where he'd be. According to Sally, the deceased visit their death spot regularly. It's as if we're drawn to that one area of our past. My place of death had been in my own john. Not the most glamorous place to die, but I've seen worse. At least I had died fully dressed, which is another important detail I'd learned from Sally. We spend eternity in the clothing we die in. My mother doesn't yet know how right she was when she harped about always wearing clean underwear. She'd be proud to know I'm wearing the silk blouse she gave me for Christmas with my Donna Karan pants.

Mike Blake had died valiantly in the line of duty one afternoon during a robbery call. The mom-and-pop jewelry store stood at the end of a small strip mall beside an alley. Mike had been first to arrive and found the suspect clutching a little girl by the hair with a gun to her throat, dragging her toward the rear exit.

The gunman had threatened to kill the girl if Mike didn't drop his weapon.

Mike had two choices: one, put down his weapon and hope the guy would let the child go, or, two, take his best shot. He never had to make the choice. When he heard the gunshot he said it didn't register right away. A solid blow hit his chest and he watched his world crumble in slow motion. The suspect fled out the back, leaving the little girl shaken but unharmed.

Standing in the jewelry store now, I walked past customers peering into the glass counters, pointing to their favorite pieces. A young couple sat with a clerk, picking out an engagement ring. The atmosphere was light and happy, yet it filled me with sadness when I thought about what had happened here. It seemed wrong that these people had no idea what a place of reverence this was as they smiled and chatted about gleaming jewels.

I spotted Mike near the back wall behind one of the counters and headed that way.

I'm not one to ask for help unless there's no other way, but I didn't know how to handle the current situation with Kate. Backing off seemed like the best idea, yet how could I leave her when she needed support and encouragement the most? I needed an impartial sounding board and felt Mike could help me out.

"Busy place," I commented.

"Pick out anything you like," he offered.

"I just can't take it with me, right?"

"Something like that. What's on your mind?"

"Why do you think that? Can't I visit you?"

"I know how you feel about this place. You wouldn't have come here if it wasn't important."

"Know-it-all."

"Is it about Jakes?"

"Kind of."

"Are we going to play forty questions?"

"Do I win a prize?"

"Like I said, take your pick."

I meandered around the counters, looking at all the lovely gems as he came up behind me.

"Diamonds are a girl's best friend," he said.

"You're getting warmer."

"What do you mean?"

"This is about my best friend."

A rotund little man walked through me just then, on his way to the register.

"This place is a little distracting. Why don't we go somewhere more quiet?" Mike suggested.

Within seconds, we arrived at my picnic spot and I immediately began pacing as he seated himself on a tree stump.

"So what's this about Kate?"

I explained recent events, and my feelings of abandonment, feeling a little petty and foolish, seeing how I was the one to leave her when I died.

"Am I overreacting?" I asked.

"Not at all."

"Then she's wrong?"

"Nope."

"Thanks, Freud."

"Kate has every right to feel the way she does. Think about it. Where can she go to vent her feelings about you? She's stuck trying to sort out her fears of dying, and seeing you only reinforces them. I think you should give her some time."

"But she needs someone in her corner. I'm glad she has Alvarez, but this is a woman thing. She can't go to our mom because it would upset her to think she might be losing another daughter. I hate leaving her completely alone."

"Kate is tougher than you give her credit for. If you back off, she'll come around."

"You think?"

"The two of you are sister soul mates, if there is such a thing. I doubt that this will harm your relationship."

He was right. Kate and I were as close as twins, even though I was four years older. As hard as it might be, I decided to make a conscious effort to stop dwelling on the whole issue.

"Have you seen Kathy lately?" I asked him.

"I took your advice and haven't visited her since our last conversation. I still walk my daughter to the bus every morning, though."

"Nothing wrong with that. Will you be all right if Katherine remarries?"

"I think so. You gave me a lot to think about, not to mention a kiss to remember."

"If any other man were to feed me that corny line I'd walk away."

"Maybe that's because you know I'm sincere. I'm really on your side."

"Yeah. Us spirits have to stick together." I smiled.

"It's more than that, Lindsay. I truly have feelings for you."

That floored me. I've had my share of relationships, but I've never had a guy come straight out and say that before. He was being totally honest. No premature "I love you." No insincere "We belong together." Right now he felt the same way I did. Nothing too solid as we both stood a little unsure about one another. Still there was something beyond friendship brewing between us, even though neither one of us knew what to do about it.

"I feel the same way, Mike. Do you think we're the first?"

"For what?"

"Paranormal romance?"

"You mean like the first Adam and Eve?"

"You're not wearing a fig leaf."

I felt his arms around my waist as I focused on his nearness. Once again my lips felt his sensation and my senses became aroused.

"If we keep this up, we'll have to create a more private place to meet." I closed my eyes, focusing on his touch.

"I've been working on that."

I followed him as he faded into the void.

We arrived at a room lit entirely by candles. Some hung mysteriously in the air, while others sat in brass holders on an antique dresser and bedside table. A huge canopy bed dressed in pale-pink satin stood to our right. The Victorian-style decor was not my usual preference, yet it touched me that he had put so much effort into our special place. No one had ever gone to this much trouble for me before and I adored Mike for it.

"Do you like it?" he asked.

"It's wonderful. But when did you do all this?"

"In my spare time." He led me by the hand to the bed and we lay down, enjoying the room's ambiance.

Another kiss had us reveling in the rise of our emotions. I stroked his cheek, enjoying the tingling excitement in my fingertips. My hand roamed to his shirt where I stopped.

Suddenly I broke the kiss. "What about clothes?"

He frowned.

"I don't think they're removable on this side." I tried to grasp a button on my blouse without luck. Apparently only our death tags were removable.

"If kissing is any indication, I'll bet nudity isn't necessary," he said.

As he caressed my body, I wondered if the feelings of arousal were from memory. How else could I explain the physical sensations coursing throughout my ethereal body?

Without warning, Mike pulled me on top of him and I took the lead, kissing him. Our tongues sought one another, as we teased, until I moaned in yearning.

Our gazes locked on one another and we didn't need to speak to know what to do next. I felt like this was my first time, and, in a way, I guess it was. And, like my first time, I didn't want to mess it up. This time took more concentration than the first.

It was as if our bodies melded into one another, so deep and pure that at first I thought I was sinking. I felt electric energy filling me as I began to move. Mike held me close as we allowed the aura to encompass us.

As our motion became more intense I sensed the familiar rise of elation threatening to take me over the precipice and I fought to hold back. Mike seemed to sense my urgency and whispered softly into my ear.

"Let's go together."

With that, I cried out as our combined energies exploded. My weightless body felt even more so and I held him close to keep from floating away. After several moments, I felt the energy ebb and I lay beside him feeling exhilarated and emotional.

"What is it?" He stroked my cheek.

"I've never experienced anything like that. It's overwhelming."

"I don't think that begins to describe it. Do you think we broke any rules?"

"Probably. If this isn't illegal, it should be."

We lay there allowing the beautiful experience to fill us. My thoughts had mercifully drifted far from my concerns and I found myself excited about the things I would discover in this new life in the beyond.

CHAPTER TWENTY-SIX

Detective Milner had phoned the day before to say Kate's SUV had been released and cleaned. Ready for pickup. She'd gladly turned in her rent-a-car this morning, anxious to feel at home again in her own ride. The fact that one of her best friends had been interred inside didn't give her pause about keeping the vehicle; instead, it stood as a strong incentive for her to solve the case.

As Gerard drove, the beautiful snowy Wisconsin landscape made Kate wish his boys could have joined them on the weekend trip. Although it was business, it would have been nice to share some time with them. The boys had grown comfortable with her, accepting her as their dad's girlfriend, including her in events like soccer games and camping trips. She had no desire to take their mother's place, but cherished their special times together, trying on the mom-role here and there. To her delight it felt comfortable and right.

As luck had it, the boys had gone with their mother this weekend, providing an unexpected couple-only getaway. Cynthia had attended AA a couple of times during the past week and had regained some sense of control. Kate recalled how happy the boys had been when they'd dropped them off at their mom's house.

Cynthia had come out to the porch to greet them, glancing at Kate in the car. While they'd never been formally introduced, Kate got the distinct impression the woman hated her. Her dark eyes stared hot enough to burn holes in Kate's skin before she turned to go back inside with the boys. Not so strange under the circumstances, Kate decided; after all, she was the new woman in Gerard's life. But she hoped they could eventually become cordial.

Kate sat in the passenger seat as the miles went by, allowing her thoughts to wander. She bit her lip as she reviewed her conversation with Lindsay. No matter how many times she went over it, she felt guilty. The look on her sister's face was all she could see in her mind and she knew Lindsay had been hurt. Lindsay hadn't appeared to her since, and this confirmed Kate's suspicions that big sister needed some space. She knew Lindsay would quickly get over it, and, in no time, they'd be back to their playful banter and competitive rivalry. It was the closest they'd ever get to normal.

She forced her mind on the crisp blue skies and the idea she had Gerard all to herself. Monday would be here soon enough and with it, a turned page in her life. She looked at Gerard as he focused on the road ahead, and smiled. Right now he was her guarding fortress.

"Just a few more miles to go." Gerard smiled.

"Great. It's time for a break. I think I heard my legs snoring."

"After we pick up the car, I thought we'd take a look at the cabin."

"Great minds think alike. I brought my snow boots."

"What? No skis?"

"I didn't want to embarrass you."

"Is that a challenge?"

"No. A fact." She grinned.

"I see. And your skiing expertise includes nursing a bruised nalgas?"

"Never mind. I didn't see that bump until it was too late.

Speaking of bruises, Nog turned over his funeral pics without a fight."

"I figured he might. Why did he take them?"

"He thought it would help the investigation."

"Well, it sure couldn't hurt, if that's his real reason. Did they show anything interesting?"

"Not really. I knew almost everyone there. One or two cars didn't look familiar, but that's not so unusual considering the crowd size. So far all of Jakes' employees have checked out and they were all in attendance. It seems another dead end."

"What did Nog say about it?"

"He realized his mistake. I guess he's just a guy trying to make a living."

"So you weren't too hard on him."

"Broken bones heal, right?" Kate grinned.

"Forget all that for now. I plan on spoiling you this weekend. You need to relax."

"Where are we staying?"

"Detective Milner suggested a cottage-style bed-and-breakfast in town overlooking the lake. He said they have a spa and hot tubs and offer massages. I told him he'd be footing the bill if it wasn't nice."

"Sounds wonderful. But business before pleasure." She nodded toward the White Crest police station up ahead.

Detective Milner greeted them and immediately led them to the garage where Kate's SUV stood gleaming under the fluorescent lights.

"Good as new," he proclaimed.

"Thanks, Pete," Kate said, accepting the keys.

"We found no other evidence inside. Sorry about the wait."

"I'd rather you be sure."

"I wish we could be more sure about a suspect."

"No leads?" Alvarez wanted to know.

A nearby squad revved loudly as the mechanic worked.

Detective Milner motioned for them to follow him. "Let's go to my office."

He closed the door behind him. "Make yourself at home. Coffee?"

"We're good." Kate and Alvarez answered in unison.

"You asked about new leads and I'm sorry to say the case grows colder by the minute. No prints, no fibers, nothing out of the ordinary. The material used to wrap the body parts was a latex casting material. The body had been covered first in a papier-mâché material. The only unusual item found was this inside the cabin." He held out a small, clear cylindrical vial containing a brown, twig-like item about an inch long.

"What's this?" Kate scrutinized it.

"It was found near the door. Crime lab analyzed it but it didn't make any sense until one of my officers recognized it as a horse wormer pellet."

"As in de-worming horses?" Alvarez asked.

"Right. Lucky for us, the officer grew up on a farm."

Kate handed the vial back to Milner. "If you don't mind, we'd like to take a look at the cabin."

"No problem. It's been released, and, as far as I know, the owners haven't claimed it. We're working on that. Feel free to look around. Have you had any luck on your end?" Milner asked Alvarez.

"I told you about the boyfriend, but we don't have enough to hold him. He rented a room in town, but all that proves is what he's already confessed to—that he was here."

"He was the mysterious Ted Burke," Kate added, knowing even as she said it that Milner would already know that.

Milner nodded. "Did Ms. Jakes have a life-insurance policy?"

"Yes, but Stevens wasn't the beneficiary. She'd named her parents," Alvarez said. "We're looking for one of her ex-employees. Percy Smith. He's an ice sculptor."

"Nice. I'll bet he knows how to handle a hacksaw."

"So far he's missing. But we'll keep you informed."

A short time later, Kate left Milner's office with a hollow feeling inside. Discussing the facts only confirmed what she already knew; Jakes' case had grown ice cold.

It felt good to be behind the wheel of her own car again as she followed Gerard to the inn. The cottage-style building, painted white with Wedgwood-blue shutters, overlooked Lake Juanita. Cozy mullioned windows completed the cottage look, providing a serene feel to the little hideaway.

Their room overlooked the spacious lake, and Kate wished it were summer with water warm enough to swim in. A fireplace sat ready with kindling and fresh wood for the chilled and weary traveler.

Dropping her overnight bag onto the bed, Kate took in the view of the lake.

"This is too beautiful. How does anyone ever leave here?"

Gerard wrapped his arms around her waist, drawing her close.

"I suppose they leave when duty calls." He kissed her neck.

"What kind of duty are you talking about?"

"Unfortunately, the kind that kills a romantic mood."

"Ah, that would be the cabin. I'll get my boots."

They followed the map that Detective Milner had drawn for them leading from the A-frame. Kate's vacation home remained vacant, making her wonder if people would shy away from the beautiful structure because of the recent incident. Her mind replayed her weekend with her friends, including the scene of Jakes in her SUV. It seemed burned into her memory. She made a mental note to touch base with the girls to see how they were doing.

"Over here," Gerard called.

She followed his gaze up a steep incline and saw a tiny dilapidated cabin fenced in by a fortress of mature trees. No wonder she hadn't noticed it.

They climbed the hill, helping one another navigate the slippery terrain. Finally, they stood only a few feet from the structure.

"This place is awfully old. I'm surprised it's still standing," Kate observed.

"Creepy." Gerard rubbed his hands together.

"And it's not even the original crime scene. Let's go." Kate led the way. "Maybe this old geezer will tell us what was."

Inside, they pulled on rubber gloves and looked around. They found the cabin as Nog's photos had shown, with overturned furniture, and a couple of blood smears on the floor.

"No blood spatter on the walls or surrounding areas. If this is the only blood, it's definitely not the murder scene. But why kill Jakes and bring her to the cabin? And then move her again to my car?"

"The killer had a message for you and probably had to wait for the right time to get into your car. Meantime, he had to have a place to hide the body."

"Which means the guy had to have been watching us like a hawk. He had to get a feel for our coming and going. I get the shivers just thinking about it. I wonder why he didn't keep the body in his car?"

"Maybe too much blood. That's what the blood in here looks like. Leakage."

Kate wished she could call on Lindsay right now to get her impression of the place. Perhaps she could pick up on Jakes' spirit or something. But she quickly shut the door on the idea after remembering her plan to let Lindsay cool off.

"It looks like the crime team did a thorough job; not that I doubted them," Gerard said.

"I know what you mean. I like to investigate things for myself. Another pair of eyes never hurts."

They made their way throughout the small cabin, checking the two bedrooms and claustrophobic bathroom.

"No one's lived here for a long time." Kate noticed the dark-stained, waterless toilet.

She double-checked the bed linens for signs of use. The bedspreads were covered with a thin, undisturbed coating of dust.

"If he slept here, he didn't use either of the beds. Although I can't imagine anyone laying on the floor in this place."

"You'd be surprised what desperate criminals will do."

"I wonder if the killer knew the cabin was here, or just happened to get lucky?"

"Milner said no forced entry, but, with an old doorknob, you could use a credit card to get in."

Kate crawled on her hands and knees in the kitchen.

"What are you doing?"

"Looking for clues."

"I think the crime team got everything. Why don't you get up before you catch something."

"Like a criminal?" She sat up holding a small object she'd found wedged under the threshold.

"What's that?"

"Another wormer pellet. I'm not sure what it means, but I do know there aren't any horses nearby."

"Wisconsin time must go faster than ours," Kate observed on Sunday morning.

"Why is that?" Alvarez asked.

"It seems that every time I spend a weekend here, it flies by too quickly."

Kate closed the rear of her SUV and took one final look across the lake.

"It sure is beautiful. I'd like to come back here when we can spend more time."

"I'd like that too. But right now we need to get on the road. We have a big day tomorrow and you should probably rest up."

Kate wished she could have erased his words as she said good-bye to the lake. Suddenly the day seemed colder and the sun less bright with the thought of her impending surgery tomorrow.

As she merged onto the highway she fought down thoughts of "what if?" She knew there were risks with any surgery but she trusted Dr. Karr. Still there was a gnawing trepidation concerning the procedure. Her real fears stemmed from the biopsy's results and what it could mean for her and her family. She still hadn't told her parents. It was too soon to put them through another crisis after Lindsay's death. Her gut told her this would all work out and they'd never be the wiser.

As the miles stretched between Kate and her weekend getaway, she bit back tears. It seemed she was leaving a safe haven to face her darkest nightmare; only, with Lindsay out of reach, she would have to face it alone.

CHAPTER TWENTY-SEVEN

Okay. I'll admit it. I'm stubborn. I don't regret it though because it has saved my ass on countless occasions. Today was different however, because it didn't do anything but serve my own curiosity. I had to know if Kate was all right, and, although I vowed to give her space, my Freudian side rationalized it away as a simple case of a protective big sister.

At the tender age of eight, Kate had been sent home from school looking like a speckled hen. I teased her unmercifully about her chicken pox, having escaped them several times myself. Then one night, I heard her crying in her bedroom and braved the quarantined area that my mother had warned me to stay clear of. I sat up most of the night trying to think of ingenious ways to keep her from clawing at her skin. She finally fell asleep in my arms and I managed to sneak back into my room before mom found out. A week later, I sprouted the telltale signs, and Mom chalked it up to airborne germs. It was worth every excruciating itch that I fought not to scratch. I'd done my duty as Kate's big sister.

I decided today would be no different.

Although Kate had only been given a local, and a mild sedative for the breast biopsy, I saw she was out. I watched the surgery without the need for mask or gown and paced behind Dr. Karr's back. The terminology and general conversation of the surgical staff kept me lost in confusion, wondering if everything was going well. Finally, I saw them wheel Kate into the recovery room and I paced some more as the nurses checked her frequently. Ask any cop who's been injured on duty and they'll tell you nurses are an officer's lifelines after a really bad day at work. Today I felt gratitude like never before and wished I could have hugged every one of them. I also knew they'd probably need a good hug after Kate woke up and started barking out orders.

As they wheeled Kate into a small room outside of recovery, I saw Alvarez waiting. He looked tired and worried.

Kate remained groggy but able to direct the unwanted traffic in her room, asking for water and her doctor.

Alvarez grabbed her hand and kissed it.

"Welcome back, cariña."

She mumbled something and pointed to her clothes.

"Not yet. They'll release you when you're ready."

"Today?" she croaked.

He glanced at the nurse taking her blood pressure.

"Dr. Karr will be in to see you later, Miss Frost. Meantime, this is your chance to catnap."

Kate started to object, but fell back asleep.

Dr. Karr's visit did little to ease my fears. She told Kate the lump had been small and she'd removed the whole thing.

"We'll do a frozen section to be sure, but I'm confident the tumor is benign. I'll have the results in about five days. If there's anything to be concerned about I will call you, and you need to schedule a follow-up appointment with me so I can check your incision."

Kate glanced down at the bandage.

"I don't want you to worry, Kate. Everything went well, and the incision is quite small. I'll prescribe a painkiller, and the nurse will fill you in on your activity levels."

"When can I return to work?" Kate asked.

"Tomorrow if you promise to take it easy. Nothing strenuous, like wrestling down a bad guy."

When Kate started to object, Alvarez spoke up.

"I'll see to it, doctor."

My hero. I know how hard it is to keep my stubborn sister down. Poor Alvarez might make quick work of murder suspects, but he sure had his work cut out for him with Kate.

A short time later, I watched them leave the hospital. I'd purposely stayed out of Kate's way. I figured she'd been through enough without feeling she had to come to terms with our recent issues. What she needed the most was zero stress and plenty of rest.

I stayed with Kate all night, watching over her. Alvarez had brought her home and tucked her in after a light supper. He'd argued that he should stay and could get his mother to watch the boys, but Kate would have none of it.

"I need to sleep off these drugs. There's no way I'll make it into work tomorrow if I don't."

"And that would be such a tragedy?" he teased.

"Yes, it would. I have a mountain of paperwork to catch up on, not to mention a murder to solve."

After further discussion, it was agreed that he would call her early in the morning and she had to promise to call him if she needed anything.

She'd agreed, but I knew she'd only done it to get rid of him. Kate could be extremely stubborn, never wanting to admit she needed help. She gets it from me. As she settled into her bed, I did guard duty and prayed for a quiet night.

During my time in homicide, I'd gone days without much more than a few hours' sleep. Now, the fact that I didn't need to sleep seemed to be just another death perk. I appreciated it now that I needed to be here for my sister.

As she slept, I roamed my old house, unable to avoid the visit to my death spot. The claw-footed bathtub where I'd been found no longer made me flinch. I'd seen life from both sides of eternity and no longer had to deal with the ominous dread of a death cloud hanging over my head. There were still unknowns and probably things I was too green to fear yet, but, for right now, I liked my existence. The fact that I could still do homicide work on both sides thrilled me and gave me a sense of purpose.

I passed the mirror just for fun, to see if I had a reflection. Logically, it couldn't happen. No physical body, no reflection. But I can't resist a challenge. It's a strange feeling to see nothing but the wall behind me whenever I do it. This time, however, I saw a fleeting shadow through the doorway slinking down the hallway towards Kate's room.

I bolted after it.

Coming up behind the tall shadow, I saw the intruder was massive. The guy had to weigh at least three hundred pounds and wore a short jacket, gloves and work boots. He was heading for Kate.

I ran ahead to try and rouse her.

"Wake up!" I shouted, trying to shake her. When my hand went through her to the mattress, I decided to just keep shouting.

She groaned and turned over, without opening her eyes.

The guy stood in the doorway.

"Kate! Get up now!" I shouted right next to her ear.

"Not now, Lindsay." Her voice was thick with sleep.

The intruder stepped right through me and stood beside the bed. In the darkness, I couldn't see his face. He reached into a coat pocket and pulled something out, placing it on Kate's nightstand. The creep factor almost reached a palpable level as he watched her sleep for several moments. Then, to my great relief, the guy turned around and went back down the hall. I heard the back door slam, and realized he had some awfully big gall to go with his size. He didn't seem to care if he was heard. In fact, the way he'd slammed the door, instead of just closing it, had almost been an invitation to "catch me if you can." Kate never flinched.

I thought about taking off after the guy to see who it was, but I didn't want to risk leaving Kate alone with the mysterious offering. I stared at what looked like a candy gift box, wondering if it might be dangerous. A bomb? Too small. Chemical weapon? Probably not, it was gift-wrapped. Another body part? Quite possible.

"Kate!" I shouted into her ear again.

Her response was a gentle snore.

I was reminded of Christmas mornings growing up. The rule was that we had to wait and open all our gifts together. So, just like all those years ago, I could do nothing but sit and wait until Kate awoke.

When the sun beamed its way across Kate's bed, I tried once more to wake her. The bedside clock read five-fifty. I figured Alvarez would be phoning by six anyway.

"Kate? Kate wake up."

Her eyes came open, blinking twice to focus. She glanced over at the clock and groaned.

"What the hell, Linz?"

"You had a visitor last night. He left you a gift."

She frowned and sat up slowly. "Man, am I sore. Was I in a fight?"

"Of sorts. Dr. Karr won."

"Oh, yeah. The surgery." She swung her legs over the bedside and saw the white box adorned with a red bow. "What the hell is that?"

"I think you should call Alvarez."

"He brought it?"

"No. Kate wake up! Someone was in your house last night

and put it there."

"Why didn't you wake me?"

"I tried. Even Jesus couldn't have raised you last night."

"Really?" She reread the prescription bottle for the pain medication she'd taken the night before. "Oops. Take *one* capsule. That explains a lot."

"Call Alvarez." I would have handed her the phone if I could. As it turned out, I didn't have to because it rang.

"Guess who?" I said.

"Frost here," she answered.

Her smile confirmed my suspicions and she explained to Alvarez about the gift on her nightstand.

"I'm fine. No . . . wait . . . I'm not . . . dressed." She hung up.

A short time later, Alvarez arrived with a crime team. The activity of police personnel in the house reminded me of the night I'd been murdered. Once again, Alvarez took charge and ran the investigation like a well-rehearsed play. In no time they'd determined the box did not contain any explosives or chemical weapons, or candy. It did contain a small noose made out of thick twine. Alvarez stood convinced it was a warning.

"You're not to go anywhere without an escort. Namely me," he announced when the team had gone.

"Did you get any prints off the back door?" Kate was fully awake after several cups of coffee.

"Nothing. He most likely wore gloves."

"Any footprints?"

"Looks like work boots. From their heavy indentations in the carpet, they're about a size ten and the guy probably weighs a good two-fifty or three hundred pounds. Not someone you'd want to mess with, even when you're feeling a hundred percent."

"How did he get in?"

"Jimmied the lock and cut the chain with something big.

Most likely bolt cutters. It looks like the guy made no attempt to hide what he was doing, except to wear gloves."

"Nice." Kate examined the damaged lock.

"What about the security system you promised to put in?" Alvarez stared at her.

"Are you putting my name in for a raise? I think I should get a guard dog." She smiled at me behind his back.

"Is your carpet Scotchgarded?" he asked.

When the house had cleared of police personnel, including Alvarez, I had Kate all to myself. The fact that she'd survived the surgery and the break-in made me want to forget our issues, and step out for a beer with her. The issues could be dealt with but the beer would be a trick.

She stood at the sink washing up the few dishes a single woman might have. I think it amounted to a coffee mug and a spoon. It took her a long time to get the items clean, and I finally realized she was crying. Her shoulders shook slightly and she sniffled now and again.

"Kate?" I stood behind her. "It's all right. You've been through a bad time." I wanted to hold her so badly, but all I could do was stand there feeling lost and helpless.

She grabbed a paper towel and blew her nose. When she turned I saw the flood works had only taken a brief respite with the telltale signs of an impending water-main break.

"I hate to cry! It's so juvenile." She blew her nose again as the tears flowed.

"It's probably the pain meds. You've been under a lot of stress. You're entitled."

"I haven't handled it well at all."

"Frankly, I think you've done quite well."

"You do?" Her nose beamed red. Rudolf had nothing on her. "But I'm falling apart, Linz. I don't carry things like you. You're the tough one. You're the one who gets the job done."

"Is that what all this about? You being like me?"

"No. But what would be wrong with that?"

"Because I'm an original—an original screwup. Never held a relationship long enough to get to the altar. I have several unsolved crimes to my credit. And I let myself get murdered in my own home. I think you need to pick a new hero. Perhaps Rambo?"

She grinned and blew her nose one final time.

"Okay. I'll give you the one about getting murdered. But Rambo? I don't have the arms for it."

"I wish things could have turned out differently. Maybe working together isn't such a great idea after all. I understand how hard it must be to see me in spirit form as a constant reminder of what's to come."

"But I need to realize that, if that's what's to come, it's not such a bad deal. Nothing to dread, really."

"So we're okay then? The partner thing still works for you?"

"It always did. We're a team."

CHAPTER TWENTY-EIGHT

The next afternoon, Kate felt the blood rush to her head as she listened on the phone to Emma Ellington, editor for *The Crier* newspaper.

"He what?" Kate's temples throbbed.

"I'm sorry, Detective Frost, but Mr. Nog hasn't worked here for the last few months. He was fired."

"May I ask why?"

Kate could visualize the woman ticking the reasons off on her fingers.

"He's lazy, doesn't show up when he's supposed to, can't make his deadlines, and . . . well . . . never mind."

"His hair?"

"Well, yes. Frankly, it was the icing on the cake."

"It's definitely a topper. So you know nothing about a reality detective story for your newspaper?"

"That's correct, although it does sound like a terrific idea. You know, spotlighting law enforcement. We'd be sure to paint you in a favorable light."

"No, thank you, Ms. Ellington. I have no desire to be in the spotlight, favorable or otherwise."

"Well, if you change your mind. . . ."

"I won't. Thank you." Kate hung up ready to level a city block. If not for Dr. Karr's strict inactivity orders, it would have been a strong possibility. Instead she dialed Gerard's number and got his voice mail. She left a quick message regarding her recent information on Nog. The guy had grated her nerves more than the stitches of her incision. It was one more aggravation she didn't need.

The past few days had been a flurry of chaos, from her surgery—and the fear that the tumor could be cancerous—to the break-in. She'd tried to put the biopsy on a back burner but had failed miserably. If anything, the home invasion was a diversion, except she felt constantly at risk and uneasy in her own home. Although she knew an alarm system would help, it wasn't scheduled until next week. Meantime she slept with her gun on the nightstand, ready to fire.

Now, in an effort to keep busy, she'd tried to follow up on the break-in with forensics, but they had little to go on. No viable fingerprints, boot prints that could have belonged to any big man in town and no witnesses. Except Lindsay. But even she had no idea who it had been and didn't get a good look at the guy.

In order to get her mind off her anger, she gave Teresa a call. She hadn't spoken with any of her White Crest buddies since the trip. It would be nice to hear Teresa's voice.

The phone rang until Teresa's machine kicked on. Kate hung up.

Next she tried Pam, thinking she might be working the early shift at the hospital.

No luck. Where is everyone?

Looking out of her small office window, she saw the murky skies threatened more snow. At White Crest, snow would have been a welcome sight, but not here and not today. Since her surgery she'd felt chilled, wearing sweaters and taking in hot soup and coffee throughout the day. Perhaps Gerard had been right and she should have stayed home, but the familiar words of her father rang in her head: "I can feel lousy at work just as easily at work as I can at home. I might as well get paid." A mailman for over thirty years; Perry Frost hadn't missed a day of work.

Someone knocked on her office door and she prayed it was Ed Nog. The door opened before her imagination could choose the best form of torture for the little weasel.

"Kate? I have that Internet info you asked for," John Turner said.

"Thanks, John." She winced when she reached out to take it.

"Are you all right?"

"I'm fine. Still recovering from minor surgery. I keep forgetting about the stitches."

"Can't you take something for pain?"

"I hate to do that. All they do is make me sleepy. I'm trying to tough it out."

"Why don't you go home?"

"No rest for the wicked." She tapped the pile of paperwork. "Congratulations on your arrest the other day. I heard Jack kicked ass."

"No kicking, but a lot of growling. He's turned out to be one of the best dogs in K-9."

"I'll bet."

"Think about those pain pills. I won't tell if I find you asleep at your desk." He grinned and left the room.

Kate leafed through the information John had looked up on marionettes and puppets. She read a brief summary on their history and how they're made, recalling the latex material that had covered Jakes' body, noting the absence of the traditional elements used in manufacturing marionettes. No correlation between the dolls and any Broadway show tune turned up in the paperwork and she tossed the stack aside. None of the pieces were fitting. She couldn't think any longer.

Kate's hand hovered over the medicine bottle in her top drawer. The pain had become distracting enough to disturb her concentration. What the hell, she decided. If she became too tired, she'd have Gerard give her a ride home. She downed one tablet with a swig of water and went back to fuming about Ed Nog's ploy.

She pulled out the card he'd given her with his home phone and dialed. His answering machine picked up after several rings.

"You've reached Edward Nog, journalist and professional photographer. If you're in need of my services please leave your number. If you're a bill collector, screw you."

Beep.

Kate rolled her eyes and tried to remain calm. She mentally amended the first sentence that came to mind, and said, "This is Detective Kate Frost. I'd appreciate it if you'd give me a call back when you receive this. It's a matter of importance to our work together. Thank you."

She left her number and hung up ready to gag, quite sure she'd be receiving a phone call soon. Nog stood more than eager to intrude on her life.

Suddenly her phone rang.

"Damn, I'm good."

She let it ring once more and then picked up.

"Detective Frost."

Her eyes went wide as she listened.

"Now?"

She nodded.

"I'm on my way."

She felt the room tilt slightly when she stood to retrieve her coat from the rack beside her desk, and closed her eyes until the feeling subsided. Grabbing her keys and purse, she left her office, passing John on the way out.

"Decided to take my advice, huh?"

"See you tomorrow." She said hurrying toward the door.

Chapter Twenty-Nine

Percy Smith haunted me but I was determined to turn that around. Sooner or later I'd find him. Something didn't feel right about a guy who pranced around naked with a hacksaw for fun. Although he'd disappeared right before the crime, the whole scenario didn't add up to a murder. So where the hell was he? I hadn't been able to locate him by my traditional focus-and-find method, and the only reason I could think of was that I'd never met the guy. Everyone I'd ever found that way had been someone I knew. Apparently having a name wasn't enough. It seemed I had to be able to picture the person before finding them. Not sure of what my other options might be, I decided I needed some help.

When I arrived at my picnic area, I found a meeting in session with Mike, Sally and Dr. Saint in attendance. Sally paced before the other two, who had settled themselves on the grass beside Mike's favorite tree stump. They all looked perplexed.

"Who died?" I couldn't resist.

When they all stared at me I mimed tugging my shirt collar and sat down beside Mike.

Tough crowd.

"I'd make you a list, but eternity isn't long enough to read it," Sally replied.

"What does that mean?" I asked Mike.

"Remember when you threatened to hang out a shingle for business?"

"Yes."

"Well, business is good."

"How so?"

"We came here to get away from the crowd," Sally said.

"It seems there are a good number of folks on this side with issues about their deaths," Dr. Saint clarified.

"It looks like *Night of the Living Dead* back at Sally's parking lot." Mike grinned.

"And they're all looking for me?"

"They asked for you by name." Mike feigned a stretch.

"How do they know about me?"

"Must have been Rico."

"But he gave up his tag and left."

"Could have been before that."

"So you left all those people standing in the parking lot?"

"You betcha. I wasn't about to start taking names," Sally said.

"About how many people are we talking?"

"At least fifty," Mike said.

"Anyone we know?" I asked.

"I thought I saw Hoffa."

"Was he standing next to Elvis?"

Sally stopped pacing and came to stand beside me. "Well? You ready?"

"For what?"

"Your public awaits you."

"They'll just have to wait a little longer. Right now we have other business."

They listened as I explained about Percy and the need to find him. Right now he was our only lead, and even that didn't look very promising.

"If we can at least establish that he's not dead. Sally? Is there a way to do that?"

She shook her head. "Not sure."

"Right. No APB system here."

"If I may?" Dr. Saint interrupted.

"What's up, Doc?" I quipped, then grinned.

"What did law enforcement do before APBs were available?"

I shrugged.

"They formed a posse and went looking. I suggest we do the same."

"I don't have a horse."

"Ah, but you do have the posse."

"I don't follow."

"All those folks waiting for you back at Sally's lot. Why not put them to work? Someone is bound to know something. If Percy is still alive it might be our best chance to prove it."

It was all I had. "Let's go," I said.

When we arrived at Sally's parking lot, I saw a small mob had gathered. No signs of anyone I knew. To be honest, I'd hoped to see Jakes. Her case had grown cold with the exception of Percy Smith.

Mike stood beside me with his arms crossed over his chest. He took in the crowd and nodded.

"What?" I asked.

"Looks like you've got your hands full."

"I didn't ask for this. I considered helping a few folks, but there are plenty of cases to solve on the other side right now. Jakes is priority. Maybe we can make this work for everyone."

"So what are you going to tell them?" He waved an arm toward the crowd.

Most of the people were young, twenties or maybe a bit older. I saw one elderly gentleman threatening the young male beside him with his cane. They all had the hungry look of people who think they ought to be first. If I didn't act soon, there was going to be trouble. Part of me was curious enough to want to hold out and see what a group of spirits would do with a mob mentality. Fortunately, my professional persona took over and I found myself making my way over to try for diplomacy.

"If you'll all just break it up a bit. I'm sure we can work this out," I said in my most commanding voice.

"Who the hell are you?" a young woman with a meat cleaver lodged in her forehead asked.

"I'm Detective Lindsay Frost. I hear you're all here to see me." I held up my badge.

A quiet mumble of voices moved through the crowd and finally the old man with the cane stepped forward.

"I'm Joel Carson. I was murdered in an alley not far from my home. They never found the murderer. Can you help me?"

A round of voices with similar stories rose from the group. I held up my hands to silence them.

"I'm not sure I can give you what you want. I'm in the same shape you are."

"That's not true. We heard that you took care of that Tanner character. Put her away. If you can do that, you can help us."

Tanner Jean Hoyt had been a sick military wannabe with a vendetta against me. We had a jaded history, one that involved revenge and murder. When she'd come after me on this side, I'd had to find a way to put her away for good. Thanks to Tanner, I'd learned the power of death tags and had managed to take hers and put it in a safe place. It seems when a spirit loses their death tag they fade into nothingness. I'm not sure what happened to her, or where she is, all I know is she hasn't made an appearance since.

"How did you find out about that?"

"Things get around. No different here than on the other side," Joel said. "Can you help us?"

I had a plan.

"I'll be happy to do what I can for all of you, but you'll have to cooperate with me. I need your help."

"Why should we help you?" Cleaver Woman asked.

"Because I'm already working on a case, and, the faster I solve it, the faster I get to all your cases."

"So you'll help us?" Joel asked.

I glanced at Mike who offered a warning grimace.

What choice did I have? If I said no, they'd all leave and I'd be back to square one. If I agreed to help them, I might get to Percy a lot quicker.

"Yes," I said, wondering what I'd gotten myself into.

"What guarantee do we have that if we do what you want you'll help us?" Cleaver Woman frowned past the wooden handle obscuring her vision.

"You'll just have to trust me."

"I trusted my husband. Look what it got me." She pointed to her forehead.

"If you know your assailant why do you need my help?" I asked.

"I don't need anything. But I've seen cops in action before and I want to be sure no one here gets the shaft."

Looking at her head, I figured it was too late, but I wasn't going to split hairs over it. At this point I felt it better to just bury the hatchet and get on with things.

"I'm good for it," I told her. "Trust me or not, I don't care. I guess you'll just have to wait and see. Besides, I'm easy to find."

"I'm in. What the hell else do we have to do around here anyway?" Joel asked.

I saw the crowd nod in agreement. It looked like I had my search party.

That evening, as night settled over Southfield Heights, I felt my restlessness awaken. My mind wouldn't shut down. Sleeplessness had become a familiar pattern long before my death, leading to an ample supply of makeup to hide the dark circles under my eyes. During my time in homicide, sleep became an occasional hobby instead of a physical requirement. Working tough cases deprived me of countless nights in my bed, and after a while I found it difficult to sleep all the way through. I started taking walks in the middle of the night to clear my head and offer the neighborhood watch an added boost. No one ever questioned my strange ways, as I'd wave hello to some of the steel workers or medical staff in my neighborhood coming or going to their jobs. Old habits die hard, and, although I no longer have the physical requirement for sleep, I maintained my need to be a watchful citizen.

I began surveillance feeling a sense of purpose. This was still my town, my turf, and, although I might not be able to stop a robber or provide assistance to a stranded motorist, I could maintain a solid vigil. I'd never encountered anything earth-shattering on my rounds, but tonight I felt uneasy. I knew I was being watched.

It doesn't take a detective to know when something isn't right. My ethereal hackles stood at full attention. In life, I would have made an unexpected turn, or hid behind a tree to see who eventually came by. But whoever was following me had to be able to see me, and that meant they were dead.

I thought of Mike, then realized it wasn't his style. As a cop he wouldn't tail a woman at night for a joke, even if she were a ghost. I checked off a mental list of all of the people I'd met in my new existence and knew none of them would play a trick like this. That's when I caught a glimpse of white across the street beside Mrs. Jenkins' house. From what I could tell, the person was about five-five and had ducked around back.

"Hey!" I called, unconcerned that I'd wake the neighbors.

I followed as quickly as my navigational skills would allow.

Mrs. Jenkins' backyard stood vacant, save for the crippled old oak and a battered shed. No point in looking for footprints, I decided, as I followed a dirt path to the small structure. The rickety wooden door remained closed and, knowing Mrs. Jenkins, most likely locked. My target had broken and entered minus the breaking.

Inside the shed, I found yard tools, a wheelbarrow and mouse droppings. No entity, only the sense that one had been here. Since I had yet to work out all of the rules and possible dangers of my new world, it unnerved me to think I'd fallen into a potential trap so easily. I knew better than to follow an unknown person into unknown territory. It could have meant my end, whatever that might be at this point.

My instincts told this me this hadn't been a coincidence. I'd been lured here, but why and by whom? The idea of a demon or a poltergeist came to mind only to be shot down by my skepticism that such things actually exist. The fact that I'm a so-called ghost should open the door to believing in all such things paranormal, but I'm still not thoroughly convinced. I have yet to see actual proof of any of those activities.

A movement outside the grimy window caught my attention and I hit the floor when I saw a gun muzzle pointed my way. What can I say?—it's a reflex. Feeling foolish I got up and hurried out into the yard in time to see a flash of white round the shed's corner. When I got there, I was met by nothing more than darkness and the eerie sound of a wind I couldn't feel.

Scanning the yard, I tried to figure out why I'd overreacted to the gun. I had been dead long enough to know it couldn't hurt me, yet the glimpse of the muzzle had sent me into a near panic. Something wasn't right about the whole episode, but any logic to it evaded me.

I had no way to trail the person; they'd simply vanished. The disappearing act didn't surprise me—after all, I'd done it many times—but it left me with the uneasy feeling that this wasn't the last time I'd be seeing flashes of white. It brought to mind a vision of an angel, a vision that had been burned into my brain from years of Sunday school. Right, an angel with a weapon. As I left the yard, I gripped my badge, wondering what it could mean.

CHAPTER THIRTY

Kate couldn't believe her luck. Her pup had recovered faster than expected and the breeder had called to say she could pick him up today. She ticked off a mental checklist of her purchases as she left the pet store: puppy food, dishes, chew-toys, pooper-scooper and Scotchgard.

As she made her way to the breeder's farm she tossed around ideas for names, finally deciding to simply wait until she saw the pup again and go with the first thing that came to mind.

She pulled into the drive beside the small house and shook off another yawn. Kate realized the painkillers were working their magic and she could move without wincing but she really wanted nothing more than to take a nap. She reminded herself to stop for coffee on the way home. Exiting the SUV, dogs barked in the distance and she decided to head toward the barn and take a peek.

She stood inside the barn, smelling hay and manure as she allowed her eyes to adjust to the dim light.

"Hello?" she called. "Anyone here?"

She moved past the row of stalls, hearing horses stomp and sputter from behind the gates.

Two adult huskies paced in a kennel near the back of the barn, and Kate recognized them as the parent dogs of the pups. So where were the puppies?

"Hello? I'm here to pick up my dog."

Kate turned around at a sudden sound.

A tall figure towered above with an arm raised to strike.

Before she could defend herself she was tackled to the ground.

Kate's head throbbed, but she couldn't recall drinking. She couldn't recall much of anything. Her bed didn't feel right either. She groped at her sides and found a hay-covered dirt floor. Somewhere in the distance, dogs barked and the wind howled an eerie cry. It was the stuff that horror movies are made of. She tried to focus in the darkness but all she could make out was her body's silhouette. Wherever she was it held little warmth but was shelter enough against the raw elements.

"Screw this." She started to get up.

A sharp twinge in her left breast forced her to lie back down and she felt the place where a bandage lay bunched up under her shirt.

"What the hell?" She couldn't make sense of this nightmare.

Her last memory remained blurred as she tried to recall how she'd gotten here. She recalled getting the call from the breeder and entering the barn. Someone came up behind her, then everything had gone black. Her memory caught on a woman's voice, no—two of them. Arguing. She'd been dragged, but had been unable to fight them with limbs of lead.

She fought the urge to sleep. Glimpses of the recovery room ran through her mind, and suddenly the bandage made sense. She wondered if she were still coming out of the anesthesia.

"Gerard?" Her voice sounded miles away. "Gerard!" She tried to call louder.

The blackness enveloped her senses and she dozed on and off dreaming that she'd returned to White Crest to find the whole episode a nightmare. Jakes called to her now that she needed to wake up before it was too late. Her eyes bolted open expecting to find that she'd overslept and was about to receive the dreaded wedgie.

"Jakes?" she called. "Anyone?"

As her head cleared, she realized this wasn't a dream. She reached for her pocket but found she'd been stripped of her coat as well as her cell phone and gun. Gone. Of course they were. The chills returned, making her teeth chatter in the cold where she knew she would be able to see her breath if there had been enough light. She rubbed her arms in an effort to create warmth, ignoring the pain of her incision. A quick check of the dressing confirmed it to be dry and intact.

Think, Kate. Get out of this stupor or you'll die!

The fact that her legs and arms moved freely confirmed her captors had most likely used a chemical restraint. Now that the drug was wearing off, it meant she didn't have much time before they came back. This might be her last chance to live.

Kate forced herself onto her stomach, hoping to crawl her way to freedom. Every inch of her body ached as though she'd been beaten. Once up on all fours, she tested each limb for steadiness and began crawling. Her head swam. She fought not to fall over, knowing what kind of pain it would bring. Suddenly she coughed and retched, grabbing her sides in agony. Tears ran down her cheeks as she wiped her mouth and tried to continue. She breathed through her mouth to avoid the strong smell of urine surrounding her. It wouldn't take much to make her vomit and she needed to save her strength.

Moonlight bled through the wooden slats of her prison, creating enough light to see she was in some sort of stall. She explored her surroundings carefully, and found a pie pan sitting beside the door with a slice of bread and what looked like dried oatmeal in it. At least her host thought enough to feed her. Her hands pressed against the hay as she crawled, and she wondered how she'd get out of this mess. She was being held captive in an Indiana barn. Now that shouldn't be too hard to pinpoint. Gerard should be arriving any moment. Except she knew that wouldn't be the case because she hadn't told him she was leaving.

Kate forced herself to keep moving until she reached the wide gate and felt around for a latch. The sudden twinge in her breast forced her back down. Lying quietly for a moment, she took in the sounds around her. She heard nothing unusual and thankfully no signs of her kidnappers. A horse whinnied not far from her stall and she wondered what kind of horse it was. Her mind wandered as she took several deep breaths to pace herself. She thought about riding a beautiful white stallion across a field, and fought to stay focused. Forcing herself to reality, she realized the effects of the drug were still working. She had to concentrate on getting out of here.

Once again on all fours, she felt her knee land on something hard. She squinted in the dark to make out the tiny object as she fingered the familiar shape of a wormer pellet like the one found at the cabin. Brushing aside mounds of hay, she felt several more in the stall. At least she could stop searching for Jakes' killer. It looked like she'd found her.

She'd been wrong to believe that Betty Carter hadn't recognized her and now it looked like she and her crazy mother had gained the upper hand.

The sound of heavy footsteps sent her heart pounding. Kate struggled to get to her feet, but, before she could move, the gate swung open, hitting her in the side. She cried out and fought another wave of nausea. A pair of muddy work boots stood inches from her face and she tried to follow them upward to see her captor. Her vision clouded on the dark blur above and she felt a sharp jab in her upper arm. Instinct made her grab for the attacker, but her arm seemed to rise in slow motion and drop again. Her body grew heavy and she fought to stay awake. One of the muddy boots pressed hard against her throat to hold her down. Eventually, she was overcome by an overwhelming loss of consciousness. The last thing she heard was the slam of the gate and tight click of the latch.

CHAPTER THIRTY-ONE

Thanks to my posse, my memories of Tanner had been brought to the forefront, reminding me of some of the most painful times in my life and afterlife. My mind replayed scenes from our violent past in a brief reel of Here's Your Life. Tanner's evil eyes burned a hole in me as I recalled the last time I'd seen her. That's when it hit me.

The reason I'd overreacted to the apparition in white's weapon is because it was familiar. It was Tanner's AR15 pistol. Although spirits can't seem to grasp anything in the physical world, we can latch on to death tags, and this spirit had somehow gotten hold of Tanner's, or one like it. In the dark, all I'd seen was the muzzle, but I knew from its outline it wasn't an average weapon. The AR15 resembles a smaller version of the M16 so it's easier to conceal if you're a sicko on the loose.

It was no coincidence that the intruder carried the same gun as Tanner. That's why I'd been lured. She hadn't been trying to shoot me; she'd wanted me to know she had the death tag.

The next morning I found Mike at his daughter's bus stop and I politely waited for the bus to turn the corner before I motioned for him to follow me.

"Good morning to you too. Where are we going?" he asked.

"Miner's Jewelers."

His eyebrows rose. "You trying to tell me something?"

"Yeah. I think they've been robbed again."

Miner's Jewelers had been the place of Mike's death, and,

although I wanted to avoid it, I had little choice. After I'd taken Tanner's death tag, I'd given it to Mike for safekeeping, and he'd brought it to his death spot. I figured as long as the gun stayed out of her hands, she'd stay out of the picture. I had to know if it was still here.

As we made our way past customers peering over glass counters, I explained my encounter with the apparition.

"Who's that?" I pointed to the stout little man wearing a wide smile under a handlebar mustache.

"Julius Miner. He's owned this place for over thirty-five years. He was here the day the store was robbed."

I followed Mike to the vault in the back.

"You put Tanner's gun in the vault?" I asked.

"Why not? Who would think to look here? Besides, my storage unit is a little full. But what makes you so sure it's missing?"

"I know that creep had her gun. There can't be too many of those floating around in the afterlife. Why else would the guy have let me see it?"

We stepped inside the vault. It stood empty.

"Shit." Mike cursed at the vacant space where he'd put the weapon. "How did he know about it?"

"Like our good buddy Joel said, 'Things get around.' "

I started moving inside the vault as I would any crime scene. Mike cocked his head in question.

"I'm working," I explained. I inspected the entire vault and came up empty. "Hard to determine an entry point when you're dealing with a spirit."

"Does it matter?"

"I don't know. This is all new to me."

"I think you have a pretty good idea who might have taken it. Your apparition in white seems like a solid suspect. Shouldn't we be laying a trap?"

"Right. I knew that. No pictures, witnesses or fingerprints necessary. I guess I'm looking for the proof that it was indeed the mysterious apparition in white and not Tanner herself."

"Could it have been Tanner?"

"Doubtful."

"Why is that?"

"Because the apparition didn't move like Tanner. And, besides, Tanner wouldn't be caught dead or alive in white. She much prefers camo."

"I think you'd be the first to know if she was back."

"You're probably right. But what's a motive for stealing an AR15?"

"I think the more important question is what does this mean for Tanner?"

"Already on that. I figure she'll stay wherever it is she went unless she gets the weapon back in her grubby little hands."

"But you don't know what the robed bandit is up to. We need to find him ASAP."

"Looks like I'm in for another midnight stroll."

This time I went straight for the shed. I'm not sure why but I figured that might be the place the apparition would most likely return to. I was right.

There was a flash of white against the darkness and I purposely stepped out into the openness of the shed to allow the guy to come up behind me.

"Detective Frost." A husky female voice cut the shadows. I could feel her presence as if we were touching.

Turning, I caught a good look and saw it was Cleaver Woman. Tanner's AR15 lay cradled in the crook of her arm.

Relief and anger burned at the sight of it.

"Give me the gun," I ordered.

"Not so fast, Detective. Finders keepers."

"Do you know what could happen if the wrong person gets a hold of that tag?" I tried to remain calm.

"I know all about Tanner Jean Hoyt. She's harmless. For now."

"How do you know that?"

"Without our tags, we're powerless. Isn't that the way it works here?"

"Let's cut the crap. What do you want?"

"I want to make sure you do what you promised for all those people. This is only an insurance policy. When it's all over, I'll return it."

"I can't let you do that."

"You don't really have a choice."

"And what will you do if I'm unable to help everyone?"

"Then Tanner gets her toy back."

"You'd have to find her first."

"I can find her easily."

"You're bluffing."

"Am I? Can you afford to be wrong?"

"It's happened before." I was close enough to reach Tanner's weapon.

"This time it could go beyond deadly."

"You don't have a clue what you'd be doing if you release Tanner."

"Not my problem. But she'll be yours if you don't do what's right."

She must have anticipated my next move because when I grabbed for the pistol, she vanished, taking it with her.

"Not this time," I called after her. Not sure where I was going and what I would find when I arrived, I followed her.

The gray void enveloped me like a thick fog and my stomach danced with ethereal butterflies, feeling that I'd been here before. When I'd first crossed over, I had found myself in a similar place where it felt like I'd been wedged between two gray walls. This time I had some navigational experience and kept to what I thought was a straight path ahead. Once again I chastised myself for following blindly into unknown territory, but what choice did I have? If that crazy bitch did know where to find Tanner, it could be serious trouble.

A shadow up ahead told me I'd found someone but I wasn't sure it was Cleaver Woman. I wasn't above asking for directions, especially since I'd yet to see a gas station here, but knew I had to use caution. As I came up behind the robed figure, I relied on my police training of distance, shielding and movement. I kept a safe distance behind knowing there wasn't much to shield myself with and hoping my movement would be quick enough if necessary.

"Hey there. Can you help me?" I called out.

The figure kept moving as if it hadn't heard me. I noted its hunched posture and thought of Quasimodo.

"I'm Detective Frost with homicide, and I need to speak with you."

The hunched figure turned my way, its face obscured by a deep hood.

Okay, now I'm thinking Satan, except I'd always pictured him taller.

I stopped and waited for something to happen. It didn't take long before I saw several hooded figures close in around me, leaving nowhere for me to go. There was nothing but blackness inside the hoods and I wondered what I was dealing with. They remained frozen in place, making no sound.

I'm a firm believer that a good defense starts with an even better offense, so I straightened to my full five-nine stature and took command.

"I need to speak with whomever is in charge here."

No one moved.

I singled one of them out. "You with the blank look, can you tell me who's in charge?"

Two of the group members broke apart to allow the tallest of them through.

"I take it you're the head honcho?"

The figure's left arm raised enough to reach my shoulder, although I didn't see a hand appear from the long sleeve. When it touched me, I felt an overwhelming pressure, a weight too much to bear and I grabbed it to push it aside. A shock jolted through my spirit form sending me crashing backwards through the void from where I'd come.

I landed hard on my rear. When I looked around I saw the familiar setting of Mrs. Jenkins' shed. Getting back on my feet I realized I'd stumbled into a territory I shouldn't have and had received a stern warning. It gave me another glimpse into my new environment where, just like in the real world, there were places best avoided.

CHAPTER THIRTY-TWO

For someone without an appetite, I sure had my plate full. From where I stood, I had two choices, work Jakes' case, or deal with Cleaver Woman. Both needed my immediate attention, but one held far more dangerous consequences left unattended. My meeting with the choirboys from hell had proven educational in the sense that there might indeed be a place of punishment for the truly wicked. It was my hope that that is where Tanner had gone, never to return. Looking back, I realized that whatever those beings were, they could have easily done what they wanted with me, leading me to believe that their message had been one of warning. They'd decided to let me go with the understanding that I wouldn't return. Not a problem.

That still left me to deal with Cleaver Woman and the fact she could make good on her threat. The question that nagged me was would she really jeopardize the hopes of all those people awaiting my help? To simply prove a point? Like most criminals, I didn't know her well enough to make that call. My gut instincts told me she wouldn't. Not yet anyway. She'd found me a second time to warn me and now it was up to me. She'd most likely wait me out to see what I did next. So, naturally, I decided to keep her guessing. I figured I had some time, although not a lot, and I wanted to spend it wisely.

The fact that I had future customers literally scouring every inch of eternity for Percy Smith left me free to focus on my search for him in the real world. In order to clear my mind, and follow up on one more idea, I revisited Sun City, where a game of Buff Bingo was in full swing in the ballroom.

Bob Ilkerson bellowed into a microphone. "I-65."

"You don't look a day over fifty," an elderly woman called back.

"Thank you, Martha." He pulled another ball from the roller cage.

I left before someone could jump up and shout, "Bingo!"

I searched the premises and found no signs of Percy. The canvas bag remained in Ilkerson's office where I'd seen it last, telling me it most likely belonged to the runaway nudist. The inside of Percy's locker looked the same. Apparently he hadn't returned. I checked the parking lot and grounds, not seeing any sign of the green Dodge that might belong to him.

I'd exhausted all the Percy places I could think of, and my dead end led me to the one place I'd always gone when I needed fresh ideas—Alvarez.

He sat at his desk reviewing paperwork and I saw it involved Jakes' case. Gone were the days when I'd have to wait for him to hand me the report. I simply stuck my head in front of his and scanned it for myself.

The interview with Percy's parents confirmed they didn't know their son's whereabouts and hadn't seen him since the Wednesday before the murder. That meant Percy had been missing for six days. This fact hadn't meant much to his parents, according to their statement, because "Percy doesn't visit that often anyway." Notations on the interview report told me the Smiths had a strained relationship with their son at best, with Alvarez writing that Percy's father had mentioned that they only see him when he needs something, most often money. Alvarez had also noted that Percy's parents displayed plenty of framed snapshots of their dog, but not a single family photo with Percy in it.

What Alvarez did find out about Percy was that he'd only attended one semester of college because he'd wanted to major in art. When his father refused to pay for an "artsie-fartsie" education, he'd quit and had started working at Wal-Mart, and then for Jakes. Since then, Percy and his parents hadn't spoken on a regular basis. It remained unclear whether his parents knew of their son's nudist activities.

When Alvarez moved his arm to reach for his coffee, I saw Percy still worked part-time at a local Wal-Mart in the electronics department. Scanning down I saw that my ever-efficient ex-partner had already interviewed Percy's boss and found that Percy had taken vacation time starting last Friday, the day Kate received the finger. He was due back at work this coming Saturday. Three days is a long time to wait if he was our guy. Even if he turned out to be innocent, the fact he was missing could mean he'd been a victim related to Evelyn Jakes. We had to find him.

"Alvarez," he answered his phone.

He listened a moment and nodded. "Yes, Detective Milner. What have you got for me?"

I shamelessly leaned my ear as close to the phone as I could, to eavesdrop.

"We found some DNA from the cabin that doesn't match the vic's."

"Anyone we know?"

"All it tells us is that it's female."

"And you're sure it's not Evelyn Jakes'?"

"Yes. Looks like we're looking for a woman."

"Normally, I'd question that because of the amount of power it would take to move a body from place to place, but with the body cut up it would make the job easier," Alvarez said.

"Even so, maybe she had a partner."

"Thanks, Pete. It gives us a new angle."

"Hope it leads us somewhere."

Alvarez disconnected and dialed Kate's home number. When he got the machine, he tried her cell. Concern etched the corners of his eyes when her voice mail answered.

"Merda," he cursed and disconnected.

I followed him to the area known as the corral, where desks and computers take up most of the space. He caught up with John Turner who was on his way out the door.

"Hey, John. Got a minute?"

"What's up?"

"Have you seen Kate today?"

"No. Why?"

"I haven't heard from her and I can't reach her."

"She wasn't feeling well yesterday afternoon and left early."

"I didn't get to talk to her much yesterday."

"Maybe she called in sick?"

"Right. I think I'll take a run over and see if she's sleeping."

"Let me know, okay?" John said.

Before Alvarez could grab his keys, I was on my way to Kate's. Nice to know I could still beat him at something.

Kate's house was dead quiet. After a quick perusal, I knew she wasn't home. Kate had never been on time in her life; she would have missed her own birth if not for the induction of labor. Her morning routine consisted of gulping down a cup of coffee after spilling sugar and creamer, a quick shower and then racing out the door. When I saw the empty coffee pot and spotless kitchen counter I knew she hadn't been home last night.

It didn't take more than ten minutes for Alvarez to arrive and use his key to get inside. I watched as he retraced my path and stood in frustration in the living room. He pressed the flashing light on her answering machine and listened to the message from the night before. I heard my mom's voice inviting her to dinner on Saturday.

Alvarez looked right at me—right *through* me, to be more accurate—and it felt like old times when we'd hit upon the same idea at once. I didn't need flesh to connect with his thoughts and realize that Kate was missing.

We both jumped when the back door rattled.

Alvarez drew his sidearm and moved along the wall toward the kitchen. The door rattled again, this time louder, and I knew it wasn't the wind. I went ahead of my ex-partner wondering what good it would do if I got to the intruder first. Old habits die hard.

I grinned at a familiar silhouette through the sheer curtains of the back door. This ought to be good.

As the door jiggled once more, Alvarez yanked it open and pointed his weapon.

Ed Nog fell inside and onto the floor.

"Don't move!" Alvarez commanded.

"Okay! Don't shoot me," Nog pleaded.

Alvarez patted him down then holstered his weapon. "What the hell are you doing here?"

"I was looking for Detective Frost. She's hard to find." Nog's gaze wandered about the kitchen.

"What do you want with her?"

"She still has my photos and I. . . ."

"The truth, asshole."

"I need to talk to her." He glanced at the mail on the kitchen counter and picked up a business card.

"About what?" Alvarez swiped the card away from him.

"Sorry." Nog's gaze followed the card. "Just looking for clues as to where she might be."

"Uh huh. What do you need to talk to Kate about?"

"Look. I only need to speak with her."

"One more time. About what?"

"I think she talked with my boss."

"You mean your ex-boss?"

"Oh. Then you already know."

"I suggest you stay clear of Kate and the station for a while. You have no further business there."

"I just wanted to explain and apologize. I'm trying to get my job back and if Kate will let me do her story I know the editor will go for it."

"I'll give her your message."

"If you find her."

"What the hell does that mean?"

"You seem to be looking for her too. Maybe I can help. Where was she last seen?"

I've never seen Alvarez remain so calm with someone so annoying.

He grabbed Nog's coat collar and firmly escorted him onto the back porch.

"Leave it to the pros. Get lost." Alvarez closed the door behind him, tossed the business card back onto the counter and left.

I stuck around a few minutes longer to see what the Nogster would do now that he'd been officially dismissed. He didn't seem the kind to back down easily. When he didn't come back around to the kitchen door, I went to the living room and scanned the block for his Sherman-tank-size Buick. Sure enough, it sat several houses down.

Alvarez's car had no sooner rounded the block than I saw Nog exit his car and make a hasty return. I bristled at the idea of him trying to break into the house and wished for a way to call Alvarez back. My options were few, so I decided to follow Nog to see what he was up to.

He retraced his steps to the back of the house and I saw him trying to peer into the window above the sink. Although his hair stood tall enough, he needed an extra few inches to get high enough and he promptly climbed onto the wrought-iron railing that ran along the steps. He cupped his hands around his face and stared inside at the countertop.

After several minutes, he pulled a digital camera from his pocket and started snapping pictures through the window. He seemed satisfied he'd accomplished his goal and jumped from the rail. I watched him head back to his car, and I wondered what was so interesting about Kate's mail.

When I took another look at it, I found the usual junk, a water bill, renewal notice for her *Vogue* magazine subscription, and a business card for her dog breeder, Betty Carter. Nothing exciting enough to take pictures of, but, then, who knows what inquiring minds find interesting. Feeling I'd wasted enough time I decided it was time for action.

Chapter Thirty-Three

"Kate," a voice whispered. "Wake up."

Kate forced her eyes open. Her mind wouldn't clear and she fought to get her bearings. Hay clung to her cheek as she struggled to roll onto her back.

The barn remained eerily silent and she figured she'd been dreaming again. Checking her surroundings, she saw that nothing had changed including the corner pie tin.

"Kate? Are you awake?" the voice came again through the stall wall to her right.

"Who's there?" she croaked over a dry throat. Her tongue felt coated with dust as it rolled over her chapped lips. What had happened to her?

Slowly her memory returned, as did the pain.

"Who's there?" she asked more forcefully.

"It's Teresa. Teresa Nielson."

For a moment, Kate had to focus on the name. What was Teresa doing here? Why couldn't she think straight?

"Teresa? What are you doing here?"

"I don't know but this sure isn't the welcome I expected."

"What do you mean?"

"Pam called and invited me to your surprise wedding shower a few days ago."

Kate forced her way up at that, pain or not. After a moment, her head started to clear and she saw by the moonlit floor in her stall that she remained untied. The memory of her last awakening brought on cold dread. If she was awake, it was time for another dose of whatever they were giving her.

Feeling the urge to pee, she had little choice but to do it in the corner of her stall. She pushed some hay into a small pile and relieved herself, trying to make sense of what Teresa had just told her.

"I'm not getting married," she answered her friend.

"I figured that out. Have any clues why Pam might do something like that?"

"I don't think Pam was involved." Kate zipped up her jeans. "How did you know I was here?"

"One of the women mentioned you by name. I never saw her before. She wears a creepy mask; at least I hope it's a mask, and dirty coveralls. Not a *Vogue* candidate."

Kate could hear the fear behind her friend's attempt at humor. She had to get them out of here. She eyed the fresh batch of oatmeal and bread in the corner and was surprised to find that it made her stomach growl in hunger. Unable to recall her last meal, she knew she'd need to keep up her strength. She reached for it, but, at the last minute, she shoved it aside, fearing the food might be laced with something.

"How did you get here?" Kate asked Teresa.

"Some woman picked me up from the airport claiming to be from the station, doing you a favor, but it's not the same woman who's been drugging me. I feel like a fool for getting in the car with her. But she was waiting for me at the airport and so I figured she was who she said she was. She said her name was Portia. I should have known something was up then."

"Like in *The Merchant of Venice*?" Kate was surprised she could recall anything from high school at this point.

"Right. She never offered a last name. But thinking about it, could it have something to do with the fact that I'm a lawyer? Portia pretended to be a lawyer in the story."

217

"I'm not sure. At this point I'm still trying to gain a clear head. The drugs they're using are keeping me in a fog."

"Me too." Teresa was silent a beat, then said, "Kate, I'm scared. Isn't there some mention of taking a pound of flesh for payment in that play? I hope that's not an indication."

Kate thought of the severed finger in the candy box.

"What did the woman at the airport look like?" Kate changed the subject to keep down the panic.

"About five-nine, slightly overweight with dog-shit brown hair. Kate what are we going to do?"

Kate decided not to tell her friend they were being held by a psycho dog breeder and her crazy mother with a grudge. She changed the subject. "Where are you?"

"I'm in a stall. Although it seems like I'm a good ways away from you. God it stinks in here," Teresa said.

"Watch your step."

"Not a problem. I can barely stand. I swear if I live through this, I'll never drink again."

"We'll get out. I just have to get my strength back and clear my head."

"How did they get you here?" Teresa sounded tired.

Before she could answer, the barn door creaked open from the other side of the stall. Kate forced her sore body into position. This time she would be ready. She crouched in the corner beside the door. The sound of boots trudged past her stall stopping further down.

Kate heard a commotion and then Teresa's voice.

"Get the hell away from me!"

After a brief scuffle, she heard her friend cry out. Kate wanted to leap to her friend's assistance, but forced herself to wait in silence, hoping to give the impression she was still asleep. The sound of dragging caused her to peer through the tiny spaces between the stall slats. Work boots clumped ahead of Teresa's body as it slid past her and out of the barn.

Kate shoved against the wooden gate with her hands. She pushed with her shoulder but quickly realized the door was stronger than she thought. Before she could come up with a solid plan, the stall latch rattled.

She stood ready. Her legs were stiff from inactivity, but she focused on her next move. When the door swung open, Kate lunged, grabbing her captor around the waist. They both went down in a flurry of dirt and hay. Horses whinnied in alarm. The woman grunted as she hit the ground and immediately grabbed for Kate's hair. Kate avoided it, slamming her fist into doughy stomach flesh. A sudden painful catch of her stitches caused her to gasp. This time it felt like she'd split her incision.

Her attacker returned the punch, clipping Kate's jaw in the dim light and sending her rolling onto her side. Instinctively Kate used her legs to knock the woman backwards. Ignoring the pain, she jumped on top and yanked her arm behind.

"Where's Betty?" Kate choked out.

The woman's silence infuriated her and she pulled the limb back.

"I swear I'll break it," she warned.

"Fuck you," a muffled voice grunted.

Before Kate could make good on her promise, an arm grabbed her from behind, yanking her into a chokehold. Pulled backwards, she saw the other woman rise up and tower over her like a growing shadow. A hideous mask obscured her face.

She felt the jab of the needle in her thigh, but continued to struggle. As her mind slid unwillingly into the void, she felt her foot connect with something close by and heard the satisfying crunch of bone.

CHAPTER THIRTY-FOUR

While Alvarez organized a search, I focused on Kate's whereabouts. I'd done it before whenever I needed to find her. All I had to do was concentrate. After several tries however, I found that I remained right where I started—at Kate's house. Something was wrong.

I tried once more, feeling frustrated when nothing happened. Desperate, I went in search of Sally.

Sally was right where I figured she'd be. Her form paced in front of the clinic where she'd died. The parking lot was eerily empty.

"Where is everyone?" I asked.

"You sent them on a hunt for Percy Smith, remember?"

"No luck yet?"

"No one's returned. And I have to tell you it's a relief for me. I don't like company in my thinking spot."

"Sorry about that. I'll have to set them straight when they get back. They'll have to find a new place to congregate."

"I'd appreciate that. Now what can I do for you?" she said in her receptionist's tone.

"How did you know I needed something?"

"You look worried. Crow's feet." She pointed.

"What?" I tried to feel around my eyes.

"Kidding. What's up?"

"Kate's missing."

"Geez. You keep losing people."

"Never mind that. I usually focus on her and voila—I'm there. Not this time."

"I've never had a reason to locate someone on the other side. As far as I know, no one in my family can see me."

"She hasn't tried to contact me either. Most of the time, I can hear her."

"Oh. That doesn't sound good."

"As in she might be dead?"

"Well, she would most likely seek you out if that were the case. Have you considered that maybe she doesn't want to be found?"

"That's not like Kate."

Sally shrugged. "I really don't know what to tell you. It's never been a problem for me. Wish I could help."

I nodded. It looked like I didn't have much choice but to wait for Kate to contact me.

"We have another problem. I know who took Tanner's death tag," I told her.

"So that's a problem?"

"It is when the person is threatening to hold on to it until I can help everyone I promised to help. And get it back to Tanner if I don't."

"That could take eternity."

"Thanks for the vote of confidence. But I don't have to tell you what could happen if the tag gets back to Tanner."

Sally had witnessed firsthand the kind of havoc Tanner was capable of and had helped in her capture.

"What can I do?" Sally asked.

"Get Mike on it. He can be quite persuasive. Tell him to hang out by the shed. That seems to be her favorite haunt."

"Where are you going?"

"Back to the station to see if I can find a way to locate my sister."

At the station, everyone worked on locating Kate. I saw a lot of commotion, but little in the way of progress. None of her neighbors had recalled seeing her or her car and she still wasn't answering her cell phone. Alvarez had visited Kate's favorite places like coffee houses and bookstores only to come up empty.

"I guess I was the last to see her yesterday." John Turner wore a grim expression. "She took a phone call and left shortly afterward."

"What time was that?" Alvarez asked.

"A little after one maybe?"

Alvarez checked his watch. "Okay, people," he announced to the corral. "It's now two P.M. Kate has been missing for over twenty-four hours. I don't have to tell you that after the first day our chances grow slimmer by the minute. You all know what to do so let's get going."

I followed him into his office where he shrugged off his suit coat and took a seat at his desk. He buried his face into his hands and let out a deep breath over the paperwork before him. Helpless to comfort him, I paced before his desk talking it out as if he could hear me.

"Okay, what if Sally's right? What if Kate needs time to think? Perhaps Dr. Karr called her with bad news."

Alvarez took a sip of coffee, which had probably turned cold long ago. He drank it anyway.

I counted the days since her surgery. Two. Not long enough to get biopsy results.

"Scratch that. Where does Kate go when she's troubled?"

My gravesite. But not for a full twenty-four hours.

His phone rang, interrupting my train of thought.

"Alvarez."

His expression tightened.

"Yes, Mrs. Frost. I did call earlier."

My mom.

"Well, that's why I called. I'm wondering if you've seen or spoken to Kate recently. I see. You left a message."

My heart broke as he proceeded to explain the problem. I knew she'd be upset beyond words and reliving the horror of losing one daughter already.

"You're right, she is tough. And I'm hoping it's all a misunderstanding. But if you hear from her would you have her call me as soon as possible. Meantime, we'll keep looking."

He ended the call and hung up, looking defeated.

Nancy Peterson stuck her head inside his office. "You have a call on one."

"Can you take a message?"

"I think you should take it." Her expression was serious.

"Alvarez," he said into the receiver. "Pam Mallard?"

I recognized the name as one of Kate's White Crest buddies.

"Yes, Mr. Mallard. I see. When was the last time you heard from her?"

From what I could hear, Pam's husband, Hank, hadn't seen or heard from his wife since Sunday night. She'd left for her shift at the hospital and according to her boss; she'd never shown up. They had tried calling her at home, but Hank had worked a double shift at the steel mill and hadn't checked his messages until Monday evening.

"And you've contacted everyone who might know her whereabouts?" Alvarez confirmed.

"I see. You'll need to come in and fill out a missing-person report, but we'll start the search immediately."

I knew that wasn't procedure, but, with Kate missing too, protocol had changed.

I followed him to Nancy's desk knowing what he had in mind.

"Nancy, I need a copy of missing-person reports in the area since last Friday."

If his hunch was right, we were dealing with multiple kidnappings.

By late that evening, I learned that a missing-person report had been filed on Nicki Jordan on Tuesday. I saw an ugly pattern forming on the corral information board in front of me. Alvarez had confirmed that not only Kate but, in fact, all of her White Crest friends were missing. Now all of their photos were pinned to the corkboard in the central office where the team working the case could view everything at once.

All four of Kate's closest friends were missing. Teresa's office had confirmed she'd gone out of town Friday, due back Monday morning. Carmen had flown into Chicago from Florida on Saturday morning. Her boyfriend said she'd told him she had to come in for a friend's bridal shower and would return Monday. He hadn't heard from her since. No one seemed to know where either of them had gone from the airport or who had picked them up. There were no rental cars listed under their names and no credit-card activity since their arrival at O'Hare.

Since Pam and Nicki lived in town, the investigation focused on neighbors, coworkers and family who might have seen or heard from them. When Nicki hadn't shown up for work at the high school on Monday, the principal had stopped by her home to find her dog, Beaver, frantically pacing and barking inside. By Tuesday, the principal had filed a missing-person report. In canvassing the area, an officer had confirmed that Nicki had last been seen on Sunday afternoon near a coffee shop she frequented.

It appeared the kidnapper had had a definite plan starting with Jakes' murder. We just had to figure out what it was, before it was too late for the rest of them.

Once again I tried to focus, in order to contact Kate or any of her friends, but gave up when all I got was a sense of failure. My feet remained ethereally planted in place in Alvarez's office. Where were Glinda and her wand when I needed her?

All my hopes of a happy ending shattered abruptly when a somber looking Chief O'Connor entered the office without knocking.

"Gerard. We have a body."

CHAPTER THIRTY-FIVE

I chose to ride with Alvarez and Detective Elizabeth Copley instead of navigating to the crime scene ahead of them. I was stalling. I needed time to think, time to try once more to contact Kate. When my attempt failed, my analytical mind told me she was dead. My heart didn't want to accept that and I tried to reason it out. But as the car sped into the night, my mind couldn't form a solid thought. I was pure emotion.

He'd partnered up with Detective Copley briefly after I'd died, before Kate became my permanent replacement. With Kate out of the picture for now, he'd called upon Copley's help once again. She had several years' experience as a violent-crimes detective, and, while she tended to be a bit anal, I respected her work.

The details were sketchy. All we knew was that a blonde woman matching Kate's description had been found in a field on the edge of town. With nothing more than that, the short drive felt like hours, and it showed on Alvarez's face. Copley remained quiet, probably wondering what she could possibly say at a time like this.

Terrorizing thoughts gripped me as we drove. What condition would the body be in? How long had it been there? What if it were unrecognizable? Would it be intact? The image of my sister on an autopsy table nearly threw me into a panic.

As the car turned onto a long stretch of road, my mind presented a brief glimpse of the future based on what-if. I envisioned my parents awash in fresh grief, only this time they would have no one to help them bear it. It would be the hell I'd been dreading. I stopped myself from going ahead to the crime scene, wanting to be there now, yet not really wanting to know. The ride seemed to be taking forever. And then the unthinkable happened when the crossing gates began to flash and lowered across the Forty-Third Street tracks.

"Merda!" Alvarez slammed his palm against the steering wheel.

As his partner for nearly four years, I'd grown accustomed to his outbursts. I never flinched. Unfortunately, with tensions already high, I thought poor Copley might cling to the ceiling by all fours. Her eyes widened and she kept her eyes on the flashing lights. A sudden horn blast confirmed the fact that we were hopelessly stuck waiting for a train.

"Can we take another street?" she asked.

"By the time I do that, the train will be gone. Better to just wait it out. From here the site is only a few streets down."

He radioed in his ETA and sat back, briefly closing his eyes.

"This can't be happening," he told Copley. "It's become the nightmare I can't wake up from."

"Take time to regroup, Alvarez. You've got to get there in one piece and thinking straight."

"You think it's Kate, don't you?"

"I don't know. There are a lot of variables to consider, and, until we know for sure, it's foolish to let imagination get the better of us. Kate's tough and wouldn't go down without one hell of a fight. The fact that hers is the only body in the field tells me it's probably not her. This guy seems to enjoy the shock value of his work. One body would hardly do it."

Alvarez nodded. "Point taken. Thanks, Copley. You've given me something to hope for. You're right. Kate's no rookie and I should give her more credit than that."

"Besides," Copley added, "if Kate is involved, it might just be what's left of the kidnapper."

I don't know if I was more shocked that Copley had made an attempt at humor, or that it had actually worked. Alvarez's tight expression eased. It sounded like something I'd say to break the tension of the job, as I'd done so many times working with him. The most I'd ever gotten had been a grunt but I knew he was smiling inside.

When the gates lifted, Alvarez drove with controlled speed making his way to Grimmer Field. At last, the Crown Vic slowed as it neared the site. Several squads stood by in the darkness and I watched Alvarez race across the snow-covered field, with Copley trailing behind. I beat him to the place where it seemed half of the Southfield Heights PD had gathered, all waiting for the medical examiner to arrive so that the body could be identified, all—obviously—fearing the worst while hoping for the best—that it wasn't Kate. Vehicle headlights burned bright to spotlight the scene and I willed myself not to look. Police personnel and the crime team stood in silence.

A pair of headlights driving slowly across the field revealed the arrival of the medical examiner, Thomas Stern. He jumped down from the van with a huff and trudged his way to the site. His paunch belly only emphasized his squat build, reminding me of an awkward toddler, but I'd yet to see him falter as he maneuvered in and out of the most awkward crime scenes. Tonight was no different as he prepared to view the body before Alvarez and Chief O'Connor.

Not one of the men formed a readable expression as they examined what was left of a young woman partially covered in snow. Either they weren't sure it was Kate or they were too grief stricken to react. I forced myself to look, wanting to know, but not wanting to see Kate. This was the toughest scene I'd ever viewed.

The nude body lay on its stomach in the snow, long blonde hair covered the face. I didn't recognize the woolen scarf tied around her neck. No other clothing items lay near by, and the snow surrounding the body looked relatively undisturbed, telling me the victim had most likely been dumped here. Two crime lab members worked with snow-print wax to secure a trail of boot prints before they were lost to the drifting snow of the open field.

Pink-tinged snow pooled to the left where her arm lay partially underneath her body. The small amount of blood suggested she hadn't bled out and that the wound most likely hadn't killed her. My bet was strangulation. Her right arm stretched out above her head with no apparent wounds, no jewelry that I could identify as Kate's. It could have been any woman's arm.

Unlike me, Kate had been spared any identifying marks like freckles or "beauty marks," and, as far as I could see, this woman didn't have any. I'd been blessed with what came to be known in my family as the Frost Freckle. It was standard issue brown, and lay etched on my inner left thigh. As a self-conscious teen girl, I'd thought it was hideous. My poor mother tried to convince me the beauty mark was something to be proud of. *Right!*

From this angle I couldn't say if the corpse was my sister. The body type and height seemed right and from the body's condition I figured she'd probably been dead about a day. The time frame fit.

The chief nodded for Stern to roll the body, and I braced myself for whatever might come. If it were Kate, I'd be off to find her on the other side, knowing there would be nothing left for me here. My gaze remained on Alvarez as the ME turned the young woman over. A brief series of camera flashes seared through the darkness as a crime tech took photos. Then, Alvarez brushed snow and hair from the victim's face. He fell suddenly forward onto his hands, his face inches from the victim's. His face pinched in sadness as his dark eyes glistened in the white light while he mumbled a brief prayer. It was then my mind caught on his last word, "Grasias."

Chief O'Connor closed his eyes shaking his head and let out a long sigh. "Great God Almighty. It's not Kate."

It was then I could look into the face of the victim, and I felt a twinge of guilt that I had been so cowardly when I thought it might be my sister. What did that say about me as a sister and a homicide detective? The woman's eyes had a frozen stare, taking on an opaque, marble look under the bright floodlights. Her blue-tinged skin lay dark against the snow, and I saw her left nostril held a tiny diamond stud. Lips that had once worn a provocative pout lay frozen open as if she'd died in mid-scream. It looked like she'd been stabbed a couple of times in the thigh but the real damage had been done by the scarf. Someone really wanted this girl dead. All I knew was that it wasn't Kate.

The release of tension seemed palpable, and the crowd of officers patted one another on the back. I saw grown men wiping tears from the corners of their eyes and nodding in relief. The brief joy was quickly replaced with the realization that now their work began. The night took on the familiar dread that went with the fact that there was an unidentified body in Grimmer Field and some young woman's parents would soon be grieving an insurmountable loss.

If I'd had tears they would have filled a bucket, and it surprised me that I felt the need to shed them so strongly. I hadn't been this emotional at my own death. I bowed my head to regain focus and let the emotions subside. As the group went to work, I decided the woman before me was in capable hands. Alvarez and his team would take on her plight for justice while I went on with mine.

CHAPTER THIRTY-SIX

Kate awoke to the sound of an engine rumbling somewhere outside the barn. Dogs barked at what sounded like a truck crunching a gravel path.

"Teresa?" she called out. "Teresa are you there?"

She recalled the events of the night before, when her friend had been dragged from the barn. Kate had spent most of the night in another drugged stupor, waking now and then to find herself shaking from the cold. She'd finally covered up with hay and drifted off to sleep.

No response came and she feared the worst for her friend.

Kate noticed her shirt's stiffness over the incision and saw that she'd bled quite a bit after her encounter with the night stalkers. The bleeding had stopped but she knew her incision had been torn open. She decided a messy scar was the least of her worries.

The truck's reverse warning signal beeped slowly past the barn. The truck was right outside!

Kate forced herself up and kicked at the wooden slats of the barn.

"Hey! In here! Help!"

She scraped the oatmeal pan back and forth along the door making a loud grating sound. The truck sounded further away now but she continued to yell.

"Help me, I'm locked in the barn!"

After a few moments she heard muffled voices over the

truck's rumbling and she strained to make out what they were saying. Bits and pieces of conversation floated over the truck's low rumble.

"Load . . . in back pole barn," the woman said.

"Signature . . . empty it out," the other voice said.

Kate continued her noisemaking then stopped suddenly when the stall door swung open, nearly hitting her.

She saw a large hunched figure, wearing grimy coveralls and a rubber mask. The twisted features were demon-like with a permanent snarl. The voice behind the mask was gruff and she detected a hint of Southern accent.

"You shut the fuck up." A large fist connected with Kate's chin, sending her backwards and onto the floor.

"Not this time!" Kate lunged and tackled the large woman to the ground. She tried to pin her but the woman outweighed her. Within seconds Kate found herself on her back with the giant straddling her.

Kate dodged another punch, sending the woman's fist into the ground beside her. Unfazed by the misjudged punch, the woman grabbed Kate by the throat and squeezed.

Kate's vision grew spotty and she struggled to break free.

The sound of the truck rumbling past the barn in the opposite direction didn't escape her as she fought for a breath. Her hope of being rescued faded along with her hope of surviving.

A welcome interruption came in the form of a shadow in the stall doorway. Her attacker let go of her throat but remained on top of her. Kate hungrily sucked in fresh air.

"I caught this bitch making all kinds of noise," the attacker drawled.

"Don't kill her, yet," Betty said. No question in Kate's mind now—this was Betty Carter, sister of the poor, suicidal man she, herself, had arrested.

"What do you want to do with her? She's a troublemaker. The bitch broke my nose the other day."

"Tie her up. No one will hear her now. Everything is almost ready."

"Hurry up with that." Betty tossed a rope inside the stall. "I have to feed the dogs."

"You can't hope to get away with this," Kate said.

"I lost all hope years ago. All I can do is the best I can."

"Do you want to spend years in prison? Is that the best you can do?"

Betty's pudgy hand grabbed Kate by the hair and yanked her head back to look at her.

Kate winced at the pain in her breast as her arm slammed onto the ground to catch herself.

"I'm already in prison. Have been for a couple of years, waiting for justice. But now it's in my hands." Spittle landed on Kate's cheek.

"You know they're looking for me." Kate felt the woman's grip release.

"Well, they don't seem to be in any hurry do they?" The masked woman finished tying Kate's hands behind her back. "If they don't get here soon I'm going to have to bring in some fresh hay for you to squat in." Her laughter followed her out of the barn.

"What have you done with Teresa?" Kate asked Betty.

"Who?"

"She was here yesterday and you took her away."

"She's safe. You'll be joining her soon. It'll be a real reunion." Betty left the barn.

The gate stood open and Kate saw her freedom only inches away. She struggled to get onto her feet without the use of her hands. Before she could gain her footing, the masked woman returned to the stall, shoving another pan of bread and oatmeal inside.

"You'd better eat. You'll need your strength for the show."

Kate wanted to lash out and kick something but refrained. Still reeling from the pain in her breast, she realized that she was hungry and that the paste-colored oatmeal looked pretty good after all. And the woman was right: she did need her strength. To kick their asses.

Hands tied behind her back, she leaned over and put her face to the pan to lap up the meal like one of her captor's prize huskies.

As the food settled in her churning stomach, her memory replayed the last few days. The last person she'd spoken to before she'd left for the breeder had been John Turner, but she hadn't told him where she was headed.

Her head finally cleared of the drugs she'd been given and Kate tried to rationalize the reason for it all. She reviewed what she knew, or what little she knew about Betty Carter. The woman had a serious grudge against her and was out for revenge. Killing Jakes had been just the beginning. *Think, Kate. How could she have pulled this off? She's not the sharpest knife in the drawer.*

The day she'd picked out her pup with Jakes, she'd made arrangements for pickup after the dog was weaned when she returned from White Crest. Betty had known she was going there because Kate and Jakes had discussed it in front of her. She'd also known how to get in touch with Jakes after learning she was in the catering business and had asked for a business card. Kate's anger burned at the manipulation. In Kate's mind, psycho Betty had motive, means, and opportunity. Now Kate had to prove it. And save herself and lord only knew who else.

Counting back, she realized she'd been missing at least two days. The department would be looking for her but she'd left few clues as to her whereabouts and had no way to communicate with the outside world. Except for Lindsay.

She focused like she had the day at the cabin, mentally calling for her sibling.

A sudden wave of nausea gripped her and she vomited everything up. Her stomach twisted into knots and she continued to retch with dry heaves until she could barely catch her breath.

Either she'd eaten too fast after having nothing in her stomach for two days, or they'd poisoned her. Her mind called out once more for Lindsay before she passed out in the hay.

CHAPTER THIRTY-SEVEN

We'd caught a break and found Percy Smith. Alvarez had checked the airlines and sure enough, there had been a Percy Smith on board a flight to Fort Lauderdale, the Monday after Jakes had died. He'd stayed at a beachfront hotel called the Pink Flamingo. After several more calls, Alvarez determined Percy's return flight would arrive in Chicago by noon.

Once again I found myself in the backseat as Detective Elizabeth Copley rode shotgun with Alvarez on the way to Percy's house. Alvarez's furrowed brow and tense lips told me he wanted this guy bad. The little sleaze probably held all the answers we needed, even if they weren't the answers we wanted to hear.

"No leads on Kate yet?" Copley asked.

Alvarez shook his head. "That's about to change."

"You like this guy for the murder and Kate's disappearance?"

"I doubt he's working alone. With everything that's happened, it looks like the work of a team."

"It would explain being able to transport the body in all that snow and how five women could simply disappear. Is there anything in the past that links him to Kate?"

"Evelyn Jakes."

"But Kate never met Percy."

Alvarez pulled next to the curb and cut the engine.

"Nice place." Copley grinned.

"From what I've seen, the pen will be an improvement in

Smith's living conditions."

Percy answered the door fully dressed. His longish black hair lay slicked back, reminiscent of a sixties beatnik. A skinny physique poked through his black skintight shirt and gray trousers. A scruffy goatee clung to his pointy chin. I felt the urge to beat a bongo and recite poetry.

Before he could speak Alvarez fanned his badge. "Percy Smith?"

"Yes."

"I'm Detective Alvarez with violent crimes and this is my partner, Detective Copley. May we come inside?"

"Violent crimes? You must have the wrong address. Try the juvenile delinquent next door."

"Were you employed by Evelyn Jakes?"

"Yes."

"Then it's you we need to speak with."

"This isn't a good time for me. I've just returned from a trip." Percy started to shut the door.

Alvarez's foot prevented it from closing all the way. "I know. We've been looking for you for days."

Percy offered a stubborn scowl and remained in place. Finally, Copley edged her way closer and offered her sincerest smile.

"Please, Mr. Smith. It will only take a few minutes and we'll leave you to your unpacking. I know how exhausting airports can be. Did you come in through O'Hare?"

His scowl smoothed into a half smile. "Yes. The place is huge. I got lost just trying to find the right luggage terminal."

"Same thing happened to me. Would it be all right if we step inside?"

Copley, you sly dog.

He allowed them in shaking his head. "Why would you be

looking for me?"

"You're a person of interest in a homicide investigation," Alvarez stated.

Percy's already pale complexion turned ashen. He plopped down in the closest easy chair.

"Have a seat, detectives," he said weakly.

"We're sorry to bring the news to you this way, but we need to speak with anyone who might have had a grudge against Ms. Jakes," Copley said.

"*Evelyn* is dead?"

I'd seen this show before. Even the guiltiest criminal can usually conjure up an Academy Award performance when necessary. I watched his body language carefully for signs he was lying. That's when I noticed his hands. They were covered with red patches resembling ringworm. As the interview continued, I noticed him scratching his shoulder occasionally and then I recalled the tubes of ointment in his bathroom.

"Excuse me, Mr. Smith. May I use the washroom?" Copley's blue eyes could have charmed the spots from a leopard. "Long drive."

"Of course. Down the hall, first door on your right." Percy watched her go.

As Alvarez grilled him, I followed Copley to see if the tubes remained where he'd left them. I knew she had no intention of touching anything in his bathroom and had used it as an excuse to look around. I'd used the ploy myself in the past; sometimes it worked and sometimes not. But Copley had a way about her. She could probably sell shoes to a snake, at least the two-legged kind.

In the bathroom, Percy's travel bag lay open on the counter revealing several more tubes, all greasy from use. Copley nodded to herself as she looked and then held a tissue on the toilet lever to flush it and the same to run the sink water a moment.

When she returned to the living room, I searched the rest of the house again, this time for evidence of Kate, or that he'd brought her here. Nothing. I briefly thought I heard her call me, and then it was gone. My imagination seemed to be working overtime.

Back in the living room, I heard Percy's voice rise in indignation.

"You think *I* killed her?"

Copley took this as an opportunity to do a quick check of the other rooms while her host defended his honor.

"Why would I do a thing like that?" he asked.

"She'd recently fired you," Alvarez said.

"Oh, that. Silly misunderstanding."

When Copley and I returned to the living room, Percy had broken out in a sweat. His cheeks were crimson with anger.

"Then she didn't fire you?" Alvarez continued.

"Of course she did. But I had outgrown that job anyway. I've already lined up a new gig more suited to my talents."

"And what might that be?"

"Well, if it will get you people off my back, I'll tell you. I'm to start modeling for an art school in Chicago. The pay is extremely generous, much more than Evelyn ever paid. She actually did me a favor. With any luck I'll be able to give up my part-time position at Wal-Mart, too."

"Why didn't you tell anyone you were in Florida?"

"That's a private matter and last time I checked I'm over twenty-one and really don't have to give account to anyone."

"That's right. But I'm asking anyway, where were you two weekends ago?"

"I don't recall."

"No one can vouch for your whereabouts for any of those days?"

"I lead a simple life, Detective. I'm no social butterfly and I keep mostly to myself. I have only a group of friends at Sun City where I'm a member. Unfortunately, I did not visit the club that weekend."

"We believe Evelyn was killed on that Friday and her body dumped into the vehicle of one of our detectives sometime Saturday night. According to our records, your flight didn't leave until Monday morning."

Percy seemed undisturbed by Alvarez's description of the body. It was a ploy that usually worked on weaker criminals. A vivid visual description, or actual crime-scene photos could turn a stubborn witness or criminal if presented at just the right moment. This time it didn't work.

"I watch *CSI*, Detective. Yes, I have what some might consider motive, and, with no proof of my whereabouts, it looks like opportunity as well. But you have no solid evidence. Why don't you get a warrant and search the place? Perhaps you'll find what you're looking for."

"And what might that be?"

"A weapon. Blood spatter." Percy shrugged.

Alvarez hid a smile. "Ah, I can see you're well versed in police procedure. And, since you're offering, we'd like to pick up your ice sculpting tools for analysis. Are they here?"

"No. I left them with the manager of Sun City. I'd forgotten them the last time I was there and asked him to keep them for me. Why do you need . . . ?" His eyes grew wide. "Did someone cut her up?"

"Yes. Would it be all right if I have an officer collect your tools from the club?"

"Of course. I'll call Bob Ilkerson."

"I'd appreciate that. You say you have a new job, yet you went to Florida on vacation? How did you manage to get time off so soon?"

"I haven't actually started my job yet. They're expecting me by the end of the month, and that is why I had to take care of some personal business beforehand."

"What kind of business?"

"That's why it's called personal."

Alvarez locked his gaze on Percy. He never said a word. I love to watch him work his magic. Some detectives feel if you ask enough questions you'll wear a suspect down, but Alvarez takes a different approach. He says nothing. His eyes bore into the suspect until they can't stand it. Then they break. This time was no different.

"Okay! If you must know, I have a rash."

"A rash?"

"Yes. I'll give you my doctor's number if you'd like. He can verify it." With that, Percy jumped up and stripped off his shirt. "It's called Pityriasis Rosea."

His back, abdomen and arms were a mass of reddish-brown scaly patches. The areas along the ribs lined up, giving his back a Christmas tree pattern.

Copley's eyes widened and she brought her hands into her lap so as not to touch the well-worn chair she sat in.

"Are you satisfied? The only way to ease the symptoms is with UV-B rays like from the sun. I need to get rid of this rash before I can model in the nude. Florida seemed like the ideal place to do that." He turned for effect.

"But as you can see, after hours in the sun, I'm still in no shape to take the job."

Alvarez straightened his tie and pushed ahead, although I detected tiny beads of sweat on his top lip. I knew he'd be cutting this interview short.

"Please put your shirt back on, Mr. Smith."

I've heard some pretty wild alibis in my time, but this topped them all. It was too bizarre to be a lie. The look on Alvarez's face told me he agreed. Percy was not our man. And if he wasn't, we had no leads on Kate's whereabouts.

In the car, Copley reported her bathroom findings with Spock-like seriousness. "Do you want me to follow up with his doctor?"

"Not really. I've seen the proof. He's not our guy."

"What's next?"

"See what the tools show, but I'll bet they'll come up clean."

"I feel like I need a bath."

"A shower and a beer sounds real good right now, but I have to get back. As if this isn't enough, I'm working the Grimmer Field case."

"Did they ever get an ID?"

"She doesn't meet any missing-person description and she's never been printed. We'll have to go with dental records."

"Sorry this Percy guy didn't work out. I really thought he might lead us to Kate."

"So did I. We're running out of time."

Chapter Thirty-Eight

I went back to my picnic area to lick my wounds and hopefully see Mike. It was time for an update on the missing death tag. Good news was what I needed the most and even if he hadn't found it, I felt I wanted to be with him.

He'd become my rock in all the chaos on both sides of eternity. Our relationship had grown and continued to surprise us both, yet it remained unclear where we could end up. It looked like his widow had moved on and perhaps that painful truth had given Mike his freedom to do the same. Whether it would include me, only time would tell. But we had all the time in the world. *And the next.*

I pulled a few weeds to keep my mind occupied while I thought about Kate. No one here seemed to know the rules, or if there were any. The fact that I could no longer communicate or find my sister could just be the natural progression of things in the spirit world. No one seemed to know. I felt the same frustrations of a dead-end case welling up inside and realized I'd become spoiled since my death. It had been far too easy to appear when and where I wanted, even taking it as far as searching a residence without a warrant. Perhaps this was my penalty for abusing my newfound powers. A niggling thought wound its way into my brain, telling me if that were the case, there had to be someone in charge dishing out the reprimands.

"You come here often?" Mike asked as he stepped over the felled tree log and took a seat.

I yanked out a large dandelion and tossed it over my shoulder.

"You're awfully aggressive with the plant life. Anything you'd care to share?"

"No leads on Kate, and Percy the nudist has an alibi. He was our last solid lead. She's been missing for two days. Time is running out, Mike. And I can't even begin to think about helping others until I find her. Tell me you have something on Tanner's tag."

He reached for me and I didn't have to concentrate as hard to feel his nearness. It was becoming more natural for us to "touch." I've never been one to run for cover, but the loss of my sister had taken its toll and I found it hard to come to terms with the multitude of feelings over it. I mentally leaned against him and pulled out a few more weeds.

"Sorry. No luck." He made the pretense of stroking my hair.

"What happens if Tanner gets her tag back?"

"We'll deal with it like we did last time. She's not God."

"No, but she gives Satan a good bit of competition."

"Stop torturing yourself. For now, let's focus on Kate."

"I feel guilty that I can't find her."

"Guilty?"

"I should be able to find her without a GPS system. I'm a spirit, and don't have the same limitations as the living. I must be doing something wrong that I can't connect with her. And then, there's this overwhelming sense of helplessness. It's worse than any dead-end case I've ever worked."

"We've all been there. You should know better than anyone that it goes with the job, only this time it's personal because it's family."

"You know, our whole lives we hear about eternal rest, finding peace, and all that. But it's no better here. We end up with stress on both sides, but can only function in one."

"Yes, but how many people here actually put this new existence to good use? From what I've seen most of them wander around doing nothing but complaining. You actually help people. You've found a way to make death worth living."

"I can't believe you just said that." I couldn't stop my grin.

"It's true. And if you give up now you'll have even more regrets."

I knew he was right. This was just another valley in the shadow of death on the way to a brighter peak.

"You're good for everyone here because you're not afraid to take action. It gives purpose to everything we've lived and died for. But most of all, you're good for me, Lindsay."

He leaned close and we kissed in our special way, sharing the electric energy between us. For the first time, I felt complete as I allowed myself to accept this new existence and enjoy what it had to offer. I'm the lucky one who has the privilege of knowing the best of both worlds. All I need to do is find a way to make them work for me.

We stayed locked together, feeling not a physical presence, but an emotional bond. When at last we parted, I knew we were together, in the sense of a couple. Neither one of us spoke the words because we didn't have to. The uncharted territory before us stood fresh and inviting. Filled with new hope for the future, I felt a renewed sense of confidence that there may just be a grand plan after all, and that I was fulfilling my part.

And that's when I spotted Sally trudging through the tall grass with Evelyn Jakes in tow.

"Jakes?" I ran toward my childhood friend.

The first thing I noticed was that her spirit body remained intact, including all of her fingers. That told me, she'd been dead before the cutting had started. The second thing I saw was the Blackberry cell phone she used as her business lifeline. It had become her death tag.

Jakes smiled her trademark impish grin, with one corner of her mouth lifting slightly higher than the other. She was still one of the most striking women I'd ever seen. At five-foot-seven, she might have been a little short for a New York model, but her dark auburn hair, green eyes and perfect milk-and-honey cover girls I'd ever seen.

"Well, I'll be damned," Jakes teased. "And I mean it, seeing that you're here, Frost."

Our mutual air hug sent her into a hardy laugh. "It looks just as corny on this side, doesn't it?"

"You don't know it, but I really would hug you if I could," I said. "How did you get here?"

"Sally spotted me wandering around some parking lot and brought me here. Wherever 'here' is."

Sally shook her head. "My death spot has turned into a portal for the spirit world. I might have to think about a move."

Jakes looked to me for an explanation.

I waved her over to where Mike sat on the log. "It's a long story. But, then, we have plenty of time."

"So this is really it? I'm dead?"

" 'Fraid so. But I've made a few friends and we're all getting through it together. You will too."

"I keep thinking I'm dreaming and soon I'll awaken late for work as usual."

"No alarm clocks here. It's kind of a perk."

Jakes seemed to be taking well the official news of her death. I knew from experience that at first it's a shock, but everything is so new and overwhelming that the reality doesn't sink in until later. At least that's how it went for me. It didn't really hit me until I visited my father. When that day of realization came for Jakes, at least I would be there for her.

After the introductions, I explained what had happened to Kate.

"I think I know where she is," Jakes said. "I wouldn't be dead if Kate hadn't introduced me to that psycho Husky breeder."

"How so?"

"Kate was so excited about her new dog and wanted me to see it. So we went to the breeder's home and got to talking with the woman. When she found out I'm a caterer, she asked for my business card because she intended to plan a surprise party. Turns out the surprise was on me when I went back to her home to set up the details. That's when she hit me on the head with something. The rest is kind of blurry."

"Probably best that way." I didn't want to tell her what had happened to her body after that. Jakes had always doted over her looks.

Suddenly everything clicked when I recalled Kate's story about the breeder's brother. She'd been the one person I hadn't thought to investigate.

"What's the breeder's address?" I asked Jakes.

"Why? What good could that possibly do you?" she asked.

Sally and Mike laughed.

"What's so funny?" She turned to me.

"Remember how my dad always said that once I made up my mind about something I was more stubborn than Satan?"

"Yes."

"Let's put it this way, Satan calls me for tips."

CHAPTER THIRTY-NINE

Kate awoke to a thud outside her stall door. She got up, hands still tied behind her back. Whoever it was, she'd be ready for them.

The thud came again, this time louder.

Seconds passed and she waited for the door to swing open like it had so many times. Who would it be this time, Paula Bunyan in the grimy overalls, or Betty the Bully? Either way, it wouldn't be pleasant.

When the door swung open all Kate's hopes for an offense vanished at the sight of a shotgun pointed in her direction.

"Turn around," Betty motioned with the shotgun. "I want to make sure you're still tied."

Kate turned, keeping an eye on her captor.

"Good. Let's go," Betty commanded.

"Where?" Kate stalled.

"You'll see. It's what you've been waiting for, 'cept you didn't know it."

"I don't know what you're talking about, Betty. Why don't you tell me?"

"No need for that. You'll see soon enough."

"What if I refuse?" Kate watched for an opportunity to strike with her foot.

"Then you die right here." She shoved the muzzle against Kate's chest. "Makes no difference to me really. Either way you're gonna meet your maker. I just figured it would be more fun to see all your friends first."

"What friends?" Kate saw Betty back away now, too far to reach.

"If you get a move on, you'll see."

"Answer me, Betty. Tell me what's going on?"

Instead of answering, she prodded Kate along in front of her to a pole barn near the back of the property. As pole barns went it was top of the line. Kate's uncle had had one similar, always referring to it as the Coach House. With actual siding and roof tiles it looked more like a quaint guesthouse than a barn. It had expansion areas attached on both sides of the main building making room for four hinged barn doors across the front. The roof came to a peak over additional loft space for extra storage, or in this case, perhaps her friend Teresa.

Although the situation looked grim, Kate was glad to be out in the open. The cold air felt good against her face and she breathed its freshness, glad to be out of the claustrophobic air of the barn. Betty kept a safe distance behind her, shotgun aimed to the middle of her back, leaving Kate no room to make a move.

At the wide barn door, Betty nudged her from behind to go inside and Kate stepped in bravely, unsure of what she'd find. After her eyes adjusted she blinked again to be sure of what she saw.

Four life-size marionettes hung from a long support beam across the barn; their feet supported beneath by a catwalk. Nine cables, like the ones that had been attached to Jakes, held each of them from their heads, shoulders, hands, knees and feet, just like real marionettes. A noose hung from the beam beside each doll. Their bodies swayed silently, with pasty white faces blank and staring. As she neared the figures, Kate swallowed her impulse to cry out when she saw the marionettes were Teresa, Pam, Nicki and Carmen.

Their entire bodies, including their faces, were covered in the same rubbery material that Jakes had been enclosed in. She could see holes in the nostril areas for breathing and realized they must all still be alive. A catwalk-style support had been built along the wall providing a place for Betty's partner to pace back and forth behind Kate's friends. Her heavy gait stomped along, as she poked at each of the women with a stick causing them to sway back and forth by their harnesses.

"C'mon on now. Dance for me!" she shouted after each poke. "Be a good little puppet and dance!"

Kate fought the urge to lunge ahead, knowing it would do her no good with her hands tied and a gun aimed at her.

"Cut them down!" she shouted to Betty.

The woman on the catwalk cackled a crude laugh and slapped her knee.

"Momma thinks you're a riot," Betty said. "Maybe you should join your friends in the show. You could be the comic relief."

She secured Kate to a straight chair with rope.

"Betty, listen to me. Let my friends go and you can do what you want to me."

"You say that like you've got a say-so in it. I'm in charge here, Missy. Not you." Betty's freckled cheeks burned red behind her anger.

"I know you're angry with me."

"You hear that, Momma? She thinks I'm angry."

Betty slapped Kate's cheek, nearly toppling her over in the chair.

Kate's eyes watered, and her cheek burned like fire, but she kept her wits.

"I remember your brother, Betty. His name was Tim Maklin. He was my arrest. I'm responsible. No one else here has caused you or your family harm."

"Is that all he was to you? An arrest? Tim was the kindest, sweetest, most wonderful man. He loved Broadway musicals and would sing all the show tunes. He dreamed of becoming an actor so he could play all of his favorite Shakespearian roles. You robbed him of that chance and took him away from me. You need to suffer, that's why I took your sister."

Caught off guard, Kate didn't know what to say.

"You know, that redhead you brought with you that day when you came to see the pups?"

"That was Evelyn. She wasn't my sister."

"You told me you two were like sisters, and that's why you wanted her to see the dog. Tit for tat, Missy. You took my brother so I took your sister. I cut her up like you cut my brother from my life."

"Why harm my other friends? I'd say we're even now."

Another hard slap burned Kate's face.

"I'll decide what's fair. You see I'm in charge now. I'm in complete control because I hold all the strings. You'll see your friends dance when I hang them by their pretty necks, just like my brother. And then it will be your turn. Now don't go anywhere. I'll be back soon." Betty grinned back at Kate on her way out of the barn.

Betty's mother strutted along the catwalk without a word. Kate tried to break through to her.

"Can I speak to my friends?" she asked.

"What the hell for?" the woman answered in a more nasal voice than before. Kate saw the oversized bandage taped over her nose and realized her own handiwork.

"I want to be sure they're all right. What harm could it do?"

The woman grimaced, then spat on the floor. "I don't give a shit. It might be interesting to see what you have to say to each other."

"Teresa? Are you okay?" Kate tried.

No answer.

"Pam, what about you?"

A muffled cry escaped the second figure as it swayed more distinctly.

"Nicki and Carmen? Move if you hear me."

By now all of her friends were swaying as they tried to communicate from behind their latex cocoons.

"Are you sure they're getting enough oxygen?" Kate asked the woman.

"Don't you think they'd be dead by now if they weren't? Not that it matters none. Won't be long now anyhow." She swung a long stick in agitation.

"I have to hand it to you, Genevieve. You sure pulled a fast one on all of us. How did you trick my friends into coming here?" Kate tried taking the attention away from her friends.

"After I got this one here"—she gave Pam a little shove—"it was easy. I had her call the others. Not too hard to do when you have a shotgun pointed at someone's head."

"Who killed Evelyn Jakes? Was it Betty?"

"We share all the responsibilities here," she said proudly.

"So she was murdered here at the farm?"

"That's right. And our dogs cleaned up all the evidence."

Kate had to take a deep breath at the thought of all those beautiful innocent puppies lapping up all the blood.

"Course they had help. Their momma and daddy cleaned most of it. So you see, Missy? No evidence. When we're finished you and your friends will all be just a memory. Like my son."

Betty's mother slapped her knee in a loud fit of laughter. "By God, let the show begin!"

CHAPTER FORTY

I had a renewed sense of strength now that I knew where I was going. Jakes had given me the address and I left her in Sally and Mike's capable care while I went in search of Kate.

The dilapidated farmhouse stood in need of a paint job with a broken-down front porch to match. I saw a large pen made of chicken wire but no chickens or Huskies. I skipped the house tour, figuring the two barns on the property would be the more likely hiding place. I checked the rustic barn not too far from the house, where several horse stalls stood empty, except for two. The horses themselves seemed a bit on the thin side, and their eyes were runny with mucous. With no sign of Kate I could only imagine what kind of shape she might be in. In the first stall, I noted a pie tin with what looked to be remnants of dried oatmeal. Beside it I saw the telltale signs of vomit.

Toward the back of the property stood a pole barn, apparently newer than the house and horse barn, with bright red siding and green roof tiles. I saw no signs of Kate's SUV but found a beat-up snowmobile and figured it might be the one used at White Crest. With no sign of Kate—or sign that she'd even been here—I wondered if this would turn into another false lead.

I never thought about running in spirit form but I guess that's what I did because I'd never arrived to a destination faster. Inside the barn, I saw what looked like life-size marionettes tethered by cable to a support beam. In the middle of the barn tied to a chair, was my sister.

"Kate!" I wanted to hug her.

Her eyes widened when she saw me and I could see the relief on her face, along with the painful reality of the situation.

"Are you all right?" I asked.

She mumbled so the large she-man in overalls wouldn't see her talking.

"I have to admit my surgery was more fun."

I saw her bloodstained shirt and knew she'd done some damage to her incision. For right now I'd take her any way I could and was glad she was still able to joke.

"What's going on here?"

She proceeded to explain the short version of what seemed a long story, but I got the idea quickly. Betty Carter was out for revenge and was taking it out on Kate's friends.

"How much time do we have?"

"Not sure. The lumberjack up there keeps antagonizing her 'dolls,' as she calls them. I'm not sure how much time they all have wrapped up in whatever that rubbery stuff is."

I recognized it as the same latex compound that had covered Jakes.

"Is there any way you can get them talking, to guage how they're doing?" I asked.

"All I've been able to determine is that they're alive. I'm afraid if I keep trying it will aggravate the situation. Mother and daughter are both a bit unstable."

"That's Betty's mother?" I recognized her lumbering frame from the night at Kate's house. She'd been the mysterious intruder.

"Yup."

"What's wrong with her face?"

"She's butt-ugly."

"No. The oversized bandage."

"I broke her nose," Kate said proudly.

"It's probably an improvement. Oh, by the way, I found Jakes. Or rather, she found me. Either way, she's the reason I found you at all. It seems our lines have been disconnected."

"I've had the same trouble contacting you and I think I know why. They've been drugging me most of the time and I haven't been able to stay awake long enough. This doesn't look good, Linz. Even though you've found me, there's no way for you to let anyone know about it."

"Don't go there. There has to be a way." I tried to sound sure of myself.

"Not unless you have an ace up your sleeve."

I took a look around the barn, moving into the side room. The expansion area housed a bathtub-size vat filled with what looked like vanilla milkshake. Beside it stood a large surgical table with leather restraints. I could visualize how Betty had created her marionettes. Materials for papier-mâché lay beside it on another worktable, and behind that stood an industrial size drum labeled Natural Latex Casting Compound. According to the label it was very flexible. First papier-mâché, then casting compound. Martha Stewart should see this.

I went back to Kate still not sure what my options were.

The lumberjack snickered and gave one of the "dolls" a poke with her stick.

"I'm going for help," I told Kate.

"What are you going to do?" she asked.

"I need to send an E-mail."

I found Alvarez in his office writing out a report. His computer was on, but he had his back to it. His computer wasn't set to his E-mail. This was new turf for me and I wasn't sure if I had to actually send him an E-mail, or simply place it on an existing message. Instead, I went to the search engine and spelled out

AKA licensed Husky Breeders in NW Indiana. It was slow going at first because I couldn't actually type on the keys, I had to focus on each letter until it appeared on the screen. Then I managed to activate the search function.

A list of breeders came up and I scanned down and found Betty's address and phone number listed. Betty's was the only one nearby as the rest were further north, near Chicago. Now all I had to do was get Alvarez to find it. No easy task when with his back turned and no way to grab his attention.

Once again I had to call upon my electric personality to come up with a brainstorm. I focused on his E-mail program and managed a somewhat garbled voice-over of "You've got mail."

He turned with a frown and then saw that his screen had something more interesting than a tropical-fish screen saver. His hand hovered over the escape button, but not before he read the title. I saw the recognition on his face and heard the familiar Spanish curse words when he realized what he'd missed.

Relief filled me when I saw him head out of his office and signal John Turner.

"Hey, John! You have time to take a run with me?" he asked the officer.

John looked up from his paperwork and grinned. "Sure. Anything to get me away from this stuff. Where're we headed?"

"Just outside Southfield. You might want to bring Jack."

I wanted to scream. Alvarez wasn't calling in the team; he was going with only one other officer—well, two, if you include Jack, the police dog. This wasn't how I'd envisioned it. But then I realized he had little to go on. In his own mind, he was only following a hunch. My tip was flimsy at best, simply a fluke of an idea that might lead nowhere. He had no justifiable cause to send in the cavalry. At this point a warrant was out of the question.

If he did find Kate, he could say he'd gone to interview Betty as a person of interest, and, with Jack along, it was almost assured that Kate would be found. My only worry now was that Betty and her psycho mother would be waiting for them. They had to assume by now that the authorities were searching. As Alvarez and John left the office, I decided to head back to the farm. This time I would have good news for Kate.

I turned to find Cleaver Woman grinning from behind the wooden handle of her death tag.

"Have you thought about my offer, Frost?"

"Yes."

"What's it going to be?"

"Take a number, bitch. You're not a priority."

The cleaver blade prevented her from raising her eyebrows in surprise. Instead, anger radiated in a glare created strictly for me.

"Then let this be on your shoulders." She stroked Tanner's weapon.

I wasn't sure what she planned to do with it but I wasn't going to give her the chance. In an instant, my head plowed into her abdomen, sending her flying backwards. My paranormal self-defense training with Mike proved beneficial once again.

Tanner's gun sailed across Alvarez's desk and landed on the floor in the corner.

It took her a moment to realize what I'd done and she scrambled after it on her hands and knees.

My navigational skills had improved enough for me to reach the corner ahead of her and I felt the rush of success as my hand reached for the weapon.

She came up behind, putting me into a chokehold but her efforts did little except to briefly hold me in place.

"In case you've forgotten, I don't need oxygen." I countered her move, sending her onto her back.

Apparently she'd had some training of her own, although it

hadn't been enough to save her life. Her leg swung out unexpectedly, knocking me off balance and onto the floor. She grabbed a handful of my long hair from behind and hauled me across the room. I can't say it hurt, but I took issue with the fact that a civilian with less training was besting me.

I clutched her hand and yanked hard enough to bring her down. I planted my rear on her chest, and pinned both of her shoulders.

"Had enough? I could use a protein drink."

"You're not going to help those people, are you?"

"Of course I am. Why are you in such a hurry? We have eternity."

"I don't. Who knows when I'll have to go on to the next level? I'm going to do this one thing before I go, because I never did anything useful in my whole life."

"Is that what your husband told you?"

"My husband?"

"Your abuser."

"He didn't abuse me."

I tapped the meat cleaver handle. "Anniversary present?"

"He killed me in a fit of rage. It doesn't excuse it, but I know what kind of person I was. Jealous. Spiteful. If anyone was abusive it was me. It turned my husband against me."

"What would make a man so angry that he'd do that to his wife?"

"I killed his bird."

She had me there. My mind searched for something supportive to say.

"With the cleaver," she added.

Shit. There is no good response for that.

"The damn thing bit me every time it was out of its cage. Came after me. One day it pecked my face so hard it bled for twenty minutes. He just laughed. So when he complained about the dinner I cooked I told him I'd be happy to fix him something else. When the bird came at me again, I grabbed it, cut off its head and threw the bird into a frying pan."

"You're no June Cleaver. But if you're trying to redeem yourself, why did you steal Tanner's gun?"

"I wanted to make sure you'd help those people. Maybe it was the one unselfish thing I could do in my existence."

"You tried. To me that proves you're not the selfish person you thought. I'm sure every one of those people appreciates it. You just needed to find a different way to help them."

"Yeah, but now that's backfired too."

"How so?"

"It's too late."

"Too late for what?"

"For you to keep Tanner from her weapon."

I toppled off of her and scrambled to the corner.

Tanner's gun had vanished.

"Where is it?" I demanded.

She remained on the floor, no fight left in her. Her lips formed a pleasant smile behind the cleaver's handle.

"Thank you, Detective. You helped me after all. My efforts to do something good have been recognized."

"No!" I cried as the cleaver began to fade. "You have to tell me where Tanner's weapon is!"

I tried to hold onto her form but my hands slipped through.

"You conniving bitch! You planned this all along!" I focused on grabbing her firmly this time but wasn't fast enough.

She winked at me before slipping away into nothingness.

Frantically I searched Alvarez's office, thinking she'd played me and it might still be there. Finally, I came to the conclusion that the evil I'd fought so hard to contain had the potential to resurface. I just didn't know when.

CHAPTER FORTY-ONE

Kate watched her friends closely for any signs of distress or that they were even still breathing. Holes had been cut into the latex masks, creating black hollows for the eyes and she saw that the captors had gone the extra mile in painting their faces to look like regular marionettes. Shakespearean-style costumes adorned her friends' bodies, creating the illusion of a larger-than-life puppet show.

She detected a minute twitch from Teresa's left hand and saw that it had a regular rhythm to it. Her index finger raised, then dropped, raised, then dropped. Kate couldn't signal back with her fingers so she nodded once with her head to match each of Teresa's movements. Suddenly the rhythm changed to two rises and a drop. Kate matched it with her nodding head. At least she knew Teresa was still alive.

Betty's mother climbed down from the catwalk and turned on a boom box plugged in nearby. She turned up the volume full blast. Kate cringed at the blaring Broadway musical show tunes echoing in the pole barn. Her hopes of striking up a conversation died with the first notes of "One" from *A Chorus Line*.

Then she saw that every time they sang the word "one," Nicki's finger would go up. She too was alive. Eventually Kate saw that all of her friends were indeed alive and performing minimal movements. She decided it was the best worst performance she'd ever seen. At the climax of the song, Betty's mother went to the end of the catwalk and picked up a hacksaw.

"I guess Betty's gonna miss dress rehearsal, girls. We can't wait any longer." With that, she headed toward the first in line. Pam.

"Wait! You can't start before the curtain goes up. You'll ruin the show!" Kate worked the ropes that held her wrists.

The woman stopped, hacksaw slack at her side. A sneer twisted her puffy pink lips.

"I ain't got no curtain. What the hell are you talking about?"

"Won't Betty be upset if you start without her?"

She stopped and thought a moment. "Naw. I'll only cut up one." Again she raised the saw.

Kate saw Pam's latex form sway as she struggled to break free.

As the saw's teeth edged close to Pam's neck, Kate wondered what was taking Betty so long.

Betty let the dingy lace curtain fall back as she stomped back into the kitchen. Visitors. The fact that they drove a police squad car meant little. She'd deal with them, just like she'd dealt with her other guests.

"Oh, look," she said to no one at all. "They've brought a dog. Maybe they're looking for a mate."

Betty squinted out the window as they passed her kitchen. "Wrong breed. The dumb-asses."

She met them at the door with her brightest smile, keeping an eye on the shotgun behind the door.

"Yes? May I help you?"

"I'm Detective Alvarez with the Southfield PD. Would it be all right if I ask you a few questions?"

Betty nodded toward the other officer with the German shepherd. "Who's that?"

"That's Officer Turner."

"No, I mean the dog. I'm a husky breeder. Dogs are of great interest to me." She knew it would seem a silly question even as she asked it, but it might serve also to distract him.

The detective's dark eyes never wavered as he spoke. "That would be Jack. Would it be all right if they stay outside while I come in?"

"Of course." Betty allowed him inside as she reached for her gun.

She allowed the detective to step past her as she coaxed, "Go ahead into the living room. I'll put on some coffee."

"That really won't be nece—" He stopped at the sight of the gun pointing at him.

"Don't even think about reaching for your weapon. You'll be dead before you do. Now open your coat wide so I can see where you're hiding it."

He did as she said and she quickly swiped it from its holster.

"Now go sit down on the couch and picture the size hole this baby will blow into your spine in case you're thinking about making a move."

The man did as she said and she perched on the arm of a love seat across from him. She kept the weapon pointed.

"What is it you want to talk about, Detective?" She smiled her sweetest smile.

"You know the officer with me will find them. You won't get out of this. It's over."

"Let him find them. I have backup, as you call it."

"Where are they?" the man asked.

"You'll see eventually. What's your name again?"

"Detective Alvarez."

"How long you been workin' at Southfield?"

"What do you care?"

"I'm just curious if you were around when my brother died."

"Was he an officer?"

"No, he wasn't a cop. His name was Tim Maklin and he died in your jail."

"I don't know anything about it. Is that what all this is about?"

"You bet your sweet ass. Too bad you got yourself caught up in it. Since you didn't have anything to do with my brother's death, I don't have no grudge against you. Just that blonde detective."

"Her name is Kate. She's a very good friend of mine. Can I see her?"

"No!" She aimed the muzzle higher. Maybe a headshot would be better. Either way she'd have to have the drapes and carpets cleaned or replaced.

"I'm sure Kate didn't do anything to your brother. If you put down the gun we can sort it out. I won't make a move."

"Right. And I'm Dolly Parton." She sneered. "It's a real shame I have to deal with you like the others. You should have called in sick today." She laughed too loud for the small room and caught herself. It wouldn't do to lose control now. She and Momma would have a celebration tonight after the show; there would be plenty of time for laughter then.

"Well, Detective Alvarez, it's almost time."

"For what?"

"You'll see. I was going to dress up a bit but now that you and your buddy showed up, I'll just have to go like this." Her worn work jeans and flannel shirt were covered with dried latex.

She motioned for him to go ahead of her through the kitchen toward the door. "Keep them hands raised where I can see 'em. I don't want you to miss your good friend's final performance. Now we're going to take things real easy as we head outside. The first thing you're going to do is tell your buddy out there to lose his gun and put the dog in the car." She motioned for Alvarez to go ahead of her.

"No tricks now if you want to live."

Betty tightened her grip on the gun as she stepped outside. She saw no sign of the other officer or his dog.

"Looks like your friend has taken it upon himself to snoop around. In my books that's trespassin'. A body could get shot for something like that. Let's go." She pointed toward the second barn.

CHAPTER FORTY-TWO

"You look over here, Missy!" Genevieve Maklin shouted to Kate.

The buxom woman glared at her from the catwalk with one hand around Pam's forehead as she yanked it back.

"I'm gonna leave it up to you, as to how you want to see your friend die. Do you pick the noose or the saw?"

"Let her go."

"Not on the list. Too bad. Guess I'll have to choose for you." She briefly let go of Pam, giving her a shove so her body swayed from the cable supporting her. Kate saw Pam's feet hang limp, no longer trying to gain footing. If her friends weren't released soon, they would die.

"Hey, Gen. Why don't you come down here and untie me? We could have it out right here, just you and I."

"I've already kicked your ass. You bore me."

"You cheated. I was drugged. Why don't you play fair this time and let me take you on?"

"Why you skinny little shit! I should kill you where you sit."

"That wouldn't surprise me. I'm tied up, you coward."

Kate worked at her ropes.

"Just wait a little while longer and I'll show you who's a coward!"

"Got a mirror?"

Kate felt the ropes give enough for her to work her hands free, but kept them in position.

She scooted the chair a little closer to the catwalk.

"What are you doing?" Gen asked.

"I asked for front-row seats." Kate scooted closer.

"You'd better stop right there, Missy."

"That's *Detective* Missy to you." The chair scraped the floor once more.

The woman tromped down the catwalk steps.

"Don't get too close, I can smell you from here." Kate felt her pulse race.

Gen reached out to grab her hair.

Kate jumped to a defensive stance. "You need a lesson in manners."

Genevieve rushed her.

It hadn't occurred to Kate that her lack of nourishment and exercise would hinder her defensive moves. Her limbs felt like lead compared to her usual workout. When the big woman hit, Kate went down.

Before she could raise her arms to counter, she found they'd been pinned by a straddling move. The woman's weight knocked the breath from her lungs.

"You . . . need . . . Jenny Craig." Kate managed, then dodged a direct punch.

A rumbling growl escaped Genevieve's lungs as she wrapped her man-size hands around Kate's throat.

"Hold it!" A male voice commanded from across the room. "Get off of her and get your hands up!"

A large dog began barking nearby and Kate saw a large German Shepherd charging her attacker.

Genevieve stood, arms raised.

The dog stopped, sat close by, growling a warning.

"You all right, Kate?" John asked, holding his service revolver in one hand and reaching for his handcuffs with the other.

"I am now. But I've got to get them down." Kate headed

toward the catwalk.

A shotgun blast exploded in the barn, echoing like a bomb.

All eyes turned to Betty as she marched Alvarez inside with the gun pointed to his back.

"Drop it!" she ordered John.

He did as she said and raised his arms.

"Momma, you take Missy there and finish the job. This is getting out of hand, and, if I accomplish nothing else today, it will be the death of Kate Frost."

Kate felt the lumberjack's large arm secured around her neck as the woman dragged her up the catwalk. She fought to break free and finally let her legs drag to buy herself a few seconds of time as the woman had to practically carry her.

"Let the others go. Their deaths won't mean a thing to me if I'm dead."

The woman grunted as she lifted Kate up the stairs.

Kate saw Alvarez inching closer to Betty as she watched her mother struggling.

"Now you'll know what it's like, Frost! I hope you burn in hell!" Betty spat on the ground.

On the stand, a thick noose slipped over Kate's head and hung heavily on her collarbone. A quick tug and it became tight around her throat.

She glanced down at the floor below and realized all it would take was a quick shove from behind. Her eyes found Alvarez. He was the last beautiful thing she would see.

Then she saw Lindsay beside her, close enough to make a move on Genevieve, yet completely unable.

"Damnit!" Lindsay shouted.

"Well, go on, Momma. What are you waiting for?" Betty demanded.

"I'm going to do them all in a row." Genevieve started down the line of women, slipping the nooses around their necks.

In her haste, she'd forgotten to retie Kate's hands, allowing Kate to struggle with the tight grip of the rope.

"This will be the grand finale of the evening. And what a show it will be!"

Kate caught a movement coming through the doorway.

"What's going on?" Ed Nog stepped inside as if he'd walked into a surprise party.

With all eyes briefly on Nog, John shouted the order for Jack to attack.

The large Shepherd leapt at Betty, knocking her off balance.

Alvarez grabbed the shotgun and they struggled over it.

"Holy shit!" Nog ducked behind a stack of barrels.

John ran toward the catwalk to undo the nooses from the women. He yanked the cables from their shoulders and helped each one to the floor, the latex starting to rip open from the bending movements. The women began tearing the compound from their faces.

Kate elbowed Genevieve in the gut, then head-butted her in the face with the back of her head. She managed to slip out of the noose in time to land a side kick into the woman's chest. Genevieve barreled back almost falling over the ledge but caught her balance in time. The woman was a powerhouse of rage as she continued her charge. Her face had grown purple as she cursed and grunted.

Betty screamed as the gun slipped from her grip. When Alvarez ripped it away, a solid shotgun blast filled the air and Jack dropped with a yelp.

Alvarez landed a bone-crushing punch to Betty's face and she went down. He quickly cuffed her and ran to see about Kate.

John shouted once again for Genevieve to stop and put her hands up.

The woman stopped, raising her hands.

"It's over, Genevieve. Time to give it up," Kate said.

"You're right, Missy. It is over." With that, she grabbed a nearby noose and stuck her head through it.

Before Kate could reach her, she yanked it tight, and jumped from the catwalk.

A cracking sound cut the air, causing Kate to cringe. She'd never gotten used to the sound of breaking bones.

Genevieve's body swung like one of the life-size marionettes her daughter had created. Her face wore the same blank expression the latex had given Kate's friends.

Betty looked up just in time to see her mother's suicide. She tried to crawl to the catwalk, her hands cuffed behind her, moaning like a wounded animal, then gave up as grief consumed her.

Kate felt Alvarez wrap his arms around her and hold on as if he'd never let go.

"Thank God." He cupped her chin and kissed her gently. "It's probably not professional, but since I'm in charge." He shrugged, and kissed her again.

His touch never felt so good, so comforting. After everything she'd been through, her only thought now was to get away from it all and recoup in the safety of his arms. But he broke the embrace saying, "I'll call for backup. You need to get to the hospital." With that he was gone.

Lindsay stood close by, surveying the scene. "Paperwork's going to take days on this one. Luckily you'll be out of the picture for a while."

"What do you mean?" Kate asked.

Lindsay nodded toward her shirt. She barely noticed that her incision was bleeding again.

"Flesh wound," Kate joked.

"You've been through a lot. Let your wounds heal properly this time before you go racing off on another case."

Kate watched Alvarez from across the barn. "I might just take you up on that."

Nog strutted over, hands in pockets. "Are you all right, Detective?"

"I've been better."

"It's a good thing I got here when I did."

"Yeah, those barrels needed protecting." Kate winced when she moved her arm.

"Not only that, but I took some really great shots of the whole thing." He nodded at the camera around his neck.

Kate briefly closed her eyes and forced a smile. "I'll see that you get a recommendation."

"Really?"

"No."

By now, John had made his way to Jack, cradling the dog's head in his lap. "You were the bravest officer I ever partnered with. I'll miss you, buddy."

Kate fought to maintain her composure as large tears dropped from John's chin onto Jack's face. She looked around, taking stock of everything, noting her friends were still peeling latex from their skin.

All things considered, they'd all been lucky. Everyone but Jack.

CHAPTER FORTY-THREE

Before the guests arrived at Kate's, I came early with a couple of guests of my own.

"Kate?" I stepped into the kitchen as she prepared a relish tray at the counter.

She turned to see me standing behind her with Jakes.

Her eyes brimmed and she tried to hug her, even though, of course, she could feel nothing.

Jakes closed her eyes briefly, and smiled. "Mmm. That felt good. I missed you too. And thanks for sticking with the case and solving it. It nearly cost you everything."

"Wait till you get my bill." Kate swiped at her eyes. "Damn onions."

"Oh, please, Kate. You never could lie. Someone get this woman a tissue!" Jakes moved on to nose around the platters of food on the kitchen counter.

I brought Mike over with my arm slipped through his, or at least made it look that way for Kate.

"I'd like you to meet my date, Mike Blake. Mike, this is my sister, Kate."

They nodded and smiled at one another.

"Nice to meet you, Kate. I've heard so much about you."

"None of it's true, I can assure you," Kate said.

"I hear you're doing a great job in homicide." Mike grinned.

"Now that's true."

Kate gave me the official "hottie" sign when Mike turned his back to follow Jakes into the dining room. I guess I get to keep him.

"Not bad for a cop," Jakes called overlooking the table setup. "You might need more ice. . . ." She stopped. "Listen to me. I guess I'll never quit being the caterer."

She wouldn't meet our eyes and it was clear she was starting to feel the reality of her situation. Death is final and takes no pity.

"That's fine by me. I prefer to be the guest and not the hostess. Advise away, my friend." Kate eased the tension.

I couldn't help notice Kate's nearly illegible scrawl on a memo pad beside the phone. Something about Dr. Karr. Without hesitation, I pried into her business.

"So did you get the biopsy results yet?"

"You're shameless." Kate snatched up the memo pad and stuffed it into a nearby drawer.

"Did you?"

Her smile told me everything I needed to know.

"Good," I said.

Later, I sat beside Kate on her couch, although no one could see me but her. She opened yet another shower gift for her new arrival; a set of silver dog dishes with Jack engraved on the fronts. Jack had survived his injuries, but they had been severe enough that he would never work as a police dog again. When it was determined that Betty Carter had never intended to give Kate a puppy, and had already sold them all, John Turner had graciously decided to give up his beloved pet to Kate. He would be training a new four-legged partner soon and knew Jack would receive the proper care and spoiling that any retired cop deserved. Kate had promised he'd receive his pension in belly rubs and dog treats.

Alvarez had sworn it was a blatant attempt for John to keep his foot inside Kate's door now that they shared joint custody.

He glowered in the corner, keeping his cynical thoughts to himself, nursing a beer.

A round of "awws" went around the room from the partygoers when Kate opened a framed birth certificate with the date Jack had come to live with her, and his new official name of Jack Frost. That was too much for me and I wished I could have joined Alvarez in a drink.

All of Kate's White Crest buddies had stayed over a few days after they'd been checked out and released from the hospital. None of them wanted to miss the "baby shower."

"Girl, you always do things in reverse order." Carmen teased Kate.

"How so?"

"A baby shower before a wedding?" Carmen glanced over at Alvarez who quickly went for another beer.

"I don't care what kind of party it is. I'm just glad to be able to stop picking that latex crap out of my nooks and crannies," Teresa joked.

"Now that's a visual I didn't need to take home with me," Nicki stated.

"The fact that we're all alive is reason enough to celebrate, ladies," Pam smiled.

"Always the voice of reason." Carmen shook her head. "But she's right."

Kate reached for another gift when the doorbell rang.

"I'll get it." Alvarez jumped at the chance to get out of the room.

He returned with Ed Nog in tow, wearing his usual coif and a beaming grin.

"Hello, ladies. Nice to see you all, minus your latex."

He took a seat beside Kate, plopping a gift in her lap.

"What's this, Ed?"

"Open it and find out. It's a little something to show my appreciation."

"For what?"

"I got my old job back at *The Crier*. Thanks to your story—"

"Wait, Ed. We never finished that story," Kate said.

"Not the detective story, the kidnapping one. Since I was there, my editor felt I was the best person to write it. She's giving me another chance."

Kate unwrapped the box and peered inside.

I didn't know what to expect. A book on mullet history? An eight-by-ten glossy of Nog himself? I prayed it wasn't anything he'd ever worn.

Instead everyone was pleasantly surprised, especially Kate, at the digital camera she pulled from the box.

"Ed, this is such a nice gift."

"I thought you might put it to good use now that you have a dog. Unless you want me to come and take some—"

"No. That's okay, Ed. I love the camera." Kate kissed him on the cheek, causing him to turn crimson.

With that, a resounding toast was raised with Nicki at the helm.

"Here's to great friends! And our trip to White Crest Mountain next year!"

When all of Kate's friends agreed, I saw Kate finally raise her glass to join them, offering a secret glance toward Jakes.

"Nice to see things look like they're returning to normal," I said to Jakes who stood in the corner smiling.

"I don't know, Linz. Not sure if I'll ever consider any of this normal. I wasn't ready to give up life yet."

"No one is. But I'm still doing what I love, only in a different way."

"I don't think there's any place for an ethereal caterer."

"You never know, Jakes. I've found both sides of eternity to be full of surprises."

She nodded toward Mike. "I see what you mean. Think there's someone out there for me?"

"Now there's a job for you. You could start a business called Second Chances Dating Service."

"Not too keen on that. But I'm sure something will come to me."

While the party went on, I turned my attention to my own future. Staring out the front window, I thought about the past and how it had brought us all to this very point in time. I wondered if everyone here really knew how lucky they were. I'd seen life from both sides and had learned too late to appreciate what I'd had.

From here, everyone would go on with their lives, remembering these events now and then until they faded into a distant nightmare. Me? It seemed I had my work cut out for me with a bunch of spirits awaiting my help with their cases. Mike, Sally and Dr. Saint had all promised to help. I felt a surge of excitement at the prospect of running an investigation again, and a little nervous at the unknown obstacles I'd face, being dead. But then, I'd already worked two cases with Kate and we'd solved both. Guess the rest wouldn't be too much different.

We never recovered Tanner's weapon and I knew it would haunt me. It would mean I'd be watching for any signs of her unwelcome return, but it's not something I plan to dwell on. Life is too short and death is too complicated.

I glanced down at my badge, still secure around my neck on its lanyard. It showed no signs of fading and that told me I still had issues to deal with—whether personal or otherwise remained unclear. Still, it gave me great satisfaction to think I had something to offer both of the worlds I haunted. It remained my shield of duty.

ABOUT THE AUTHOR

Scarlett Dean has been a true horror and mystery fan since childhood, always creating her own dark worlds and characters for fun. As a full-time author, she has four published novels and has published her own quarterly fiction magazine. She enjoys motivational speaking to promote the gift of writing. Scarlett lives in northwest Indiana and is currently at work on her next novel. For more, see www.scarlettdean.com.